Book One of The Universe of Entropy series

James Lee

Alien Erratum

To Gaz and Shelby

Hope you enjoy

reading my book

James Lee

Message from the author

This is a story that I have always wanted to write. I hope you enjoy reading my book, as much as I enjoyed writing the book. Thank you to everyone who supported me throughout this whole process, especially Christine for the editing.

In loving memory of my mum, Annette.

Chapter One

There was a huge explosion. The gates to the base blew straight off their hinges. Smoke was everywhere in the grounds. The life forms surged in on flying motorcycles. The creatures looked like they were integrated into the bike. Mean alien-looking creatures with long faces, long curved heads, and sharp needle shaped teeth. They were extremely thin and wiry, with a glowing energy surging through them. Behind them were beings of all sizes and colours. Some were flying and some were running. They all looked incensed. The alien-looking creatures on the bikes flew straight towards the base, with blasters from the bikes blazing. The creatures screamed loudly in their own language.

The boom of the gates awakened Captain Archer and he was up onto his feet in seconds. The door to his room abruptly opened and his Sergeant ran in. Sergeant Cundill was shouting directly at Archer. Captain Archer put his finger up and Cundill came to an immediate stop in front of him. Archer would have usually put a soldier in the cells for this complete lack of discipline, especially a soldier with Cundill's experience. That would be for later though, as Archer suspected by the mayhem outside that he would need all the soldiers possible at this time. Archer quickly got dressed into his uniform. His uniform was crisp and almost new looking. It was his everyday uniform. It was red and burgundy camouflaged trousers and shirt, along with shiny black boots and a red beret. He was close to six foot tall and broad, so looked quite intimidating. Cundill told him what was happening outside. They left the room, and outside in the corridor it was chaotic. His soldiers were running around everywhere. Archer was disgusted by their actions, as they were trained soldiers. He decided after this was over they would all be severely reprimanded.

He screamed to his men at the top of his voice, 'Form up outside and prepare for the fight.'

He glowed now, and with his shield up was looking forward to the fight, as he had never had the chance of doing anything like this before. On his way to the parade ground Archer grabbed one of the lieutenants and told him to get a squad of men, and told them to take the families to the ships. The ships were old, rusty wrecks that had never been flown in his lifetime. They were covered in moss and dust. He was disgusted to think that he would need to use them, as he fully thought he would win this fight. No good soldier would put lives at risk though. He just hoped the ships would start if they really needed them. Archer told the lieutenant it was imperative to stay with the families and protect them. The lieutenant wasn't happy, as he wanted to be part of the fight, but knew he had to do as commanded. Archer got to the parade ground door and headed outside with long, marching strides. He couldn't believe what he saw. Smoke and dust everywhere. Not too far in the distance was a huge crowd coming their way. He looked to the side and Cundill had got the men together. There were around five thousand strong men. Cundill was at the front yelling at the men in his own unique way, which was boorish and condescending. The men hated Cundill, but Archer loved him, and that's all that mattered. Archer took a quick glance around and some laser bolts shot past them and hit the barracks. Archer looked across and saw some flying bikes firing at them. The bikes seemed to be in disarray. The shots were bad, as not one of his men got hit. Archer was going to get his men to attack, when suddenly the bikers all seemed to veer off and go to the right. Archer knew straight away where they were heading, so he told Cundill to send some squads after them, as they were going to destroy the shield generator. He thought they wouldn't be able to get through the protective shield for the generator itself, but could not take the risk. Off the men went to protect the generator, and others remained on the parade ground ready for battle.

Archer turned around and the alien-like creatures were nearly on them, and he could see them for the first time. He was taken aback. They were alien. Not just one species. Some were huge. Some were small. There felt like thousands of them. The front few thousand were in a regular military formation pattern. He could not see the others properly behind them, but it felt like they were less regimented and in disarray. Archer stepped to the back of his men and left Cundill in front. One of the huge aliens ran towards the men. The alien must have been ten-foot-tall, with four arms coming out of his upper torso. Two from his shoulders and two from above his hips. The alien appeared to have full armour or it could have been his skin, as Archer had never witnessed anything like these creatures before. Archer also noticed a helmet on the creature with what appeared to be a red slit across, where his eyes could be.

Cundill ordered one of Archer's private soldiers to step forward and engage the alien. The alien hit him with maximum momentum and repelled him back about ten feet, punching and kicking the private with all its force. The private regained his balance and was going to attack, when the alien suddenly pulled a bar from behind his back. The alien shook the bar and it turned into a huge glowing spear. He aimed the spear straight at the private. Archer thought the private would be dead, but the spear just hit the private's shield and seem to stick in it. The alien looked shocked and angry by this. The private swiftly pulled the spear out and somersaulted himself over the alien's head. The alien turned to hit the private, but this time the private caught one of its huge arms. He launched the alien fifty feet, over the on-rushing crowd of aliens. The aliens stopped immediately, and Archer hoped seeing this sheer feat of strength would deter them. There was a pause and they just stood for a few seconds. Then Archer was sure he heard something shout in their language. The aliens went crazy and began their assault. Cundill screamed, 'Attack', and the soldiers rocketed into them. The aliens flew everywhere, and the men scattered the first few ranks of aliens. The aliens kept coming. Some fighting hand to hand with the soldiers. This didn't go well for the aliens. Some aliens had lasers, firing laser arrows and throwing bouncing laser balls at the men. They hit the men's shields with quite a bang. The balls and arrows would return straight back to the aliens, who had fired them.

3

Archer was pleased with the way the battle was going. Slowly but surely, they were pushing the aliens back. Then all of a sudden, the front of the aliens retreated back. The soldiers stopped and cheered at the amazement of their efforts. They then noticed the aliens had actually retreated a hundred yards behind a new set of huge aliens. Archer noticed that in the front, leading the way, was now the alien the private had attacked and thrown over the crowd earlier. He looked shaky, but the alien had regained his composure and seemed to be in charge. The alien gave out an order and the front row of aliens stepped forward, pulling bars out from behind their backs. This time, instead of holding them vertically and making the spear, they turned them horizontally and all at once the bars linked up and a huge laser shield was produced. It must have been twelve-foot-high and went all the way along the row of aliens. As soon as the shield went up, the aliens slowly moved forward again. Archer knew the shield would make this battle much more difficult and more drawn out than he was hoping for. Corporal Nineham's unit was just starting to catch up with the aliens on the flying bikes. The aliens were bombarding the shield generator. The shield generator was just past the housing sector, in a little courtyard of its own. It was in an unremarkable, corrugated iron building with a small door to enter it. Laser blasts were bouncing in all directions off the shield protecting the generator. It looked like chaos. They were flying in and out blasting it. He thought to himself that they will never get through the shield that way. However, as he got nearer he thought he could hear a banging noise. He couldn't put his finger on what it was or where it was coming from, but there was something. He would come back to that, but the first thing he had to do was engage the biker aliens. The unit was about to engage, but to their surprise they were bombarded by laser bolts from above. There were so many bolts, it looked like rain. They were now being attacked by hundreds of flying aliens. These were new! They weren't so large. About four feet long and quite thin. They had little pointy heads, short arms and legs. Their wings were long and elegant, and as long as their bodies, and they were flying at speed. Some of the men

4

jumped up to grab them, but these flying aliens were just too quick and out of their grabbing range. They seemed to be firing some sort of sling shot, where laser bolts would appear and they would rain down on them. To the alien's dismay, the bolts bounced off the men's shields. This slowed the men, but annoyingly had no other effect.

Corporal Nineham always knew that he had been strong in his younger years and could bend steel. Punching steel had been more difficult for him years ago, causing him to shatter his hand and break his arm. He never tried that again until later in life. He was taught that when he hit, he would gain a force field around the whole of his body that was impregnable. It was millimetres away from his body and whatever he was wearing, and he could smash through anything knowing he would not get hurt. He felt unbeatable. All the men had these force shields. They all followed orders without question, even when they didn't agree with them. They never knew why, but that was the way they had always been since their teenage years. Nineham snapped out of his reminiscing.

The bikers had noticed Nineham's unit coming and turned their attention to them. They turned their bikes around and attacked. The Corporal thought, at least they have stopped firing at the shield, with a slight chuckle to himself. Due to the huge volume of aliens, the Corporal ordered his men to take cover behind the houses along the street they were running up. The men did not like this, because they thought their shields were protection and didn't need to hide, but they obeyed orders. Before they could get to the houses, a bike caught up with them and Nineham. The bike was long and smooth, with legs going down towards the ground, and handle bars at the front. There were blasters both sides of the machine and they were blasting at them. Nineham could only just see the alien with its half-moon crescent head. It was coming directly for Nineham now. To give his men time to get to cover behind the houses, he stopped and turned around. However, the flying coloured aliens above them kept flying in and out towards the men, and Nineham wished they would go away. Nineham held his ground as the biker flew at him, blasters firing and bouncing off him going far and wide, but he could now see other bikers heading towards him. There were hundreds, if not thousands. So, he decided this was his only chance to side step this alien, pull him from the bike, jump on it and scatter the alien bikers. This should give his men time to reach cover behind the houses. This did not go as planned! He side stepped the bike and ripped the alien from it with sheer force. It felt like the alien was glued to the machine, but as soon as he managed to pull the alien from the bike, the bike lost power and lost all energy. He looked at the alien now in his hands. It was long and extremely thin, and as he looked directly at the alien it looked like it had an ever so slight glow to it. He didn't have time to inspect it further, so quickly knocked it out and threw it to the side. The other bikes were now flying directly at him. Fifty of them blasting continuously. Nineham side stepped some blasts and his force shield deflected a few. The bike of the alien, he had dragged the alien off earlier, was still lying on the floor. He twisted round and with his immense strength picked it up with ease. A couple of bikes were nearly on him, so he changed his grip with this bike, swivelled round and used the bike like a baseball bat. He swung the bike round, smashing it into the one of the oncoming bikes that then caused it to veer and collide with the other one. Nineham smiled to himself. With what he had left of the bike in his hands, he tossed this towards the onrushing others. It hit a couple and made many of them run into each other, and then caused an explosion of parts and debris. In turn, a big cloud of dust erupted. With decreased visibility, Nineham knew that this was his chance to get to cover before the attack could continue. He was about to turn and run, when he noticed the thudding noise again he had heard earlier. He knew he needed to find out where this was and what it was. He ran towards the cover of the houses to find his men. He got behind one of the houses, trying to regain his breath, when the blaster fire started again from the bikers. He could also hear the coloured aliens overhead. They weren't firing now, but hunting for Nineham and his men. He contacted his men through their earpieces to find out where they were hiding. He headed to them. When Nineham arrived, the men were chuckling to themselves.

Nineham asked, 'What are you laughing about?'

Abbott, who was one of the privates said, 'We are just laughing, because we can't believe you used that bike as a baseball bat!'

Nineham smirked, 'It just came to me!'

The men liked Nineham, and could have a laugh and joke with him. They didn't feel the same way about Archer and Cundill though. Nineham asked Abbott how they had evaded the flying aliens. Abbott told him that as soon as the squad got to the houses they seemed to lose the aliens. He remembered someone saying once that the shields had some way of concealing them, when being chased. Some called it dark mode. As they had never been attacked before, they never knew the shields were able to do this. Nineham thought this was incredible and very helpful. He got all the men into one of the houses, then got them together and asked if they had heard the banging noise. Sherlock and some of the others said that they had, and thought it was coming from the other side of the yard. Nineham took it upon himself to find the source of this sound. He went outside with a pair of binoculars and had a look around, and all appeared to be clear. He could still hear the bikers and flying aliens around looking for them, but he had to take the chance and find the source of the noise. He bent a little and then launched himself up onto the roof. With his strength this gave him and the others the opportunity to leap huge distances, so the roof was no problem. Up there on the roof he could see the bikers going in and out the side streets, and the flying aliens around the skies still looking for them. He took the binoculars out and looked across the yard to where Sherlock thought the sound was coming from. At first all he could see was a couple of bikers. Nothing surprising. Then one of the bikers moved back a little, and he could definitely see where the sound was coming from. There were sparks coming from the shield, and a sharp device with what looked like a surge of electricity constantly hitting the shield. The shield was colourless, and so you could only see it from certain angles or when something hit it. At the back of the device, to his amazement, were some tiny aliens no bigger than his hand. Little stubby creatures with flat faces. They seemed to be pushing all the buttons on the device. Some were standing guard. He couldn't see what the guards were holding, but presumed they had some kind of weapons. Nineham came off the roof and went to his men and told them what he had seen. He told them they must destroy the device, as this is how he suspected they had got through the main shield. He formed a plan. Himself, Abbott and Sherlock would go and destroy the device, and the others would draw the aliens away by breaking cover. They would somehow lose the aliens and get back to the ships. So, off they went on their separate missions. Nineham, Abbott and Sherlock would have to get to the houses closest to the shield and then improvise. As the other men broke cover, there was a huge commotion. The flying aliens began diving from all angles in the sky towards them to attack. Nineham felt guilty using them as decoys, but had to get to the device somehow. He suspected that even in dark mode, himself, Abbott and Sherlock might get seen in the open space of the yard. So, when they got to the nearest house to the generator producing the shield, they all jumped onto the roof. They could see a few bikers, which they knew would not be a problem, but more biker reinforcements would come quickly. There, to one side, was the device. Sparks flying from the shield were visible now and quite large. Nineham knew he must get to it quickly. He had a quick look around, but from this distance and with the big open space he knew they would be seen before they got to the device, even though he could jump great distances. Then an idea came to him.

He turned to Abbott and Sherlock and said, 'If this works, follow me!'

Abbott said, 'If what works?' but Nineham was already up on his feet.

He ran across the spine of the roof, as quick as he could, keeping his balance at this speed. He got to the end and launched himself off the roof. In mid-air he thought to himself, 'I really hope this shield is a dome like the outer shield for the base, because if it's flat this is going to look really stupid!' With the shield being invisible he had no way of knowing this. He was starting to lose momentum and was coming down in the air, when all of a sudden, he hit something. He was just able to keep his balance, and looked down to see that about thirty feet below him was the ground. He thought, 'Thank God this worked!' He had no time to think though, as the bikers were screaming in their own language as soon as he landed, and so he started running. Behind him, Abbott and Sherlock landed. Sherlock only just made it, being weaker than both of them, and landed on the up curve of the dome and nearly fell backwards. Abbott was just quick enough to grab him.

Over his shoulder, Nineham bellowed, 'Take care of the bikers. I'll destroy the device.'

He was on the down curve now. It was so disconcerting, feeling like you are running in mid-air on this invisible shield. He could barely keep upright, as the gradient increased on the downward curve of this shield. So, he thought that's enough and jumped on his rear and started to slide. On the way down, he noticed he was going to land right on top of the device. He thought, 'Great, I'll crush it under my foot.' He then took a glimpse at the tiny aliens. They were screaming something in their language. He thought they were pointing to him and shouting the bikers over, but to his surprise he could see laser bolts. He thought with the size of the aliens and probably the tiny little guns, then why bother firing at them. Within milliseconds of them firing the laser bolts, the bolts doubled in size through the air. The bolts expanded in width and length as they shot through the air, and were as wide as fists and long as forearms by the time they got near Nineham. He was grateful the aliens weren't a good shot, as instead the blasts were hitting the shield with a huge bang and not him. He knew the other aliens were aware of him, Abbott and Sherlock, and wished he could slide quicker. He landed on the device, which knocked it back off the shield, and the sparks stopped. He kicked the device across the courtyard. It took out some of the tiny aliens on the way. They were still screaming, and hitting Nineham with a few laser shots. The shots were the most powerful things he had ever felt. They weren't getting through his shield, but they were stopping him in his tracks, which was annoying him because they needed to get out of there. He could hear a massive amount of noise coming their way and knew the bikers and flying aliens would have given up looking for all of his other men, and were now coming back to protect their device. Abbott and Sherlock were down now and off the shield and were just about to engage the bikers, when the bikers did something strange. One flew directly for the two soldiers. Abbott side stepped the bike, grabbed the back of the bike and flung it back to where it came from. It landed with a thud and appeared to be dead. The other bike flew at Sherlock. Sherlock was ready for it. At the last moment, the biker swerved to the side and went straight to the shield. Nineham thought this was suicidal for the biker as surely it would explode on the shield, but to their surprise the biker went half way through and just seemed to get stuck. Nineham knew then that the tiny aliens were not screaming at him, but to the bikers as they thought the shield was weak enough to get through. With only half the bike through, the alien was able to start blasting at the building containing the generator.

The bike was slowly, but surely, starting to get through now against the shield's resistance. Nineham shouted to Sherlock to pull it out of there. Sherlock ran over, but was too late. The bike was through and getting closer to the building, and they knew the iron cladding of the building would not last very long. At this point, it would be able to attack the generator. Nineham needed to get in there. He ran at the shield as well. He hit the shield and it slowed him, but he got through. As soon as he got through there was an almighty bang, and the explosion knocked him off his feet. The main generator was gone and the shield that protected it was also gone. The outer shield must have gone down for a few seconds too, as in the distance he saw some huge blaster shots rain down. This meant there had to be some big ships up there in space. Luckily the backup generator kicked in. It wasn't big and had a shield on it, but the shield was only surrounding the generator and didn't come out as far as the main generator. Knowing the old, worn out condition of the backup generator, he knew they didn't have long. Then the moment he was dreading. His earpiece buzzed and Captain Archer's voice came through.

'What was that, Corporal?' he said.

Nineham quickly explained the situation and could hear the hatred in Archer's response.

'That's very disappointing Corporal. I will deal with you later. Just get you and your men back to the ships.'

Nineham thought that this was strange. He would want them to join back up with the other men who were fighting the aliens, but he did as he was ordered.

He turned to Abbott and Sherlock and said, 'Let's get out of here.'

The tiny aliens had got their senses back after the explosion and had started firing again, but the three men had made it back to the houses and had disappeared into the shadows.

Back at the main battle, it wasn't going well. The huge aliens were starting to push them back, because of the huge difference in numbers. Thousands of other aliens had joined them. They just seemed to keep coming. Some of the men tried to jump the shields, but when they did so some eight-foot aliens would fly up and push them back, and as the men were in the air they could not use their strength. The aliens were big ferocious creatures with huge wings.

Archer was dismayed with the news of the generator and how bad things were going. He thought this battle had been lost. He felt sick to his stomach. He needed a new plan and quickly. He got Cundill and told him that they needed to retreat. Cundill wasn't happy and said that they never retreated. Archer threw him a look and Cundill shut up immediately.

'We have to retreat, Sergeant,' Archer said. 'We have to keep fighting, but get back to the barracks. We will have to try and lose them in the buildings, so that we can get back to the ships. We will lose here, if the backup generator fails. We will get attacked from the sky as well. Even our shields can't repel that kind of firepower.'

They slowly inched their way back to the barracks, getting bombarded from everywhere. The aliens were getting braver now. The enormous ones coming from behind their shields, stabbing and slicing at them with their huge spears, but still not getting through the soldier's shields. Archer could see the aliens were trying to outflank them to slow their retreat back to the barracks. The alien numbers were increasing rapidly. The front rank holding the shields, twisted their bars vertically and all of their shields changed to become glowing spears again. They charged forward towards them.

Archer sensed that was it and ordered all the men to return to the ships at once, as the planet had been lost. In their haste, the squad had splintered into small groups, but they all made it back to the barracks alive and uninjured. They would have to use stealth now rather than brawn. They went through the back streets. The aliens were everywhere. Aliens of all different shapes, sizes and breeds. Most of the time with dark mode on their shields the men could evade the aliens, but when they came to open ground they had to out manoeuvre them. They could not take the chance they were being followed, because if the aliens found the ships before they got there, their families wouldn't stand a chance. Archer, Cundill and the group they were in got to the outside of the hangar with the ships in. There were some aliens within the grounds, but they hadn't found the hangar. The hangar was well hidden underground, within a cave system. Archer gave the order to fire up the engines and the lieutenant gave him the great news that all the ships had started. The ships were a little rusty and beat up, but good to go. Archer looked at the aliens and decided that they needed to get past them, without the aliens getting reinforcements. He was considering what to do, when from the other side of the yard he saw Nineham. Nineham and his men caught the aliens off guard, knocking them out and dragging them to one side. Then Nineham went over to Archer.

'We could see you in the shadows and we got the jump on those things, so we took our chance.'

Archer just looked and said, 'That was foolish of you, Corporal. You could have got us all killed, and this won't help you with your reprimand when this is all done.'

Cundill barged forward past Archer, trying to knock Nineham over, but Nineham was too quick and dodged him. Archer and the rest followed the huge man. Nineham was seething. He hated the two men.

Archer, over his shoulder, said to Nineham, 'Are all the men here yet?'

Nineham replied through gritted teeth, 'Not yet, Sir.'

Archer replied, 'They better hurry up or we leave without them.'

Nineham was disgusted by this, 'You can't leave without all the men.'

Archer replied, 'You best go find them Corporal Nineham, and be quick about it. We will leave in an hour.'

Nineham was going to argue, but thought what's the point. In his opinion, Archer was a self-centred, arrogant man and he hadn't seen Archer or Cundill lay a finger on an alien yet.

Nineham communicated through the earpieces. There was one group of men left to make it back to the ships. The aliens had found them and they had been cornered. One of the men explained through the earpiece that they were trapped. The aliens were firing on them with huge blaster shots. Nineham knew which of these aliens they were immediately. They were the tiny aliens he had come across earlier.

'Give me your location, private. We will come and help you.'

Nineham took the men with him to the location given. There was blaster fire everywhere. He knew it would be hard to find these tiny aliens that were doing the firing, as they could hide almost anywhere. Their firing was erratic and badly placed. They could never hit their target. Nineham could tell from his own military training that these aliens had not been trained like a normal soldier would be. They were just fighting in their own way. The only way they knew. They were making such a noise, and this concerned Nineham that they were trying to attract the attention of more aliens to join them.

Nineham got all the men together. They needed a solution and quickly. Time was short. He said they needed to find where this firing was actually coming from and isolate it. They created a plan. It wasn't subtle, but it would have to do. They went into dark mode, and crept up behind a wall leading to the courtyard.

They could just spot the muzzle fire from the guns. It was in one of the empty houses, adjacent to the canteen, that the men were in. So, Nineham, Abbott and Sherlock positioned themselves behind the house. They got ready and then just ran through the back door. They took it off its hinges and headed straight through the wall and into the living room, where they found the aliens. The shock on the alien's faces was comical, but they had no time to laugh. The aliens scattered, some going under furniture and into vents in the walls, and a few escaped getting out the house where the men had entered. The men just kept running. Abbott and Sherlock first through the wall, now running across the courtyard to the canteen to get the trapped men. Nineham was just behind to one side, when he noticed one of the aliens. He thought he was going to fire at him, so quick as he could he raced over and grabbed the alien. He put it under his arm like a rugby ball and ran towards his men. He caught up with the men at the canteen. They were there with the other men.

He went over to them and Abbott said, 'What's that under your arm wriggling?'

Nineham just shrugged and said, 'I will show you back at the ship, private. Let's go.'

Nineham could hear the aliens mobilising down the way and knew this would be a chase all the way back. He would have to give away the location of the hangar, but this didn't matter. Either they got to the ships and out, or captured and possibly killed. These were the only two outcomes. They took off running, as fast as they could. Faster than normal humans, but not as fast as these flying aliens or biker aliens, so hoped they weren't about. To his relief he could hear them, but it sounded like they were in the distance. The ones actually chasing them were the huge aliens, with some new breed of alien he had not seen before. The latter was not so quick, but the huge aliens had more pace than expected, but luckily not as quick as the men. The men all got close to the hangar entrance without injury, not before the aliens had attempted to stop them. Noticing where the men were going, the aliens threw their spears towards the cave where the hangar entrance was. The cave entrance started to collapse with the force of the spears hitting it. A few rocks hit the men, but they got through the entrance and not a moment too soon. As they got into the hangar, one of the ships was in the air and on its way out. He bet that would be Archer's ship. He was right. Then suddenly another ship rose into the air. That left one last ship. Nineham and his men just made it by diving on the ramp, as the ship's ramp was starting to elevate. As they reached the top of the ramp Nineham looked at his watch. He had five minutes left. He thought that Archer left early on purpose! He grabbed the co-pilot in his ship and asked him who gave the order for the ships to leave. He said Archer had given the order to leave, as it was getting too dangerous for the men, children and women to stay, but our pilot disobeyed the order to give you time to return. Nineham went to the pilot and thanked him, as he knew he would be in trouble for disobeying such an order. Nineham went to the back of the ship with the others. The women and children were in another section of the ship.

Abbott went across and said, 'What is this thing you were going to show me?'

Nineham looked at him and was going to say, 'What are you talking about?' Then he suddenly realised, in the haste of their escape, what he had been carrying under his arm was now curled up in the crook of his arm in a tiny ball like a baby. There lay a tiny alien curled up.

On Archer's ship, Archer was stood with the pilot on the flight deck. The flight deck was large enough for a group of people. He was as calm as ever, telling the pilot to get them out of there.

The pilot said, 'The course is set Sir, but we won't get far with the shield up.'

Archer said, 'Don't worry about that Captain.'

He went to Cundill.

'Sergeant. I want you to overload the generator, so that it hopefully destroys the base and kills some aliens. It will bide us some time.'

Cundill went over to the computer.

'Not yet,' Archer said, 'We must time this just right.'

15

The pilot said, 'It is about twenty seconds to the shield, Sir.' Archer gave the order to overload the generator. It would be tight, but it had to be. The other two ships were right behind them now. Ten seconds from the shield, the generator exploded. The shockwave was intense and it pushed all of the ships forward, but the pilots thankfully regained control. Archer looked out of the window, but couldn't see much in the big smoke cloud and red dust caused by the blast. He hoped he had destroyed the whole base, but could not be sure. He told the pilot to head to the nearest moon, as they would need more speed. They would use the gravity of a moon to slingshot them around towards the programmed co-ordinates. As they climbed higher, Archer looked back. He was saddened that his home of fifty-two years had gone. If he got the chance, and survived this, then he would get his revenge. One last look back towards the Mars base, and Archer thought it was gone. They could see the alien armada now on the other side of the planet. There were ships hurriedly going to and from the planet, so most of the aliens had clearly survived to Archer's dismay. There were some enormous alien ships, possibly a few hundred of these ships. They must have been a hundred times bigger than their three ships. There were also some very small ships, scuttling about them like mosquitoes. All of the alien ships seemed to be different shapes and sizes. They were gradually heading round to face the three ships trying to escape. They had been spotted. Archer speculated that the alien ships would be much quicker than the old rust buckets they were in. These were the old ships that got them to Mars many centuries ago, and looked a little old and outdated compared to these alien ships. He just hoped that it would take them a while to pick up all the aliens, before they could chase after Archer and the other two ships. Archer and the other two ships were heading to the outer atmosphere of Mar's moon Phobos. They circled around the peninsular and tripled their speed. The chase would be on once momentum was lost from this slingshot effect. Hopefully they could get back to Earth and safety. Sensors on the flight deck were picking up a huge amount of movement in the distance now, and they had gained a sizeable lead on the alien's ships. However, they were starting to lose momentum. They could now see another moon in the distance and a little bright blue speck that was the Earth. Archer hoped Earth would be as beautiful as he had been told. They would have to get to Earth's moon and then slingshot around, before heading towards the Earth. He was hoping second time is the charm! The sensors were now detecting all the alien ships and they were in pursuit. They were a lot quicker than them. He suspected the alien ships had light speed, though they couldn't use it in the solar system. Archer's ship and the other two ships had utilised their head start on the alien ships, and Archer hoped this would get them to Earth. His ship at least! They were coming up to the moon. One last swing around and they would be there. They flew as close as they could to get the best momentum, but this time they didn't come out quite as quick as the first time. The race was truly on. The alien ships were gaining with each minute. Earth was getting larger, but they were still a way off. The alien ships started firing. They were out of range still, but doing it to frighten the three ships they were in pursuit of. It had the desired effect on Archer's ship as Archer and Cundill cowered in the corner of the flight deck, and the women and children were heard screaming and crying. Even some soldiers were crying and visibly upset. When fighting in their shields they felt protected, but when in the cold, darkness of space then this was a totally different scenario.

Nineham's ship was a completely different environment. He was petrified himself, but he knew he had to keep everyone's minds off what was happening outside. He got his men to do all different kinds of things. Some sang, some played games and Nineham would entertain and clown around in front of the children to distract them and make them laugh.

The three ships were reaching the upper atmosphere of Earth and they were starting to experience turbulent air. They also had laser fire from behind them from the approaching alien's ships. With the two effects, it was making it harder to keep the ships on course. Archer gave the order to send the code that they had been given decades ago, to hopefully allow them to

enter Earth's atmosphere. He hoped it worked, as he had never had to use it, having never left Mars before and never needed contact with Earth. The silence was deafening and he thought going to Earth could be a bad idea. Then all of a sudden, a young pompous kid came over the speaker.
'Who is this and where did you get this code?' he said.
Archer was quick to reply.
'We are from the Mars base Alpha and we need sanctuary. We are being chased by aliens and they are determined to destroy us.'
The kid came back, and with a chuckle over the speaker said, 'Mars base Alpha? I've never heard of it. I say again, where did you get this code?'
This riled Archer and he screamed into the speaker, 'Look kid, we have women and children on these ships. We need help.'
Again, the speaker went quiet and seemed to take minutes, but was probably seconds. Then there was a crackle and the kid came back.
'I've just spoken to my supervisor and he has given the clearance, because you have a code. A very old one, but still ok. Follow the coordinates I send you and do not deviate, or you will hit the shield.'
The relief on Archer was palpable and he said thank you through gritted teeth, but knew him and the kid might have words in the future. All three ships got through the atmosphere and the clouds, and they could see Earth for the first time. The blue colour of the sea and the white fluffy clouds were beautiful to their eyes. It felt bright and cheerful to them. This was not like the dark days and red sands of Mars. Archer believed he was going to love it here, but at that moment he was brought back to Earth literally! Some small alien ships fell through the clouds firing at them. As always, most shots seemed to miss, but a few did hit Nineham's ship. Luckily the armour plating kept them safe, but they knew they couldn't get hit many more times and couldn't get hit by the bigger ships at all. They accelerated for the coordinates they had been given. The small alien ships were in pursuit. They could see the land in the distance. It was green and felt very bright compared to the

browns and reds of Mars. They could see some white areas, near the blue edges of the sea they were approaching. As the sun glistened on the blue waters, Archer could also see a strange glowing outline, about half a mile from these white cliffs. He assumed this must be the Earth's shield. They were still following the co-ordinates, which were still a distance away from this glowing outline. It was even further to the greens and browns, of what they presumed was the land. Archer thought the kid had purposely deceived them. Then the sensors on their ship detected a large object coming through the clouds, which Archer assumed was a large alien ship. It was detecting a large surge of power from it. Archer was just about to give the order to get out of there, but where to he did not know! He knew they couldn't get hit by a laser bolt from that ship, otherwise their ships would be destroyed. Archer cleared his throat and was about to speak, when a huge pipe shot out of the water below them and sucked their three ships in. As they accelerated through this pipe, it appeared the small alien ships had been left behind. He heard a loud noise from behind them, where they had entered the pipe. Had they just avoided a laser blast from the huge alien ship? Before he knew it, his ship and the other two ships were safely in a huge hangar.

The now familiar and distinctive voice of the kid came over the speaker, 'Do not leave your ships, as our troops will attack you. Someone will be there shortly to assess you.'

Archer was about to abruptly reply to the kid, when he stepped outside the flight deck to be sick. On his way out, he could see Cundill had been crying and was sitting in the corner. After Archer was sick, all he selfishly thought to himself is at least I'm safe. No consideration for others or the families.

Chapter Two

Two days before this alien attack on Mars, Chantelle had been woken up by her alarm. The radio was playing one of her favourite songs. She was out of bed and into the shower in seconds. She was looking forward to her day. She had just started working and loved it. All of her life Chantelle had wanted to join the armed forces, but Miss Che was adamant that she shouldn't, and Chantelle did not want to upset Miss Che. So, Miss Che was not happy when she got a job in the Ministry of Defence as a scientist. Miss Che was Chantelle's mothers' best friend. When Chantelle's mother passed away, when she was aged five, Miss Che took on her guardianship as she had no other family. Miss Che did not want her going into foster care.

As Miss Che always said, 'Chan, you are special.'

Chantelle knew she was extremely strong, despite only being five foot tall and having a slight stature. She could pick up a sofa by herself at age five. She seemed to get stronger through the years of adolescence, and discovered some sort of force shield around her that she could not control at first. Miss Che seemed to know Chantelle would develop this over time, and kept her out of school and away from others until she had it under control, which was aided very quickly by the help of Miss Che. She had lots of questions from her friends about her absence from school for that long, but she could not tell them. Miss Che said, 'No-one can ever know your secret!'

When Chantelle finished her shower, she went back to her room to get dressed and get her bag packed ready for work. Her room wasn't very big, but it was immaculate. Everything was where it was meant to be, and as always, she made her bed before leaving the room. Chantelle wasn't your usual seventeen-year-old. She wasn't into trinkets. The only thing on her wall was her diploma in scientific theory and practical. She had finished in the top ten in her school for academic results, which given where she started in life was a great accomplishment. She hadn't had much growing up, but she had never let this be a barrier to her. Miss Che needed to hold her back a little, as she could have done even better, but she didn't want her to be in the limelight for others to see her academic rigor. She could decipher languages just listening to people. With her bag on her back, she grabbed her phone on the way out of her room and walked down the hall to the kitchen and living area. Miss Che was sitting at the table having her breakfast. 10.16 robot was milling around doing it's chores. The room's settings today had been programmed to be in a late eighties style. Shag pile carpets, wood panel walls and a massive tube TV in the corner with a black leather sofa in front of it. That's what they thought the eighties looked like anyway! Miss Che didn't like the style of today's twenty third century. As soon as Chantelle got into the room, she pressed a button on her phone which changed the phone into her own robot. This was a 5.8 robot. Much less sophisticated than Miss Che's 10.16, but with Chantelle just starting work the 5.8 was all she could afford with robot prices and insurances being so high. Miss Che could afford hers, because of her great pension. What Miss Che did for employment in the past Chantelle did not know. It was never spoken about. She never told her, but it must have been good as Miss Che was only in her late forties. Miss Che was of Oriental descent and was an imposing woman. She stood six-foot-tall and for a lady she was quite broad. She was a stunning looking woman as well. Her hazel eyes would burn through you if she stared at you. She had great cheekbones, with a little scar below her right eye. This apparently, she got from protecting herself using her martial arts training. She taught these three different styles of martial arts to Chantelle.

She had noticed Chantelle walk into the room.

'Morning Chan,' she said. 'Would you like 10.16 to make your breakfast or would you like 5.8 to try again?' with a sarcastic chuckle.

The first time 5.8 had tried to make breakfast had not gone well. Having not long been activated, the robot had to learn, and must have used the wrong data in its system. It had burned everything, nearly setting the apartment on fire.

Chan said, 'No, I will do it today. 5.8 can just get the rest of my things ready for work.'

Miss Che's mood changed immediately and she said, 'You know I don't like you working there. I think you can do better than that with your background in science. You should be in nanotech companies or graphene industries. I just don't get your infatuation with the forces.'

Chantelle just rolled her eyes at Miss Che and said, 'I'm not having this conversation again Che. It's my choice and I really enjoy it.'

Miss Che was tempted to respond, but thought better of it today. She was an imposing woman, but was a soft touch with Chantelle and Chantelle knew she could manipulate her. They chatted a little longer, but Chantelle noticed the time and knew she had to get to the other side of London to catch the train. They said their goodbyes and she shut down 5.8. She grabbed her visor and helmet and headed towards the back of the kitchen. As she did so, she would use the helmet to change her hair colour from the green streaks to pink, as she thought this might look nice.

Miss Che shouted to her, 'You better use the door today,' but Chantelle already had her feet hanging out the window and was on her way.

From the bottom up the building had a curve in it up to about the fifth floor, and from there went vertically up for about another thirty floors. Chantelle was on the sixth floor, so just dropped out the window each day. This drove Miss Che mad. Chantelle dropped a floor down the curve and her hover skates would then propel her, and she would speed down the curve onto the streets below. She had adapted her hover skates, so she could get some high speeds out of them. She skated up the street at around thirty to forty miles per hour, which wasn't a problem nowadays as cars were about fifty feet overhead. The car lanes up there were incredibly busy. On the ground, market stalls were being opened with fresh fruit and vegetables being put out along her route. The produce was plentiful nowadays under the shield covering the United Kingdom, as the temperature could now be controlled. The shield went up decades ago, as they were told the ozone layer had nearly gone, and the country needed protection from the sun. The protection from this shield, which resembled a greenhouse, was great and temperatures could be adapted within it to suit the growth of produce. In some cities, such as London, they controlled the temperature to be around twenty degrees during the day and slightly cooler at night.

Chantelle was racing on her skates through the streets. She loved hover skating early in the morning. She had many of the streets to herself. She had to be careful though, even in these days of well-developed technology, as there were still areas of bad poverty and robberies went on in these areas. If the robbers tried anything with her they wouldn't get far with her strength and martial art training. She could hear the river now, as she sped down the streets. 'Not far from London Bridge,' she thought. Her head set activated, but she couldn't take the visual on her visor at the speed she was skating at, so she selected audio. It was her best friend Bronwyn.

'C,' she said.

C was her nickname for Chantelle.

'We're out tonight, if you're available after work? Maybe you can tell us about your day!' she chuckled, knowing Chantelle could not talk about her Ministry of Defence work.

Chantelle knew they would mainly talk about property they had sold, as most were estate agents, and what lovely new cars they had with their large salaries. Bronwyn and her friends sometimes made fun of Chantelle for not having a car, but she didn't mind as she loved hover skating and could not afford a car. She liked to catch up with them though. She loved being around them.

'No problems, I'll see you at the bar later,' she said.

Bronwyn said, 'Great. I'll call you later to let you know which bar we are in.'

Chantelle said goodbye and signed out of the audio. As Chantelle reached London Bridge she could see the city in all of its glory. There were massive buildings with the enhancement of graphene now infused into their structures. Buildings had got bigger, thinner and structurally stronger with the graphene, but the Government always said old buildings like St Paul's Cathedral and the Houses of Parliament should be visible from anywhere. The scientists had been clever. When no one was in the buildings and the lights went off, the buildings became transparent. Cars never collided with the buildings, as the cars had sensors which corrected their course, along with road signs in the mid-air lanes for the drivers to see. The sun was now shining along the River Thames, and the sun's glow reflected off the buildings showing them in all of their glory. The buildings shone in many colours. Chantelle stopped to admire this. She paused to marvel at how beautiful London was. She stood there for a minute taking in the view this morning. Then she quickly remembered she would miss her train if she stopped any longer. She fired up her blades and was off again. The people were landing in the city now for work. She saw a huge car land not far from her, and a big man in a nice suit got out. He pressed the side of his car and it turned back into his phone. She thought to herself, 'Nice. The rich just get richer.' She skated up through Farringdon, and headed towards Kings Cross. She had noticed a lot of graffiti on the walls leading up to the station in recent days saying, 'Let us out,' which she thought was activists talking about shutting the ozone shield down. She thought that this was crazy, as scientists were monitoring the ozone layer, and there was very little of the ozone layer left. Chantelle always trusted science, and thought the activists were just ignorant and did not have the knowledge to know what they were talking about. The cleaning robots would be arriving shortly to clean the graffiti off these walls, and Chantelle was glad.

As Chantelle reached Kings Cross station she tapped her heels together, which shut the blades off, and they transformed into her comfortable work trainers. She pulled her helmet and visor off and her hair had pink flecks in it, as she had wanted. Her new helmet was great. It kept her safe, but she also enjoyed having the ability to do her hair any colour and style she wanted that day. She thought this was marvellous. She stored her helmet into her backpack and walked into the station. Chantelle loved the train station, especially the hustle and bustle of the early morning commute. She would just stand and observe people's actions and mannerisms. There were people running here and there, in a rush, probably late for work. With technology, tickets were easier than ever to get, but still some people forgot to get them. It always made her laugh how people forgot this! Then there were the easy-going people just taking their time, looking relaxed and possibly just going on their holidays. She waited a few minutes, before her train was called. This was the 8.10am to Lincoln. The train only took a few minutes to reach Lincoln nowadays. She got into her section on the train and it was quite full this morning. At 8.10am the train departed. It travelled through the tunnel. There was no track. The tunnel transforms in front of the train in a transparent cylindrical motion. She thought it was amazing what nanotechnology and graphene had done to transform travel. Travel was faster and cleaner. As soon as the train went through the tunnel, the tunnel behind it disappeared, so there was no trace of it as it sped into the distance. It gave nature a chance to grow, as the train moved swiftly through the landscapes. Chantelle would have liked to see the huge trees and lush fields of greens and yellows, but the speed of the train always meant that this was just a blur as they travelled by. Before she knew it, they had reached Lincoln. 8.12am precisely today.

Lincoln was a little station with one platform. The station had an early nineteenth century appearance, with a short platform and old features on the station exit. It had seen better days and was a little run down. It still had a corrugated iron roof over the platform, with many holes in. The entrance to the station had an eye-catching old-style front, which Chantelle liked. She liked the older styles and architecture. She exited the train and went through the station. She could see the cathedral immediately. The buildings in front of the cathedral were huge, but the local authority had said you must be able to see the cathedral from all angles in the city. There were curved buildings, cylindrical buildings and some transparent buildings. They had been built with the ultra-thin graphene girders they could use now. Chantelle tapped her heels together, the hover skates appeared and she was on her way again. At speed, she skated up the empty roads on her hover skates. Cars were overhead all around her. It was busy this morning. Her military base was just out of the town, but it didn't take her long to get there. She got to work and through the security check point with time to spare, so headed to the break room. There were lots of soldiers in there and her work friend Joan was sat on her own eating her breakfast. Joan was always early, as she lived in Lincoln. Joan noticed her and waved her over. Chantelle sat down next to Joan. They chatted about everyday things like most people do, including the weather. They had also commented on the larger number of soldiers in the room today. Joan remarked, 'I like your hair today. Have you changed it again?'

Chantelle just laughed and said, 'Yes, it's easy these days.' As Joan was an older lady, she had not grasped the new technology, so did not know you could change your hair colour so easily with the helmet system. Chantelle thought she would have to encourage Joan to use some of these newer technologies gradually. They finished their breakfast and went their separate ways.

Joan was the personal secretary for the General, and Chantelle worked in the science laboratories. When Chantelle got into the lab there were a few people already in there. She knew their names, but they were just colleagues. They didn't say much, just got on with their work. Chantelle worked in innovations, mainly improving the sensors that detected objects that could hit the Earth. She mapped the progress of these objects on the star charts. She also worked on the shield, but there was not so much work on that nowadays. Actually, the shield was gaining strength, but no one could work out why. The universe amazed her. The only problem she had was her boss! Dr Simmons was so pompous. He would walk into the room like he was the most important person in that room. He would always be telling Chantelle what to do, as she hadn't been there very long. Chantelle knew a lot more than he credited her for. She was very intelligent, but Miss Che had told her not to make her intellect too obvious to managers or colleagues, so she just did as Dr Simmons asked. Here and there she would do things, but most of the time she let him believe he had made the discovery. Dr Simmons was really well thought of by the General of this base, which inflated the ego of him even further. Chantelle spent her day working on a sensor and checking telescopes for object activity above the shield. She had been following one object for quite a while now. Although it should miss the Earth by quite a distance, her boss told her to keep observing it. This object she was watching was heading past Mars, so not much longer until it would go past Earth. While she was watching the object passing Mars she thought she saw a light flash from the Mars surface. She looked at the data and she definitely thought it was a flash of light, and quickly passed it to her boss, as it was nearly the end of the work day for her. Simmons, in his usual egotistic way, dismissed it outright. She argued with him, but he continued to dismiss it, telling her it was an anomaly and it was nothing. She should just leave it and not pursue it. She went back to her laboratory and collected her belongings. She clocked out and headed home. All the way home the light flash on Mars was on her mind, and what she had just seen from the Mar's surface. She knew the next day she had to check her data again. There was definitely something happening there and she wanted to find out what. She got back into King's Cross and it was starting to get dark. Bronwyn had messaged her with the bar they would be in, so Chantelle put the co-ordinates into her visor and off she headed. She didn't know this bar, as it was new. The visor gave her directions and she went hover skating through the streets of London. She could see the directions, and how fast she was going displayed on the top of the visor screen. Coming up to Oxford Street was great. There were lights on buildings, and holograms on the top of some too showing adverts. There were holograms on the streets as well. It was awesome to skate through. Sometimes you would think the advert characters were actual people. Then they would try to sell you something! She headed south towards the Thames and arrived at the bar. It was on the waterfront and had great views of the Thames and its bridges.

It was a cocktail bar, which was what she expected from Bronwyn. It looked like the group were set for the night. They had had a few drinks before Chantelle had even got there. They were already talking about their sales and targets, so Chantelle just sat there with her drink. She was pretending to listen to them, but really her mind was still on what happened at work at the end of the day.

Bronwyn said, 'Are you listening?'

Chantelle replied, 'Yes.'

Bronwyn said, 'Did you hear what I said about the writing on buildings saying 'Let us out'?'

This peaked Chantelle's interest, so Chantelle told everyone about the science of the shield and the ozone layer, and all the information she was allowed to from the scientists who went outside the shield. Bronwyn agreed with her, but had noticed the graffiti was getting more frequent. Chantelle told them not to worry, as it was only in London where all the graffiti was. Nothing like that had reached Lincoln. Chantelle stayed a while longer, but wanted to get back home to talk to Miss Che. She hugged Bronwyn and said her goodbyes. It was 7pm and totally dark now. She knew she had to be careful, but would be home in minutes. The street lights and glow of London was good enough to hopefully keep her safe and visible. She got home and rushed into the living area. Miss Che was there on the comfiest sofa she had ever seen. Miss Che had changed the style of the room again to a 2000's look. There was now an L shaped sofa with a large TV screen on the wall. The wood effect had gone and now replaced with magnolia and grey walls. There was still a big kitchen table, but this was now a glass table, along with white panel cupboards. She was amused by Che's continuous change of styles. Chantelle had other things on her mind though.

Miss Che noticed that Chantelle was thoughtful and asked, 'What's on your mind?'

Miss Che had a sixth sense when it came to Chantelle. Chantelle hurriedly told her about the bright flash from Mars and her boss dismissing it. Che had to calm her down.

She surprised Chantelle when she said, 'Your boss is probably right.'

Chantelle told her all of the data, but unusually Miss Che did not agree with her on this matter. Chantelle was going to keep arguing her point, but Che was stubborn and said, 'Drop it. Don't push it.'

She didn't want Chantelle to be noticed by the General and officers at the base. Chantelle was not happy and she didn't speak for the rest of the night. Che tried to lighten the mood, but Chantelle's mood would not be changed. She excused herself and Che let her go to her room. Miss Che knew she wasn't the only one who was stubborn and she wouldn't push Chantelle. In her room, Chantelle mulled over what she had seen. She looked through her own telescope, but it was limited, and could only see the red glow of Mars. She was determined to find out what was going on. She went to bed, but struggled to sleep. Her brain was too active thinking what the explanation could be.

The next morning, Chantelle was up earlier than usual for a normal working Friday. She was even up before Miss Che for once. She had her breakfast and was about to leave, when Miss Che came out of her room.

Che said, 'You're up early. Are you going into work early today?'

Chantelle replied, 'Yes.'

Miss Che told her to leave what they had spoken about from the previous day and not pursue it. Chantelle agreed, but had no intention of not looking into it further. Che probably knew this, but could not control what Chantelle would do. Chantelle was out the door and she was gone. She really did arrive at work very early that day, but weirdly Joan was still there before her. They exchanged their usual morning pleasantries, as Chantelle did not want to be rude. Joan noticed yet again Chantelle had changed her hair to blue streaks!

Chantelle just smiled and said, 'I just like the change.'

Joan smiled and Chantelle headed off to look at the telescope, well before her shift was due to start. To her disappointment, there was nothing of interest looking through the telescope.

29

She kept 5.8 looking through the telescope, while she worked on other projects during her shift. She thought to herself that something must happen. The day was dragging. She was trying to stay focussed on her work, but her mind kept wandering back to that flash of light the day before. 5.8 reported nothing was happening. At lunch, she even went back herself to check 5.8 and the telescope. Her work was important to her, so all day she ensured it was still done to a high standard, even with this other distraction in her head. At 3pm her visor started flashing. Chantelle answered and there were only beeps and noises of all kinds. She quickly went to visual mode. There was 5.8 going crazy and gesturing to her to come. This was a time she really wished she had been able to afford a voice box for 5.8. Chantelle left the laboratory as soon as she could and headed to the telescope room again. 5.8 was waiting for her excitedly. Chantelle had a quick look through the telescope, but there was nothing there again. 5.8 plugged into the computer next to the telescope and there on the screen was an enormous flash of light, this time definitely from Mars. It looked like an explosion. Chantelle and 5.8 went straight to Simmon's office with this screenshot. She was hoping he would take her seriously this time. He didn't look happy to see her at first, but as soon as he saw the footage he was on the phone to the General of the base. The General was busy, but agreed to see them. Sitting outside the office, Simmons told Chantelle he would do all of the talking. She thought to herself that he was desperate to take all of the credit for this. Chantelle didn't care about it, she was just doing her job. They waited a while to be seen. The General had a habit of making people wait. Then Joan came out the office and said that the General would see them now. Chantelle acknowledged Joan on the way in. Chantelle was the last one in, so shut the door. They had barely sat down before Simmons was telling the General what had been happening on Mars over the last few days. The General just sat there and listened. He didn't move a muscle.

When Simmons was done, the General turned to Chantelle and said, 'What was your involvement in this?'

Chantelle said, 'I had set my 5.8 unit to monitor the sector.'
The General looked at Simmons then. Chantelle looked at
Simmons too. He didn't look happy.
The General looked back at Chantelle and said, 'Good work,
my dear.'
Chantelle didn't like the 'my dear' comment, but knew the
General was from an older generation.
The General then said, 'I will need to talk to Dr Simmons in
private about this. So go home now, and again, good work.'
Chantelle didn't know why he was sending her home, but then
realised it was 5.30pm. It was past her clock out time. She
thought time flies when exciting things happen. When she was
leaving the room, she was wondering why he wanted to talk to
Simmons on his own. Simmons was the head of their sector,
so she guessed this would be the reason. Joan had gone
home by the time she left the office, so she went and got her
backpack and went home.
It was now the weekend and Chantelle had plans with friends.
She watched hoverball during the day, a very popular sport,
and one Chantelle was very good at. Miss Che wouldn't let her
play though, because of Chantelle's gift of strength. In the
evenings, she spent it with Che watching movies and old TV
shows. A nice relaxing weekend. Chantelle loved it. It was a
shame the weekend was so grey and overcast in the skies,
which wasn't the usual weather for this time of the year.
Monday morning, Chantelle was up bright and early again. This
time she waited for Che to get up. Che's 10.16 was up and
about in the apartment and wanted to make breakfast for
everyone, but Chantelle wanted to do it herself today. The
droid was not happy, as it was set to serve. Miss Che was
happy, which was all Chantelle wanted. She hated fighting with
Che. Che sat down at the table and gave Chantelle a quizzical
look.
'What is this in aid of? Have you been up to something?' she
smirked.
'No,' Chantelle said, trying to look hurt. 'I just wanted to do
something nice, after our disagreement the other day about
Mars.'

Che had a huge grin and thanked her for her thoughtful gesture. They ate their breakfast, having a laugh and joke together, and then Chantelle left for work. The train ride was not quick enough for her today. She could not wait to get into work. To her surprise, it looked like the security had been increased. More security seemed to be on the gates. She got into the building, but was early and so walked to the break room. There was no-one in there. No soldiers. Why was this? Then she saw Joan in the corner. What had happened?

Chantelle went across to Joan and said, 'Where is everyone? I've never seen this room so quiet.'

Joan looked up and said, 'I know! It never has been before. It was like this when I got in, and what's with all the security?!'

Chantelle shrugged and said, 'I have no clue.'

They chatted a little more and then had to go to their work areas. Before Chantelle could get to the telescope room, her visor buzzed and vibrated. There was a visual of Joan.

'The General wants you in his office immediately,' she said.

Chantelle thought it would be a conversation about what had been reported on the Friday afternoon. She sent 5.8 off to the telescope room, whilst she headed to the General's office.

Whilst she was walking, her visor activated again. She wouldn't usually take it, but it was 5.8 and he looked really agitated. He couldn't speak, so tried to show her. There was security at the telescope room door and there was never security on this door usually. They wouldn't let 5.8 in. That got her mind racing. She just thought these are security, why not soldiers. What's happening?

The General would usually make her wait, but didn't today. He greeted her at the door and said, 'Please take a seat, my dear. Would you like a drink?'

She looked and said, 'No, thank you. I've just had my breakfast.'

He closed the door behind, not before telling Joan he was not to be disturbed. He went around his large oak desk, and sat in his huge and comfortable looking chair. He was an old man, and looked a little dishevelled today. His grey hair was not combed back, as it usually was, and he hadn't shaved. She hadn't seen the General lots before, but had never seen him unshaven.

He said, 'I hope you had a pleasant weekend?'

Chantelle just smiled and nodded. After what just happened to 5.8 she was not going to make small talk. Chantelle was straight to the point, and asked why her droid was not allowed in the telescope room. The General smiled, which annoyed her further.

'Straight to the point. I like that,' he said. 'Ok. When you left on Friday, myself and Dr Simmons had a conversation as you know.'

Chantelle interrupted and sarcastically said, 'I know.'

This time the General's demeanour changed. He was not so friendly then.

He leant forward at the desk and said, 'We decided Dr Simmons would take over your duties in the telescope room, and keep an eye on all of the anomalies. This will give you more time in the lab to work on your sensors.'

Chantelle was disgusted and hurt by this. She tore into the General saying, 'You said I had done a good job, and it was not a problem for me to do two things at once.'

She was struggling to keep herself calm in this moment. She wanted to jump over the desk and throttle the General.

The General said, 'It was Dr Simmon's decision and I agreed with it.'

Chantelle knew it. Simmons always wanted the credit. Then the General made another remark to her.

'You're too young to have so much responsibility.'

This made Chantelle extremely angry. She looked at him straight in the eyes, and was on the edge of showing him her frustration at his comment. Then noticing this, he looked away and could not look at her anymore.

The General quickly held his hand up to her and said, 'Before you say anymore and get into trouble, I have made my mind up. You're just working on your sensors. You're dismissed.'

She sat there a few seconds longer thinking should she say more, but knowing the General's reputation for being stubborn, she got up and angrily walked out of the room. Joan tried to say something, as she walked through the office, but Chantelle was too angry for small talk. When she got outside into the hallway, she believed there was more going on here than he was saying. She suspected it was to do with what she had observed on the Friday. She went through the yard and back to the laboratory. She was planning on seeing Simmons as soon as she got there. Off in the distance, she noticed what she believed was hangar fifteen with a few soldiers around it. This was strange, because she couldn't remember seeing soldiers around that hangar in all the time she had worked there. Admittedly not that long, but this still didn't feel right. She kept walking and stormed into the laboratory. She was ready to confront Dr Simmons, but he was nowhere to be found. All of her colleagues were at their desks working, so she decided not to disturb them. 5.8 came in and she sat with him. She just stared at her computer screen and said to herself, 'What just happened?!'

It had been a weird day. People in the laboratory, who usually barely spoke, seemed to be interacting more with each other. Lots of rumours were being discussed. One rumour about an uprising in the north, which apparently was where many of the soldiers had gone. Another rumour saying some soldiers had travelled to the south, apparently to prevent the people starting an uprising to have the ozone shield taken down. All these rumours sounded preposterous to Chantelle. She did not think the armed forces would have anything to do with any new uprisings. It reached lunchtime and she went to the break room to remove herself from the laboratory, and the continuous generation of new rumours. There was still no-one in the break room. She couldn't believe it. She began to wonder if one of the rumours could actually be true. She sat down and Joan walked in. Joan walked over to Chantelle quite sheepishly.

'Sorry for what happened in the General's office. I could hear it in my office.'

Chantelle looked at her and said, 'Don't worry. It's not your fault.'

Chantelle knew Joan was trying to be kind in her own way.

Joan said, 'When the General's mind is made up, he will not change it. The General has been acting weird all day. He has been in and out, and his Captains have been visiting his office for meetings all day too. He has had a lot of meetings this morning.'

Chantelle then said, 'Did you hear anything about hangar fifteen?'

Joan's demeanour changed, when she mentioned the hangar number. She realised she had said too much and excused herself abruptly, getting up and walked back to her office.

Chantelle was curious about hangar fifteen now, and wanted to investigate what was really going on at the base. Was this all linked to the flash from Mars? Was this just a coincidence? She had her lunch and went for a walk around the base. She had never done this before, and was concerned she might get questioned about her movements. It was very quiet, until she reached a few hangars before fifteen, and she saw a squad of soldiers coming from fifteen. They were dressed in battle armour and to her trained eye had their shields up. She felt a little nervous and wondered if she should put her own shield up. She didn't want them to know she was one of them though. Che had told her never to reveal herself. She crept along past the hangars, trying to remain out of sight, and wanted to reach hangar fifteen. There were soldiers everywhere. They had dark mode on, which made it even harder to know where they were. She was positive there was something important in the hangar fifteen. With so many soldiers around she was tempted to give up, and go back to the laboratory to work out a better strategy to get to that hangar.

Suddenly she heard a voice from behind her say, 'What are you doing here?'

She turned to see two soldiers looking at her. She pretended she was out for a walk, and hadn't been at the base very long and so had got lost. The soldiers didn't believe this. The soldiers would not leave their posts, which made Chantelle even more suspicious and curious of the whole situation. The soldiers called for security to take her away. Luckily, security believed her story and gave her a warning and told her to stay away from the area. They said they wouldn't report it any further, which she was thankful for. I don't need to see the General again she thought. She returned to the laboratory and continued with her work, still with rumours and chatter among the others distracting everyone. The end of the day couldn't come quick enough. On her way out, she saw Simmons. He was walking to the General's office, but she was too far away to catch up with him. On her way she kept thinking about how she could try and catch up with Dr Simmons. She knew there would be no way her or 5.8 could break into hangar fifteen, without being noticed. She could easily break through the door, but smiled to herself thinking that they would notice that! Chantelle wondered if she could buy a nano-spy robot. They were expensive though, and she would have to buy one on the black market. She knew a couple of people, one called Atkins, but was not sure if he would help. He seemed terrified of Miss Che, whenever he had met them. Chantelle never really knew why, but hoped money might persuade him into a sale with her. She set up a meeting with Atkins, a low-ranking member of the gangs, who had his sources. They decided to meet in a part of London, where very few people frequented, to keep the meeting more secure and less likely to be policed. She hovered in on her skates to where she was meant to meet Atkins and he was nowhere to be seen. She waited and waited, but it felt like she had been stood up by him. She had waited for so long that she was going to leave, when suddenly she heard a faint voice.

'Over here. Not in the middle of the street where we can be seen.'

Atkins was not a tall man. He had short brown hair, wore a little pair of glasses, and was always smart but casually dressed. Today he had a polo shirt, jeans and black trainers on. Chantelle's only dark clothes were her work clothes, so she had told Che she was going for drinks with some work friends. She didn't like to lie to Che, but Che would not have approved or let her go to this meeting. Chantelle did not know Atkins very well, but she had seen him on nights out. He was always bragging how he could get anything. Her friends gave her the contact details for Atkins, to set up this meeting. Chantelle went over to where the voice had come from.

From the shadows he said, 'Have you got the money?'

'Yes,' she said. 'Have you got the item I want?'

Atkins came out the shadows and said, 'Not quite.'

With a quizzical look, Chantelle said, 'What do you mean by 'not quite'?'

'Well a spy bot is top of the line, and what you're offering is nowhere near enough money,' he replied.

Chantelle was not pleased.

'You told me the price. Are you trying to rip me off?'

Atkins quickly backtracked, 'No, no. I still have something for you if you want it. It's a medical bot instead.'

Med bots, as they were known, were similar to spy bots but they had no sound, and the camera was not the same quality as the spy ones. Med bots were only supposed to be used inside the human body. Chantelle debated whether to walk away, but she was desperate to know what was inside that hangar at work. Atkin's replied, seeing Chantelle seemed to be debating whether to buy it.

'You can integrate the med bot into your current droid and give it a bit of an upgrade.'

Chantelle paused for a few seconds to think and said, 'Go on then, I'll take it. I want ten percent off the price though.'

They settled on five percent. Atkins gave Chantelle a little box. She opened it and there was a very tiny object in there. She lowered her visor and magnified the box, and there the med bot was, approximately the size of an ant. It had a red front eye, which was probably the camera, and a tiny laser used to cut dead cells out of a body. Atkins said that it could be linked to her visor or her phone, and that is how she would manoeuvre it. In the body, the bot could go into an automatic mode, and use its software to navigate the anatomy of the body. It could also automatically go into this mode outside of the body, if it was not moved by the controller. Chantelle gave Atkins the money, and they were just about to go their separate ways, when all of a sudden there were bright lights everywhere. The opaque wall, they had been behind, had now become transparent by the police's gadgets. There were red and blue lights from the police cars on the other side of the wall.

'Stop where you are,' a policeman's voice echoed over a tannoy.

Chantelle and Atkin's hands went up instinctively.

Atkins looked at Chantelle and said, 'You idiot. You must have been followed.'

Chantelle thought Atkins was more likely to have been followed than her, given his criminal past. They stood there, as the police car manoeuvred around the wall, which gave Atkins the opportunity he needed. He pressed a button on his phone and threw it into the air. Before it landed, it turned into a sporty-looking car. He jumped in and was off, shouting something to Chantelle which was indecipherable. The police car sped around the wall and dropped a drone out of the window.

'Stop where you are,' the policeman shouted again towards Chantelle.

The police car went in pursuit of Atkins. The drone just hovered in front of Chantelle. Chantelle looked at it and was thinking, 'I'm in big trouble here.' Instinctively, she tapped her heels together, her hover skates came to life, visor down and she skated off. She was not waiting for the police to come back. She accelerated along the street with the drone in pursuit. Its blue and red lights flashing on it and the sound system saying, 'Stop citizen.' Chantelle was travelling at high speed and was gradually pulling away from the drone. Every little side street she went down the drone made the lower half of the building's walls go transparent, so she had nowhere to hide. In the distance, she could hear more sirens, which meant more police to evade. She needed to get off the streets and somehow onto the other side of the river. The road leading to the Tower of London was blocked by a huge, moss-covered object. At the speed Chantelle was going, she skated up the side of the wall of the Tower of London. She was going so fast that she was at a horizontal angle to the wall. Her momentum stopped her from falling off the wall side. She came to the end of the wall and somersaulted off, landing on her feet and was away again. She then remembered reading about the historic tunnel network, that used to be part of an underground system of trains, that had shut down decades ago. She hoped the tunnels would still be intact, as this could be her way of escaping the police chase. She accessed some old maps on her visor, and knew this would be her best option to avoid arrest. On the old map, the nearest entry point to a tunnel to get under the river was at Blackfriars. This was about half a mile from where she now was. Her speed was still increasing and she was navigating various obstacles. She was having to jump bins and dodge people. She was zig zagging her movements to avoid the drone, which was firing tracer units towards her. If one of them attached to her, then she would have nowhere to go. They could trace her anywhere. Blackfriars was coming up and not too soon. The police sirens were louder and she was not sure how long she could keep up this pace. Blackfriars tube station had been closed for years. It was a shell of a building. An old delipidated looking building, with dirt on the walls from years of neglect, and clearly a lot of smog in the past. There were old boards outside, with future plans for the building on them. As she skated towards the boards she was thinking, 'What should I do here? As she slowed towards these boards, the drone would have an opportunity to close the gap. She did not want to smash into the boards and show her strength. She couldn't get caught, but this might be her only option. As she was about to hit the board, she noticed a hole in one of the boards. It was small, but she judged it would be just large enough for her to get through. She advanced towards it and slid through. It was actually only just wide enough. She was now going towards what was the old entrance. The drone flew over the boards. The Blackfriars entrance had most of the glass smashed out and debris everywhere. Chantelle had to swerve around this debris and fallen items. She ducked under a frame of a smashed-out window pane and straight into the main building. To her surprise, there were families everywhere, all over the main concourse. She skated past them, and it seemed the people had also confused the drone for a moment. Not for long though, as it soon located her once more. Chantelle could not believe all of the homelessness in this era, but she supposed where there was money then there was always a chance of poverty. She came up to a barrier, hurdled it and skated to what looked like a steel staircase. Right now, it felt like the drone was slowing. Was it losing power? Was the battery draining? Was she just hoping for this? If it was, then that would be great news for her. She sped up, as much as she could, towards the steel staircase. The stairs were steep and it looked dark down there. She knew she had to head into the depths of these tunnels to escape. She activated the night vision on her visor and hopped onto the smooth metal handrail. Her hover skates would work great on here. She dodged old signs on the rail, which read, 'Keep to the right.' This was great fun, but she had to remain focused. She gained velocity going down the rail. The floor at the bottom came quickly into her vision. She slid off the end of the rail and skated quickly towards a board with North and South on it. There were many names on the board and what looked like many routes on the map. In the corner of her visor, it was flashing 'Go South.' She had to be quick, as the drone seemed to have caught up with her, and was trying to tag her again with a tracer. It only just missed this time. Through another tunnel she went and she was now on a platform. Posters on one side, and the other side had Blackfriars written into the wall. On the edge of the platform was a drop of about four foot. At the bottom of this drop there were thin metal rails on top of gravel and concrete. She went to the end of the platform and then hopped down onto the gravel area. Her hover skates helped her, as she could hover and avoid concrete and metal extrusions coming up from the rails. She hovered just above the rails and was at the start of what appeared to be a long, dark tunnel. She was about hundred yards into the tunnel, when a light from the drone showed up in the darkness. She wished it would go away. This was not fun and she was getting more worried about being caught. With her night vison, it appeared there was something blocking the tunnel further down. Her visor told her, from the archives programmed into it, that this was a derelict London underground tube train. She was following the tracks of

40

one of the old tube lines. Taking a second to look at the archive maps, she had an idea. She had now reached the back of the train. With the drone being far enough back and around a corner, she ripped the train door off its hinges and threw it onto the track. She jumped into the train. The old carriage was damp, fusty and covered in cobwebs. The seats had been torn out and the metal poles were rusty and cracked. She went through the first carriage to the next door. Opening it and skating into the next carriage, leaving the door open behind her. Was this a mistake? Did she do it on purpose? Halfway down the carriage was yet another set of doors. This time she slid them open and closed them behind her. She hid by the side of the train. The drone light came down the tunnel and stopped at the end of the train. It was buzzing around it and was very confused. There was not enough room for it to fly over the top or down the sides, but detecting the open door it flew through. It flew through the first carriage and then into the next, where Chantelle had left the door open. She decided that this was her opportunity to the trap the drone. She kept low and made her way back to the back of the train. Then she powered up her skates and jumped back into the train, and headed down the carriage as quick as she could. The drone turned around and darted towards her. She just got to the door before the drone, and shut the door trapping the drone in the carriage. Thinking it did not have much charge left, she observed it could not smash its way out. She went back down the carriage slowly, as she was also lacking energy and was drained herself. She got out of the train, where she had originally entered, and shimmied down the outer shell of the train. She went back towards the carriage the drone was trapped in. She could see the light of the drone, buzzing around like a captive wild animal. She got past the end of the train, leaving the train and drone behind her. Perhaps if anyone found the battery depleted drone they could sell it on, she surmised. Either way, as long as it was no longer chasing her, that was a relief. She kept moving down the track until she reached another station, which her visor told her was on the other side of the river. She jumped up onto the platform and made her way to the exit, following the tube exit signs above her, along with her visor information. There was a final, long metal staircase again to go up, before she then saw the boarded up front of the station. She got near the boarding, and took the case out containing the medbot. 5.8 had turned back into her phone, and linked immediately with the medbot. There was an image on her phone screen now, and a cursor to pilot the medbot. She knew 5.8 could fly it, but she wanted to have a go at operating it herself to check the workings of it. She got the medbot airborne and found a small hole in one of the boards next to her that it would fit through. The camera quality was not great, but good enough to see what was outside this station. It was dark outside. Where were the police now? Did they know how far along the line their drone had got? So many questions were in her head. The medbot flew through the hole and the images around the station looked clear. There did not seem to be any activity. No police at least. Chantelle went into dark mode on her shield, just in case. She did not want to be detected by any infra-red cameras that could be hidden out there on the streets. In the dark mode, she would not be seen by the naked eye, unless they had these infra-red cameras. She tore a piece of boarding down and hopped through, putting the medbot back into its case on the way out. She hover skated down a few streets in dark mode. She did not think she was being followed, so deactivated the dark mode. The rest of the skate home gave her a lot to think about. How stupid had she been to trust Atkins? She would never take that risk again. She just had to know what was in that hangar.

Thankfully it was an uneventful skate back home to her relief. When she got into the apartment, she was greeted by 10.16. It was very late now, so she did not expect Miss Che to still be up. The room was bright and modern, now with the LED ceiling lights. Miss Che hated bright and modern, so this did not feel right. Miss Che was sat at the table.

Chantelle went over and said, 'Is everything ok?'

Miss Che looked a little rattled and a bit sweaty.

'Yes, I am fine. With you going out, I thought I would too. I didn't have time to set the room up, so chose this modern rubbish! Did you have a good time with your work friends?'
In amongst everything that had just happened, Chantelle had forgotten she had told Che this story about going out with work friends. At least she had put her hair back to green again, otherwise Miss Che would really have questioned the black hair look!
'Yes, it was good. It was nice to get to know some of them,' Chantelle said.
Miss Che looked up at her and said, 'That's good. Glad you got back safely. Best get to bed now, as you've got work in the morning.'
Why was Miss Che saying about being back safely? Chantelle wandered off to bed wondering why Che made this comment. Was Chantelle just paranoid after everything this evening or did Che know something?
The next day at work Chantelle tried to focus on her work, but was distracted by her thoughts of her plan to get the medbot into that hangar fifteen. She had managed to get through the gates this morning and the scan. It only detected 5.8 in the phone mode and they made her transform 5.8 back into robot mode. Thankfully they did not detect the medbot. Her plan was to get as close to hangar fifteen as she could herself, as security was still very high everywhere on base. She did not want the medbot to fly too far, as a light wind could blow it off course. She got to lunchtime and decided to put her plan into action. There was a storage room around the corner from that hangar. She walked around the site, planning to get to the storage room. There were soldiers everywhere and they all still had their shields up. Chantelle aimed for the closest hangar to hangar fifteen and looked around to see if anyone was about. She could not see anyone and hoped there were no soldiers in dark mode restricting their visibility. She thought that perhaps soldiers in dark mode was how she had been caught the first time she tried to get to the hangar. She went into dark mode herself. She knew in daylight she could be seen in dark mode, but it was harder to be seen and she would look like a blurry

outline. She kept to the shaded areas, as much as possible. She had to dodge a couple of units of soldiers, but reached the storage shed by hangar fifteen. The door on the shed was locked and usually it would have had a padlock on it. However, for some reason a keypad lock had been installed on it, which needed an alphanumeric code. If she had her visor with her this would have helped her get into the lock, and would have been an easier task, but she had left it in her locker. She got her phone and tried to look at all of the codes she knew for other buildings on the base. None of them worked and she was starting to panic. She could hear a unit of soldiers nearby and they sounded to be getting closer. She tried old and new access codes, even old ones not used for decades according to the records on her phone. Nothing seemed to work. The soldiers were nearly there. She was about to give in and run, when suddenly one of the codes worked, the door beeped and slid open. She rapidly entered, and the door slid shut just before the unit got around the corner. Chantelle just stood there sweating and shaking, listening to the soldiers walk by. Then it fell silent and they were gone. She stood there for a moment feeling the exhilaration from what she had done. She deactivated dark mode and removed the medbot box from her pocket. She got the medbot out and turned it on. It flew out of one of the vents of the storage room and towards hangar fifteen. Chantelle chose the nearest vent she could see on hangar fifteen and directed the medbot into it. There were lasers and security bots inside the vents. She knew this would be difficult. She had to fly the medbot around the vent for quite a while, dodging security bots and laser beams. When she evaded all of this security, she was now able to view the hangar from the vent. She saw from the medbot's camera what appeared to be a laser shield all around whatever the object was in there. She knew her medbot would not get through this laser shield, so she flew the medbot slightly out of the vent to get closer to this shield. She did not want to set the alarm off, but wanted to try and detect what was beyond this shield. The laser shield was blocking the cameras vision and was sending back a grainy image to her phone. On this image, it appeared there were outlines of large objects at a distance within the hangar. Were they ships or could they be buses? Could they fly? It was difficult to tell. As the medbot's camera adjusted to the laser shield, it then detected some soldiers just on the inner perimeter of the shield. She thought she had seen them in the work's canteen in previous weeks. One of the possible ships looked like the door was open on it, as the image showed a lighter area.

Chantelle waited, holding the medbot steady at the edge of the vent, whilst viewing the laser shield. She wanted to see what might come out of the door. She waited for half an hour and knew her lunch break was nearly over. She set the medbot down on the edge of the vent and put it into standby. If anything moved, the medbot would record it. She left the storage room and went back to work. Another little challenge for her, avoiding soldiers and security on the way back. At the end of her shift, she needed to go back to retrieve her medbot. It wasn't easy again trying to dodge security.

On the train home, she was so excited to find out what the medbot might have captured. Though the train ride was two minutes, it seemed to take longer, when she was desperate to get back to view the medbot's recordings. She got back home and went straight to her room, with a quick hello to Miss Che. She would say sorry later. She was so excited to see the recordings, she did not have time to chat right now. She got 5.8 out and inserted the medbot into him. It started playing the larger images onto her wall. Hopefully she could see what the medbot had recorded with a larger image, as she knew the images had been a little grainy originally. She started to play the recording, but nothing seemed to happen. No movements from the ships. She forwarded through the recording for hours, until something happened. To her surprise there was movement out of a door, from what appeared to be a ship. To her shock and disappointment, it was not an alien or anything suspicious that she had hoped for. Instead, it was an average size looking human with two legs and two arms, but she could not see any further features, as the image was poor and distorted. She thought to herself, 'Why all of the security? Why

45

had the base had so many soldiers patrolling it? Why had they been sent to the hangars, and not been seen in the canteens as usual?' None of this made sense to Chantelle.

She shut off the recording and laid back on her bed completely disheartened. All she could think is that she had risked everything for what felt like nothing. There had to be more to this.

Chapter Three

Archer was starting to become annoyed now, as they had been on Earth for two weeks and were still being held in the hangar. The first week was ok, because Nineham had been showing him the little alien he had captured before escaping from Mars. He had not been so bothered about the alien and just wanted to kill the thing, until Nineham told him about the powerful weapon technology the little aliens had. Archer really wanted that technology, so that he could get his revenge on all of the aliens that had attacked them and driven him from his home. They had interrogated the little alien for a week, but they could not understand its responses when it 'talked'. They tried different tactics for three days to attempt to get it to communicate, from being nice to aggressive to torture, but it still did not give them anything useful that they could use. Nineham wanted to know why they attacked Mars, but Archer cared less about that and never asked the question. Archer would not let Nineham do the questioning, as he blamed him for the loss of Mars. Archer locked the alien in a cargo container on the ship, as a makeshift cell. He would not stop the interrogation until he got the information on the weapons technology. Archer got Cundill and his immediate staff together for a meeting. They all decided enough was enough and wanted a meeting with this General of Earth that they had heard about, but not actually met yet. This was aggravating Archer immensely, as he was the one who usually gave the orders, and did not like to be in this situation of receiving orders from an unknown General. He wanted to do something about this, but he would deal with that in the future.

He walked down the ramp into the hangar and said to one of the soldiers guarding the hangar inside, 'I want to speak to Captain Habersham now.'

He had disliked Habersham on the radio, and disliked him even more when he met him. Habersham was the name of the soldier that was on the communication system they used, as they tried to escape Mars. He nearly did not let them through the shield to Earth, as they desperately tried to evade the alien attack. Archer had to deal with Habersham as soon as they arrived in the hangar that day two weeks ago. Archer could not deal with the fact that Habersham was the same rank as him. Habersham would listen today though, as Archer was determined that him and the men would all be getting out of this hangar today. The other men stood on the ramp behind Archer, ready and waiting for Habersham to arrive.

The soldier said, 'Habersham is on his way.'

Archer waved the men down the ramp towards him. The soldiers inside the hangar and guarding the exits looked worried, and quickly sent a message for more support from the others outside on the base. They formed up ranks, as slowly more soldiers arrived and joined, acting on the message received. Archer liked to see well-drilled soldiers. He would like to be in charge of them in time.

One soldier stepped forward and said, 'What's the meaning of this, Captain Archer?'

Archer replied, 'We have been here for two weeks in this hangar. We need to get out and get on with our lives.'

The soldier replied back, 'That is up to the General, Captain.'

They all squared up to each other. It would not take much to ignite the situation. Archer knew Nineham and Abbott were good when it came to confrontation. They would throw punches first and ask questions later.

It felt like it was going to escalate, when he heard a voice shout, 'Stand down, Captain.'

Archer knew straight away that was Habersham, by the squeaky pitch in his voice. The man walked straight past his own soldiers, who let him through. Habersham was about five foot eight inches tall, with an army issue haircut. His uniform was perfectly ironed and there was a shine on his boots. His face was small, with a large nose and hazel deep set eyes. He went straight up to Archer.

'What's the meaning of this, Captain? We gave you safe passage through the shield and away from the aliens, and this is your appreciation to us?! Trying to provoke us. Not very polite is it?'

Archer was taken aback for a few seconds, but then shuffled forward slightly and gritted his teeth.

'We appreciate what you did Captain, but we've been here two weeks and we have not seen the General yet, who you said we would have seen by now. We see him today or we get out another way.'

Archer's demeanour became passive aggressive. Habersham held his hands up.

'Easy men, let's not do anything hasty. The General has been very busy, but I will call him and see what he says.'

With piercing eyes aimed at Habersham, Archer said, 'Well do that then.'

The two men glared at each other, and Habersham went to the back of the hangar. He seemed to be talking for quite a while. Then he came back through the soldiers.

Habersham said, 'The General's not happy, and does not like your attitude Captain, but he will see you and one other at his office at 3pm today. You need to swap your Mar's uniforms to our uniforms. He does not want the whole base to know where you came from. It could unnerve many on the base.'

Archer thought this was all a little unnecessary, but if this was the only way to see the man then he would do it.

'That's acceptable, Captain. We will stand down for now.'

Archer's men turned and walked back up the ramps into the ships. Habersham scurried off and the guarding soldiers went back to their original posts inside the hangar. Archer smiled to himself. He never planned to fight. It was all bravado.

Back in the ship, they had another meeting. Who would want to come with him? This could be interesting. Archer was taking Cundill no matter what, so there would be no debate anyway in this. He was in charge and would take Cundill, as he wanted protection and Cundill was intimidating in both size and demeanour. He thought Cundill was an idiot, but this didn't bother him. Archer had had enough of debates today. He was in charge now and he would make the decisions, whether the men liked it or not.

The uniforms for the base arrived at the hangar at around 2pm. They were delivered nicely folded by one of the guard soldiers.

Archer and Cundill really did not like the uniforms at all. The material felt weird to them. It apparently was material which worked with your body's movements. The guard soldier said that the uniforms would get more comfortable the more they wore them. This was new technology to them in materials that they had never seen before. Although Archer did not like the fit, he wanted to know more about the materials used and technology embedded within them.

A unit of soldiers appeared at the hangar doors to escort them to their meeting with the mysterious General. Archer noticed the soldiers had their shields up. Cundill was going to put his shield up too, but Archer stopped him.

'No. Let's go friendly this time. We don't want to upset the General. If we go with shields up it looks bad.'

Cundill wasn't happy, but the good thing about him was he took orders without question. The two men walked down the ramp and met up with the unit of soldiers waiting for them at the bottom. They acknowledged each other with a salute, and Cundill and Archer walked in the centre of the men. The laser shield was down to let them through and out of the hangar. As soon as they went through the laser shield, it went back up. At the hangar door now, they waited for clearance, as Habersham slowed the process again. Was Habersham getting joy out of this? As the hangar doors slowly slid open, the sun came blazing down on them. It was blinding at first, as their eyes slowly adapted to this brightness.

Archer turned to his left and said to the soldier, 'Shields up, is that really necessary?'

The soldier just turned and said, 'The General's orders.'

Archer thought this General was a little excessive, and anticipated they would not get on very well with each other. As they walked through the yard, Archer was sure he could see little objects flying around above them, and asked the soldier what they were.

The solider looked at him bemused and remarked, 'They are just security bots.'

They didn't have these on Mars. Archer thought that the technology here was well beyond theirs. He couldn't believe the vibrant colours and smells on this land, compared to Mar's red sands and stagnant air. They could never go far on Mars either. This was a whole new experience. The two men walked with weird smiles on their faces. The warm sun warmed their skins. They were both thinking they would enjoy it on Earth. In the far distance they could see flying cars, possibly fifty feet off the ground. Cundill and Archer had never seen anything like that before and were amazed. Nothing seemed to be going up into the atmosphere though. Was nothing leaving Earth? Archer found this strange with what appeared to be very advanced technology. Why would they not be travelling to other planets? Archer was taking everything in on this walk. He could have spent hours walking around if he could freely, but he needed to see the General urgently. They reached a hangar, which had a large sign displaying 'Hangar One'. It was very busy with soldiers going in and out and civilian workers, such as cleaners, scientists and administrators. The soldiers escorting Cundill and Archer stopped at the door. To not look suspicious, the soldiers stayed at the door and directed the two men down the corridor to the General's office. The General's office would be at the end of the corridor. Archer looked at the soldier with a scowl. He was not used to soldiers talking to him in this way. Archer and Cundill went through the doors and into the packed corridor. People everywhere chatting with each other. Archer knew Cundill would love this, as the big man would knock people flying, as he bumped into them accidentally on purpose! Cundill knew these were just civilians and would not have the strength of the two men. He enjoyed hurting people. It was his bullying nature. Archer could feel the eyes on them both as they walked down the corridor, but because of the uniforms they appeared to go quickly back to chatting in their groups. The two men walked down the corridor. They could hear the whispers of, 'Who are they? Where have they come from?' as they strolled through. Archer just smiled and thought, 'They will get to know me very quickly!'

Cundill bumped a lady, who looked like a cleaner, and she flew across the corridor bumping into others. He laughed out loud.

51

The lady got back to her feet looking dazed and shocked. She scowled after them and Archer heard them say, 'What a jerk!' Cundill was just behind Archer, as he tried to barge a few more people, but people were aware of him now and just dodged the big man. Archer then heard a weird noise. He stopped and turned to see Cundill across the room on his back.

Archer said, 'What are you doing, Sergeant? You are making a scene.'

Cundill jumped to his feet and his face was bright red with embarrassment. Archer could see people laughing and a woman walking away with bright orange highlights in her hair. 'What happened?' said Archer.

Cundill did not know what to say at first and then blurted out, 'Well I went to bump some really small girl, who was in conversation with an older woman and didn't see me coming, but I obviously didn't hit her. I must have hit a wall or something, as it didn't move and I went flying.'

'I see,' Archer said, as he quickly looked back down the corridor, but everyone seemed to have scattered. 'Interesting Sergeant. We must look into that, but not now. We need to see the General.'

Archer was just thinking that they would try and find this girl at a later point to see who she was. They got to the office door and Archer lightly knocked.

He heard a voice say, 'Come in Captain and take a seat,' as the door slid open.

He was going to ask the lady behind the desk how she knew it was him, but he could see her desk was full of screens and all sorts of gadgets. This must have been how she knew him. She had probably been watching them come down the corridor all the time. Archer and Cundill took a seat outside the General's office. As they sat and waited other staff in lab coats and soldiers were in and out of the office continuously. They sat there waiting for a least a quarter of an hour and at that point he went over to Joan, the secretary, asking when they would be seen.

Her answer, 'In a minute.'

Archer sat back down. A quarter of an hour became half an hour and then a full hour. Still people went in and out, but they were ignored. Archer was getting more irritated thinking 'I am Vinson Archer, Captain of Mars. I don't wait like this. The General will find this out first hand.' Archer was just about to get up again and ask Joan what the problem was, when the desk buzzed.

Immediately Joan said, 'Captain Archer, the General will see you now.'

'About time,' Archer sarcastically said as he got up.

Joan just ignored him. The door slid open as the two men reached it. They entered quite a small office. A huge desk in the middle seemed to take up most of the space. The General sat in a very comfortable looking chair. It looked the most comfortable chair they had ever seen, and Archer wanted it. The General was an elderly gentleman, round faced with rosy red cheeks, short greying hair and he also looked a little overweight. Archer thought this would be easy from the look of the General.

The General's booming voice came over the desk, 'Take a seat, gentlemen. Can my secretary get you anything?'

Archer and Cundill sat down and Archer replied, 'No, General.'

The General then apologised for taking so long, because he had been so busy. Archer did not believe him and his excuses.

'How can I help you, Captain?' the General said.

Archer thought this is my chance.

'Thank you for seeing us General and permitting us through the shield. You have saved a lot of lives.'

The General interrupted, 'I would do that for any humans that needed help.'

Archer did not like being spoken over when he was talking.

'It is General. We have been here two weeks, and we're still locked away in that hangar. We want to get out and start our lives again.'

The General interrupted again, much to Archer's irritation.

'You're not locked away, Captain. We just had to make sure everything was ok with your ships, but I understand. I will start proceedings to have your people tested and to see if we can

53

get some accommodation for all of you. Unfortunately, this will have to be on the base at first. I would like it if you didn't tell people where you all came from.'

This further increased Archer's annoyance.

'Tested for what, and why do you not want people to know where we are from?'

The General shot back, 'You're from another planet Captain and you've never been to Earth. We don't know what your bodies have, or what ailments you have from Mars that we don't have here on Earth. Also, you might not have immune systems that can defend you from our viruses. I also don't want people to know where you are from, as it might start a panic. To know you are from Mars is bad enough, but to know why you were driven away would be even worse. I will not have rumours and panic starting on my base!'

Archer understood, but he was not happy about it all.

Then the General went to stand and said, 'Is that everything gentlemen?'

Archer was taken aback by this and said, 'No, that's not everything Sir!'

The General sat back down and was getting frustrated himself with Archer's tone towards him.

Archer said, 'What are we going to do about the aliens that attacked us? Those things drove me away from my home, and I want to wipe them out from this universe.'

The General sat back in his chair and looked directly at Archer. 'We are not going to do anything, Captain.'

Archer was furious at this comment and screamed, 'Nothing! But they tried to kill us. If you're too old and frail to do something, then give me some men and I will do it.'

The General sat forward at this and in a measured voice said, 'You will not speak to me like that, Captain. You might have been in charge on Mars, but here on Earth I am in charge. From what I've read from your reports you were negligent. You had no guards on the gate and you were outflanked, as you had no patrols. You got complacent.'

Archer was steaming, 'We have to do something General,' he shouted and then he stood up. Cundill stood up too to look intimidating.

'Sit down, Captain,' and he gave Cundill a piercing glare. 'You too, Sergeant. You don't intimidate me. I've known about your little outpost for years Captain, but never thought I would ever have any dealings with it. Now I will not go to war for you, Captain. We are more than safe behind this shield. They will never get in. Nothing has.'

Archer's face was red raw and said, 'You're wrong about this, General. We have to wipe them out.'

The General put his hand up and said, 'Enough Captain. That is my final word on it. You and your people will be tested and relocated around the base. This meeting is over.'

Archer sat there for a few seconds and was going to scream something else, but thought what's the point and got up and stormed out with Cundill hot on his heels. Joan tried to say something to them, but he ignored her and kept walking back down the corridor, where the guard soldiers were ready to escort them back to the ship. In minutes they were back at the ship, and they were furious. They went straight to the meeting room in the ship.

Archer turned to Cundill and furiously said, 'If that crusty old fool won't do anything, then I will. I will bide my time and wait until he's dead or sooner! I will kill every single one of those aliens and get my revenge!'

Archer's people were all tested in the following weeks and then relocated with cover stories and new identification. Archer went along with the story given to him by the General. Archer was playing games a little. He had started engaging and manipulating some of the higher-ranking officers to try and grab a favour. He was going to climb the ladder as quickly as he could to displace 'the old fool' General, but he knew he was being watched at every turn. He also wanted to know more about the sciences on the base, and find that mysterious girl with the orange hair that Cundill bumped into and sent him flying.

Chapter Four

General Blasius, the Omorfi Stvar leader and elected leader of all of the alien races in the fleet, was on the main deck of the flagship looking down on this little island. The main deck was enormous. It housed about a thousand different aliens. There were scanners and computers being manned everywhere. At the very end, there was a huge window viewpoint area. Pilots sat in chairs suspended from the ceiling. Blasius stood on the platform looking out of the window. They had been pounding the UK's shield for days now and not getting any results. The Tilluke people didn't seem to be getting the same results that they did on Mars, when they used their energy drill. They would not give up though. They wanted to get their most senior scientist back, who was also their friend. They didn't know what the soldiers from Mars would do to him. General Blasius knew that his men would be getting restless, as they were in orbit waiting for orders from him. A lot of people thought they should be going to look for other places to live and not wasting time on this ridiculous mission. Blasius did not like the thought of just sitting here waiting, but did not want to leave the Tilluke scientist in the hands of the humans. He hated the humans and still wanted to get his hands on them literally, knowing they would be out to get revenge on him after he attacked the humans on Mars. Sometimes he wished he hadn't attacked the humans on Mars, but he decided too, and all the alien races trusted him. At the time Cecillio also said this was a bad idea, but Blasius ignored this and then would not let Cecillio join the battle in case he jeopardised it. Blasius stood on the deck by himself, just thinking what a beautiful planet Earth was. It reminded him of his own planet, but a lot greener and more beautiful. He just smiled to himself.

He was taken unawares by a sudden movement behind him. It was his junior officer.

In the Omorfi Stvar language the officer said, 'We have scanned the planet and there are life forms everywhere.'

Blasius was taken aback by this information, but thought immediately that he did not want them communicating with each other and said, 'Jam them now.'

The officer said, 'But that's the thing General, there seems to be nothing to jam. Apart from the shield down there, that is the only technology we can detect.'

Blasius said, 'What, no more shields? That can't be right. Go check again.'

The officer replied, 'No need, General. We have checked five times and there is nothing.'

Blasius knew this was his opportunity to wipe out this race. 'Send for the Captains. We need to start our attack now.'

All the Captains gathered in the meeting room. Blasius marched in.

'Our time to attack is now. We can hit everywhere. There are no more of these shields to slow us down. We are going to hit each continent. Each Captain will have a platoon of soldiers. I'm going to stay here with the Tilluke and keep an eye on their progress, and make sure nothing happens to them. You will get your orders shortly. Good luck to everyone. You will need it!'

Captain Cecilio got his orders and he could not have been unhappier. He got the Mbalame flying aliens in his platoon, but also got the Gogortasanas. They were huge beast-like creatures, which Cecilio did not get on with. They always made fun of him.

Cecilio got in touch with command and they just said, 'That's your platoon Captain. Deal with it!'

He just had to hope they listened to him this time. He got the Mbalame and Gogortasanas together and they were making fun of him. When he gave them the orders they soon quietened down and listened to him. They wanted to get their gruesome hands on the humans. Cecilio's platoon were going to be the first ones on the ground to see what they were up against. They knew the humans didn't have shields, but did not know why, which unnerved all the commanding Captains as this was unprecedented. Cecilio was confident though. Yes, he did not get on with the Gogortasanas, but they were good fighters, and the Mbalame took orders and could attack from the sky. He said his farewells and off he went in the drop ships. As there were not many of his race here, the Omorfi Stvar, most were made Captains as they were the best warriors.

Chapter Five

Two weeks earlier, Vaughn was making his way through the forest. It was a horrible place to be in these days. The trees were massive. The redwoods were around five hundred foot tall. Many of the lower plants were toxic and very deadly. You did not touch anything in here if you didn't know what you were doing. Not only were the plants going to get you, the animals were too. There was one bear that was always after him. It was a big old thing. It was about twenty feet in height, when it stood up on its hind legs. Vaughn had a very good knowledge of the forest. With his shields up, he was impervious to the plant's toxicity. He almost had free reign of the forest, as normal humans stayed away. Too many died over the years from plant scratches or eating the wrong things. Vaughn was in here finding the resources for his medicines that he would sell at the local market. He had helped so many people survive this harsh world. With his high intellectual ability he could decipher what kinds of plants and animals would help with certain ailments and diseases, that had developed over the years in this society. He would also hunt for meat, while he was picking up these ingredients for his medicines. He would take the meat and medicines to the local market, so he could barter for things they simply couldn't get. The rest of the village hated him going to the market, as the people of the village wanted to stay reclusive and not to let people know who they were. Vaughn disagreed with this, as he thought as long as you didn't give away details as to who they were, it was nice to see other people. He got on with many others, but loved being around Annette from the market. She was his favourite. He continued his hunt for resources, including tracking a deer for hours. He could not pause and get distracted by his dreams, as there were animals that would stalk him too. There were tigers in the forest that were large and hard to see in the dense undergrowth. He had his trusted bow and arrows ready and was in dark mode, so he was less easily detected in this dense forest. He caught a glimpse of the deer in the distance. He was always wondered how the deer ate this toxic grass. Had its body adapted to the toxins? The animals seemed to find their way around these difficulties nowadays. He stalked up behind the deer and upwind to hide his scent. He readied his bow. He would have a good shot at this range. He took aim and was about to release the arrow, when suddenly there was an extremely loud noise in the distance. The noise echoed through the trees and the deer bolted. Vaughn was concerned, as he had never heard anything like this noise before. What was it? He ran towards the nearest tree, and then quickly jumped up. He must have reached at least fifty feet. With his enormous power and strength, he could have got even higher, but the branches slowed his ascent. So, he climbed the rest of the tree to the top as quick as he could. He thought he would see some kind of object in the sky, but to his disappointment there was nothing there, except a possible movement in the cloud further away or was this just his imagination running wild? Had he not been quick enough to see what actually made this noise? His mind was overthinking. From this distance, and without his binoculars, he didn't want to guess what this movement in the cloud could have been. He did not want to tell people about something that might be nothing of concern. He would tell them about the noise and see if anyone could decipher what it was he had heard.

He climbed back down the tree, and the deer had returned a little further away from where it had been startled. It was back down the woody trail. He tracked it and eventually killed it, and also got the plants he needed for the medicine ingredients. The noise continued to occupy his thoughts on the way back to the village. The village was on the very edge of the forest, where no one ever went. His reclusive people liked living there. If anyone did venture near the village, they often hid in the forest in dark mode with shields up. Vaughn hated hiding like this, but understood people would not like them around. The village was small and only about four hundred people lived there. It was a tight community, which it had to be for survival. As he got back towards the village, he was spotted by his son who ran over to him.

'Hey Dad. I wish you had taken me on the hunt today.'
Vaughn sighed, 'The forest is no place for you son, until you
get your shields and learn the dangers.'
His son was only ten years old, so had a few years yet to learn.
Vaughn stored all of the meat and medicinal ingredients in the
outside storage shed. He went to see his wife. If anyone knew
what the noise was, then she would. He found her in the village
hall talking with others. Vaughn went over and made
pleasantries, then excused his wife and himself from the
conversation. He wanted to know what she thought. They got
back to their cabin. It was nothing over the top like some had
built, but just a modest cabin. It had two bedrooms, living room,
kitchen, and a bathroom at the rear. He went inside and sat his
wife down.
'The strangest thing happened today, whilst I was hunting in
the forest,' he said.
She sarcastically replied, 'How can you possibly tell in that
place!'
He knew his wife was sharp witted, which he loved about her.
She said things as they were. He smiled and explained about
the huge echoing noise. He told her how he thought it could
have been some kind of object in the distant sky moving away
from the area. His wife sat back in her chair.
'I'm not sure, but when I was a kid I used to hear stories about
sonic booms from aircraft,' she thoughtfully said.
Vaughn knew this was impossible, as there had been no
aircraft for decades. He had heard old stories about aircraft
and the UK from his parents, passed down by previous
generations, and this was the reason they lived here in
America and not in the UK.
He said to his wife, 'I hope they are not up to something that
will affect us.'
She concurred with him.
The next morning Vaughn was up early at sunrise. He was
going for one more hunt before the market the following day.
He was not overly keen to go back into the forest today, but
needed more ingredients for some of his newly developed
medicines. He went in, shield up again, and looked for the

plant he needed. Pulling it from its roots, he quickly gathered a good amount. All of this time, he had an uneasy feeling that he was being watched. He had experienced this feeling a few times before, but had never been attacked. He looked around to try and see who it was, but it must have been an elusive character, as there was no one there when he looked around. He ventured back to the village and him and his wife had a lovely meal together. It was an early night for Vaughn, as he had a long trek to the market tomorrow.

Early next morning he hitched his wagon and filled it with meat and medicines. One of the people in charge of the village came over and tried to stop him leaving, as they did not like him conversing with others from other places. There was no stopping him though. He was taking his medicines to sell. People needed them. His wife and son joined him on the wagon as he set off, with many glaring looks from the people of his village.

His wife said, 'Take no notice of them. You're doing the right thing, as you always do.'

As they got to the edge of the village his wife and son got off, and said their goodbyes and returned back to the house. He headed off into the distance. It was quite an arduous journey, as the market was in the mountains. There were only two ways into the market. To get to the market he had to go between two sheer rock faces, that were twenty feet apart. This led him into a large prairie, which then led to an area of higher ground. Once here, there was another rock face. Many years before, the people must have blasted this rock face with dynamite to make a huge hole in it. A gate had been erected in this hole, to keep the people safe. After the gate, the track then led into a large, dried out lake bed, twice the size of the prairie below. The market sat on the lake bed. It was surrounded by mountains, and a cave system towards the rear of the market where people lived. This meant if they were ever attacked, they could quickly get back to their village they had set up inside the cave for sanctuary. They were always excavating the caves to try and make them bigger for their growing population. The people in the market used anything they could for their safety.

Vaughn admired their ingenuity and will to survive in this harsh world. There was only one way into the caves and it could be closed off if they were attacked.

The other entrance to the market was a smaller pass, just above the market, a few miles back. You had to travel through the rocks of the mountains to get through it, and it was incredibly narrow. Only a few people side by side would get through, and it was definitely not wide enough for a wagon. No one dared to go that way anymore, as there were rumours years ago that there had been gangs sent that way to raid the market, and these gangs had been attacked themselves. They had been attacked by something they had never seen before. One gang was around ten to twenty strong, and this unknown being had pulverised them all. The gang couldn't remember anything of this encounter, but then they found themselves back at the city. They were battered and bruised, but did not remember anything. The gang leader had said that pass was now off limits. That was the story and the rumours that had spread among everyone.

Vaughn rode his wagon towards the main gate. It was a steep incline, but he had a good strong horse. He remembered back when he first found the market, which was by accident really. He had just come to the mountains for a break and to do some hunting, and accidentally stumbled across this market. He remembered how on this first time it had took him a while to get into the gate, as people on the gate thought he was from the city where the gangs came from. He only got in that time, because he had some meat with him from his hunt. They needed different food and this is when he started bartering with them. He had secretly enjoyed that. Today, as he got to the gate the people just waved him in, before he even had time to announce himself.

He then heard someone from the gate shout, 'Vaughn is here. Open the gate.'

The gate creaked open very slowly. The people there were always wary of gangs from the city trying to get in and steal from them. The gangs had not got in recently, but not for the want of trying. The gate opened enough to get his wagon through, so he hurried in as the gate opened slowly, but then the gate would close quickly. He got through before it slammed shut behind him, as usual. Vaughn liked to sit on his wagon and watch the bustling market with stalls everywhere. Some of the stalls had been built into the rock face, when they had the opportunity to do so. Some stalls were made from wooden posts with drapes over the top.

Vaughn stored and locked his wagon away in small barn in the rock face, as he went to barter with the people in charge of the market. He was always aware that there was a minority element at the market that would try and steal his load in the wagon. It was valuable to them, so he didn't want to take any risks with it. He walked straight through the market, which was always tricky. The market was always busy. Today was even busier. There must have been lots of other villagers come to check it out. There seemed to be children running around everywhere. Vaughn did not have time to stay and look around right now, but would after his meeting. He always enjoyed the vibe of the market.

He reached the entrance of the cave, and went down towards the little meeting room they had built just on the edge of the village. It was a bigger room than most of the little dwellings in the cave system. It wasn't very well done, but suited its purpose. Further into the cave, builders continued to excavate and make the village larger. They had learnt as they had gone along, and the newer buildings were more sophisticated than this original meeting room. Vaughn had been taken to see some of the newer buildings, including a new hall for the villagers. It would be glorious and the hall would be the new meeting point for market business.

The market leader was waiting for him at the meeting room. He was called Cirius. An odd little man in looks, balding, hunched over a little, with quite a rounded body shape and head. Despite looks, he was very intelligent. His wife was very similar and he often conducted meetings with his wife there too, who could be quite fierce when she wanted to be. He greeted Vaughn with a huge hug and smile on his face.

'It's great to see you again, Vaughn. It's been a while. I hope you have that wonderful medicine of yours, as we could really do with it.'

They sat at the stone table, and Cirius's wife immediately started to conduct the meeting. They met for an hour. It was a little fiery at times, but they agreed an amicable deal eventually. Vaughn got most of what he needed for his village too.

On the way out of the room he asked Cirius why there was so many people in the market today. He just said they had had a good crop of vegetables this year. Other villages in the area had struggled for crops and so had come to the market to do some deals. Vaughn also asked why there were so many children running around the market. Cirius just smiled. They are in an epic game of hide and seek. They have been at it for hours. Vaughn laughed and this gave him heart that in these days with so many orphaned children, the children could just be children occasionally.

As they got to the door leading out of the meeting room Vaughn asked, 'Any news from the city?'

Cirius grimaced and said, 'Yes. Still over run by gangs with drugs, gambling and prostitution. All still going on. They're leaving us alone at the minute, but I'm sure they will try something again soon enough, when they run out of food and materials. We are always on our guard.'

Vaughn said, 'I'm glad you're safe for the moment,' and shook Cirius's and his wife's hands.

He was walking back out of the cave, when he heard a scuffle. He looked over and there was someone on the floor with four men kicking him. He thought he heard someone say, 'What you doing here again?' Vaughn's instinct sent him over to intervene, when out of nowhere a little child came running over, grabbing at the men and shouting at them to get off him and leave him alone. One man stopped to face this female child and the child held her ground. Vaughn knew who they were immediately.

The man was Charlie Oakenshaw and he said, 'Annette, go away. This is nothing to do with you.'

She just looked at him and said, 'That's my friend on the floor, Charlie. He's done nothing wrong. Leave him alone.'

Charlie laughed and said, 'We told him not to come back.'

Annette came back with, 'Who put you in charge, Charlie Oakenshaw? Now leave him alone, you idiot.'

Charlie looked furious at this statement and said, 'You're pushing my patience, Annette. Now go away or else.'

Annette just stood there and laughed, 'Or else, what Charlie?'

At this comment Charlie grabbed her. Vaughn was over there in seconds. Everyone had stopped now and was looking at Charlie and Annette. The man on the floor was still squirming. Vaughn got close to Charlie and said, 'Is there a problem here, Charlie?'

Charlie grunted, 'Nothing to do with you.'

Vaughn calmly said, 'I can make it something to do with me if you'd like? Now let her go.'

Charlie let her go and swung round, but quickly realised it was someone younger and bigger than he was. He put his hands up, with a shocked look on his face.

'No, no, no problem here friend,' he said and backed off with his three friends.

Annette sarcastically shouted at him, 'That's a good boy, Charlie. You coward. Go off home now.'

Charlie paused for a second, but never turned around. He just kept walking. Vaughn stood there looking at Annette. She was tiny, about four foot two inches tall, with long dark crumpled up hair that really needed washing and combing. Her clothes were worse for wear as well. She had been orphaned at an early age and did not have much. She turned to Vaughn, looking up at him with her small face and tiny nose. Her eyes were hazel brown. She did not look happy.

'What did you do that for, Vaughn? I had everything under control.'

Vaughn just looked her up and down, 'Yes I could see that, but I just thought I would come over and see what was going on.'

Annette, with her hands on her hips and still staring at him trying to look stern, then gave him a massive grin. Vaughn loved her smile. It was so warm. She moved closer and hugged him.

'Great to see you, Vaughn. It's been too long.'

She turned her head to one side to see the crumpled, mess of a man still on the floor. She let go of Vaughn, and stormed over to him, admonishing the poor man the whole way.

'Jimbo, how many times have I told you to stick up for yourself with those guys? They're just bullies. I won't always be around to protect you, you know.'

When she got to him she was a little gentler and more sympathetic, trying to help him to his feet.

'Are you alright? I hope they didn't hurt you too much?'

Jimbo was an average size man with scruffy sandy coloured hair, a bushy beard and a tanned complexion. It was hard to distinguish his features under all this hair, but he appeared battered and bruised from the event. Jimbo looked Annette straight in the eyes. She was the only person he would do that to.

'Yes, I know. You're right Annette. I will do so someday. I promise. Thank you for your help. You are always there for me.'

Annette just shrugged nonchalantly and said, 'Anytime Jimbo. I can't stand that Charlie bloke. He's just a bully. You will have to thank Vaughn, as he helped a bit too.'

Vaughn smirked at that comment and moved over towards them. Jimbo looked towards the ground, looking uncomfortable with Vaughn's presence, rubbing his feet nervously from side to side. He did put his hand out though to acknowledge Vaughn, and Vaughn gently shook his hand.

'Thank you, Vaughn. That was very kind of you,' he said. Vaughn nodded and said, 'No problem.'

Jimbo turned back to Annette and said, 'I'll be on my way, Annette. Thank you again.'

Annette hugged him and smiled up at him, 'Be careful Jimbo.' His face mellowed. This just seemed to make his day. He limped off into the market with Vaughn and Annette watching on. Vaughn thought to himself, 'I'm sure I know that face from somewhere.' He was certain just before he turned the corner he had stopped limping too, but he could not think at all where he had seen his face before.

Vaughn looked down at Annette, 'I'm going to have a walk around the market and get some things for our village. Do you want to join me?' he said to the small girl.

She just looked up and said, 'Naah. I can't. I'm in a game of hide and seek with the other kids and I had better get back to it. Will you still be here later?'

'No,' Vaughn said, 'I have to get back.'

The young girl looked disappointed at this, so Vaughn told her he would be back in a few days with more medicine.

She smiled, that beautiful warm smile, and said, 'You better,' and ran off to hide.

Vaughn lost track of her in seconds and thought, 'They'll never find her!' Vaughn spent the rest of the day eating, and bartering for goods around the market. He then headed back to his horse and wagon, having said his goodbyes as always. He wanted to get back before it got dark. Even with his strength and shield, the dark was no place these days for just one man.

Chapter Six

Otax looked out at the destroyed city and thought to himself, 'This is my city.' Otax, was the head of the biggest gang in what was left of New York city, and he loved it. He was a large man with broad shoulders and quite a wide nose. He had a huge scar down his left cheek. He had been in this broken city all of his life, although not many people lived in the city nowadays. He had set up a penthouse of sorts in lower New York in one of the larger buildings. Most of the building was just a frame now, as much of the glass had been shattered. Not what it used to be many decades ago sadly. Most of the area around the building was moss ridden and overgrown, but he liked it. He liked to call this home. Otax was a powerful man. He was an enforcer at first because of his size, but was very shrewd, and rose through the ranks to become the gang's leader. He thought he was a good leader and fair on his members. He could be savage if he needed to be.
Otax always got up early and today was no different. He liked to have a walk around the streets in the peace and quiet before others rose. He went outside his building. It was a bright, sunny day. He began to walk along the streets. There were a few feral dogs, that were definitely not pets anymore. He carried a sword with him and his trusted walking staff, so he wasn't too nervous. He was always alert and keeping an eye on the dogs. He walked to one of his bars. He had quite a few bars. He walked past rotten relics of yester years. He did not know what most of these relics had been and what they had been used for, but they were part of the landscape now. He got to his closest bar and kicked someone awake, who was laying on the floor outside.

'Time to go home, buddy,' he said. 'We've been closed for hours.'

The man just looked up and said, 'Home. What home?'

Otax looked down and said, 'Well you can't stay there all day, man. So, move on.'

The man looked up again and was going to say something, but noticed who it was, got up and trudged off. Otax then banged on the makeshift door.

Someone from inside shouted, 'What do you want? I told you to go away. We're closed.'

Otax smiled and said, 'No, it's Otax.'

You could hear the person behind the door hurriedly trying to get the door open, when he heard this. Everyone knew Otax did not like to be kept waiting. One person did once, but never did that again. The door flew open and the manager came rushing out.

'Sorry for that, Sir. I thought I better check, as I didn't want your bar to get robbed.'

Otax said, 'That's fine, but if anyone knew who owned this bar, they wouldn't dare. How did we do last night?'

'Ok,' the manager said. 'A bit of gold and silver, some land and food crops.'

Society did not have any money now. People paid for drinks and services in other ways.

'Great,' Otax said. 'My men will be happy. They will have to go plough for food again,' he said sarcastically. 'We need to get into that market though. It's a goldmine. I will find a way in somehow soon.'

Otax wandered off and went around some of his other establishments. They were all very similar. All were little man-made bars at the end of a room, and then whatever they could find for tables and chairs. They just had to make do. Otax then returned to his penthouse. The families that stayed in the city were starting to get up. Kids coming out to play hide and seek. Lots of places to hide made this ideal. Otax met some of his men on the way back. He called them his soldiers, but really, they were just thugs. He was nearly home, when he heard a booming noise, and something huge flew overhead. It seemed to start blasting the buildings further up the city, with some kind of weapon he had not come across before. He ran inside and got some gear together, and was back out in seconds. The object overhead seemed to have gone, but in the distance there were booming noises. The soldiers he saw earlier came running up.

'What was that, Otax?' one said.

Otax said that he didn't have a clue, but he would find out. His men went off to get their weapons and alert other men in the gang to help. They gathered in a small courtyard, and off they went towards where the noise had been coming from. Otax had ordered everyone who couldn't fight, or was too old or young, to follow his men to the south side of the city where there was a monument. Very near the monument, they would find a huge, hidden, underground tunnel that would lead them out of the city. He told the people to pass this information on to others and get themselves to safety. He had found these tunnels, when he was a child playing in the city streets. They were huge and he thought they were miles in length. He could never see the end of them though. They were big enough to fit horses and carts in them. He had later found out that a mad genius had built them, as an easier way to move around the city. These tunnels had helped Otax from time to time to get ahead of his competitors. He then encouraged anyone who could fight to join them, as they went through the streets, as he thought they would need more people. They went running up the avenues, block by block. The noise was getting louder and louder. Some children ran out of an alley and nearly into the men. Otax stopped them in their tracks.

'What are you running from, kids?'

They looked at him petrified.

'I don't know, Sir. We've never seen anything like it. A ship or something landed, after it blasted some of the buildings over there. The door came open and these multi-coloured creatures flew out, and started blasting the adults.'

Otax was taken aback and said, 'Just the adults?'

One of the children said, 'Yes. One flew up to us, stopped, looked me up and down, and then flew off. He shot my teenage brother though. I was scared for my life. I went over to my brother. He wasn't dead, just stunned. We dragged him to safety.'

71

Otax left the children with one of his men, and moved on in their mission to get to this noise. As they reached the corner of the street, where the children had described seeing a ship land, Otax peered around the corner of the building into the square. The child was correct. There were multi-coloured alien creatures flying around everywhere. They were shooting at anything that moved. They were flying in and out of the square at different angles and trajectories to avoid being brought down. Otax watched for a while to see their strategy. There really didn't seem to be one! They would just fly in and try to shoot any adult or larger person they could, but the people were becoming wise to this. The people were taking cover, in what was left of the buildings and rusted wrecks. Anything they could hide in really. Many were trying to drag the stunned bodies of their partners and friends to some sort of cover. They hoped they would regain consciousness, after the stun blast they had received had worn off. Otax noticed these aliens would not fly into buildings after people or get too close to them. It seemed to him that they were afraid of the people, which was strange to him as they appeared to have the superior firepower. Otax had enough of waiting, so ordered some of his men into a few of the buildings. He thought they would have a closer shot at these alien creatures. He told them not to go too high into the buildings though, as their ship could bring down the building with one shot, and he did not want to lose good men. The men went in and Otax gave them time to get into position. He came around the corner with his trusted bow drawn ready. He was usually a good shot and he didn't miss too much, so he let a few arrows go. Unfortunately, the aliens saw him coming and were able to avoid his shots. They were weird looking creatures, but they were amazing flyers. They soared so high. His men fired from the buildings also, but these shots just flew into the sky with no results. The aliens just flew high enough so they couldn't get hit, so for a while there was a stand-off between the men and the aliens. They could not hit the aliens, but as soon as anyone moved they knew the aliens would swoop in and stun them. All of the time Otax was thinking that the ship was sitting at the end of the avenue looking menacing, but just watching this all taking place. Otax thought the ship would not remain this uninvolved forever. Whatever was in there would probably act soon he expected. He needed to try and get the people out the buildings as quick as possible for their safety. Otax was not trying to be a hero. It was all about the wealth. No people would mean he would have no wealth from the bars. He really did not care about the people, but if they did not survive that would mean no profit for him. No one to spend their assets. He found some more families nearby and told them to pass the following message on.

'Go to the South side, where my men are showing people the vast underground tunnels. Here you can get out of the city and head to the market in the mountains.'

Otax hoped the people would be safe doing this. Some seemed to know of the mountain pass rumour and were worried, but followed what Otax said.

'It's the quicker way. We have to take the risk, and hopefully won't be attacked there.'

He left everyone with the instructions. He could hear the aliens getting frustrated up in the sky, screeching and hollering. Suddenly, the ship opened. It must have had enough of waiting for the flyers to do their job. A ramp came down and a legion of the biggest alien creatures he had ever seen marched down the ramp and formed up at the bottom. Otax knew this was going to be a big problem! There were some creatures that must have been around six foot five inches tall. These were the shorter ones. There were many more that were about seven foot tall. All were about four foot wide. It looked like they had huge heads, but Otax was not sure as he thought they could also be wearing helmets. They had two massive arms that reached down past their hips, and two very short legs. They looked like they were mainly just upper torso, and muscly with no fat on them. He could not be sure again whether they had skin, or some sort of outer armour covering them. They all held powerful looking weapons in their hands too. Otax definitely did not like the look of those. Otax and his men, still in the nearby buildings, hurriedly tried to block the avenue with anything they could find. They dragged wrecks and any other large objects into the middle of the avenue. This was made more difficult, with the flying aliens above swooping and trying to stun them. They could not afford to be stunned, as these large beasts were ready to attack, having been gathered at the end of the ramp. The men tried to block as much as possible, in between sheltering in the nearest buildings. Otax knew he had to get out of there really, but had to lay down cover so as many people as possible could escape. He got all of his men and told them to hold their ground as long as they could, as he suspected they were going to get pounded heavily. He said that if the ship takes off though they should get out the building and make a run for it. As he finished telling them their orders, there was an almighty sound. He quickly ran to the nearest blown out window and looked down the avenue. The beast-like aliens were going mad. There was an enormous one at the front. Was this the one in charge? It seemed to be whipping them up into a frenzy, which in turn did the same to the flying aliens above. Then suddenly it stopped. Everything was silent. Otax was sure this was a bad sign. Another sound came from the ship. Presumably this was an order to attack, as the large beasts started moving from the ramp into the street. They were not quick movers, but their weapons were powerful. Firing in all directions towards the people, who were running for shelter. The buildings were being battered, but for the moment withstanding the onslaught. Otax knew they needed to get closer, if his arrows were to have any effect. He looked down at his sword, but did not think this would be any use, as he did not wish to be that close to the creatures. They looked so powerful, even at a distance from him. They were! A couple of them just threw an object out of their way, that would had taken ten strong men to move earlier, but these two creatures did it with ease. However, Otax did notice that their aim with their weapons was not very accurate. Some people that were breaking cover and making a run for it were not actually getting hit. The shot directions seemed to be very erratic and ill-placed. Did the beasts have bad eye sight? Were they not trained soldiers? Was it instinct that they used to fight with? Did they just not want to kill them? So many questions, but Otax did not want to find out any of these answers. The beasts were getting closer to the building, where Otax and his men were positioned. Otax was waiting for the right time. The flying aliens were still overhead and swooping in towards the street level. Otax and his men could not waste their arrows on the flying aliens. They were needed for the beasts. The beasts were pounding up the avenue. Objects that had been put in the way were not obstacles to these beasts, and were not slowing them down in their pursuit of the people. If their weapons did not move the objects, the objects were just lifted and flung out the way by the sheer strength of the beasts. Otax smiled to himself and was thinking they would definitely make good security for him one day. The beasts were nearly in range now, just a few more feet needed. Then Otax gave the order to fire.

All of the men let the arrows loose, and to their utter shock the arrows bounced off the beast and fell to the ground. Otax immediately knew they had to get out of there. They could not stop the beasts. Him and his men took cover further inside the building, as the beasts took aim with their mighty weapons and bombarded the building even more. There was laser fire everywhere. Thankfully no one was hit. Otax got to his feet and told his men to break cover. The city was lost.

'Make for the tunnels. Take as many people as you can with you,' Otax shouted.

The make shift door for the building was taking too many hits. It was about to be broken. That door did not last long! The door shattered and the beast stormed into the building. Luckily for Otax and his men, the beast were slow and cumbersome, so Otax and his men ran out the back of the building evading mighty blasts coming from behind them. They could not break cover totally, as the multi-coloured flying aliens were still out there. If they got stunned, the beast would catch them and most likely kill them. It was a slower process for Otax and his men to reach the south side of the city. They were running building to building, taking cover all the way with beasts behind firing and aliens overhead. Otax lost where the ship was, and wasn't sure if it had moved at all. He had to stop to take a breather in one of the houses in the city streets, but was not there for long. These beasts were slow but relentless. It seemed like they wanted to capture them and they were not going to stop until they did. If felt like this chase was forever. Sometimes Otax and his men would stop and fire their bows, just to try and slow the beast down a little. In turn, this just made the beasts angrier. To Otax's relief, he could see some buildings he knew well. He knew they had almost made it back to the area where the tunnel entrances were located, but they needed to try and lose the beasts before they entered the tunnels. If they didn't lose them, this would have been a pointless exercise. He sent the vast majority of his men back to the tunnels, keeping just a few of his best men alongside him. As they ran, he told them they would divert the beast away from the tunnels as far as they could, and then circle back to get themselves into the tunnels. He got the attention of the beasts by firing some arrows at them, which focussed their attention on him. He could not stay there for long, as the flying aliens kept swooping in and very nearly stunned him. He only just evaded that one. Otax had had a secret passage made under one of his bars, that led to his penthouse. He would try and evade the beasts using this. On the way they would try and take shots at the beast to encourage them to follow them, and not the other men. It worked well. It felt like this annoyed the beasts enough that they just wanted to get their hands on Otax and his few remaining men. Otax sent one man at each block back to the main tunnel, so that he was the only one left, as he knew the passage was not too far away now. This terrified him, which was a strange feeling for him, as he had never felt scared of any human before. This was the first time he had not been the biggest or strongest person in a fight. It unsettled him to know this. He was just around the corner from the bar with the passage in. The entrance to the passage was just big enough for him, but the beasts would not fit through. He let a couple of arrows go towards the nearest beast, the big one that was in charge. He hit it with his shots, and thought it's definitely time to get out of here. He ran into the bar, and hoped the beasts did not see him go in. Straight through and down into the basement. The entrance was hidden under the floorboards down there. He started to rip the floorboards up, as quick as he could to expose the entrance. It was only small. He squeezed into it. It was tighter than he remembered, but he was only a young man when he originally constructed it years ago, and had put on weight since then. He was scrambling through as quick as he could. It was not an easy job. He was sure he could hear the aliens in the bar, so he did not have long. He just got through to the more open section, when blaster shots ran down. They just missed him. As he looked back, he could just make out the beasts. They were going crazy at the passage entrance. They could not fit through, but they were determined creatures, smashing at the entrance while others appeared to be blasting at it with their weapons. He knew it would not take them long to get through, so he got himself together and made his way along for about a mile. He would come out a block or two away from the main tunnel entrance. As he got to the end of the passage and climbed out, he tried to sabotage it, so they couldn't follow. With their power this might not work for long. The passage ended in the basement of his building, that housed his penthouse. He was desperate to go and save some of his riches, but this was not the time or place to do so. He looked around outside the building and could not see any beasts. They had not discovered the main tunnel, where he had sent his men and people too. His plan to divert them to his hidden passage appeared to have worked. Otax stayed in the shadows, as he ran out of the building towards the main tunnel, as he was unsure where the flying aliens had gone. He hoped he would not have to deal with any of them again. He made it to the main tunnel without any incidents, where he was met by his men who were protecting the entrance. They hugged him and thanked him for what he did. They saw his bravery and heroism. They were saddened that they had left people behind though.

Otax said, 'We did all we could,' and walked off into the tunnel. At that instant, there was a blood curdling scream that stopped him in his stride. It seemed to come from the direction of the

77

beasts. They must have realised they had lost him. Otax smiled to himself, but knew this was just the beginning of the ordeal. They had many miles to go to get to the market yet. Otax caught up with the people in the tunnel. There was a torrent of applause and pats on his back for losing the aliens, and getting them safely out the city. There were around a few hundred people, which shocked Otax. He thought more would have escaped. One of his men saw the shock in Otax's face and put his hand up to reassure the man.

'Don't worry. There were already thousands of people in here before us.'

Otax looked surprised at this, as he thought he was the only one who knew about the tunnel.

His man said, 'A lot of kids told us where to go and told the people they could lead them to safety. One of the kids is leading the way now. He's called Nittil. He reckons he's been down there many times, and all the way to the end.'

Otax was not happy with this. He wanted to be the saviour and to get all the recognition for it. Otax had found this tunnel, but had never reached the end of it. He did not know where it actually led to. He took some solace in the fact the aliens would take a long time to find the entrance, if they found it at all. Otax did think that there must be a large amount of people still in the city though, as they were definitely not all in here, and hoped they had gone to ground. With all that had happened to them in the past the people were good at hiding, and it would take days if not weeks for the beasts to find them, but hopefully they would find their way out of the city and to safety before that happened. Otax and his men caught up with the main group. Otax stayed at the back, as there were so many of them already filling the space in the tunnel ahead. This is not where he wanted to be. He should be leading them to safety, and not some child. They walked for a good few hours, until the smells in the tunnel began to change. There was a fresher smell from somewhere up ahead. There was a buzz among the people now. Less moaning about it taking too long and the aliens finding them. Instead, everyone had started to smile and laugh. There was positivity among the masses now.

Nittil had passed the message down that they were coming to the end of the tunnel. He had stopped everyone at the front, so he could get out and see if it was safe out there. They seemed to wait for quite a while, but it was probably only a few minutes. Word spread that it was safe, but people were told to stay with Nittil and his other child guides.

The forest was a dangerous place these days, but the children knew it well. Otax had heard of forests, but had never been in one. From what he had heard about forests, he never wanted to go in one either. Otax's group were the last to get to the open door. It was old and rusty. It had about five locking mechanisms on it and was about five inches thick. Not much would have got past this years ago. A child was at the open door. Otax was not good at working out ages, but hated kids. He guessed the kid was around ten to twelve years old.

Otax went straight up to him and said, 'Kid.'

The kid looked up with a smile. Otax did not like this. He thought the child should be scared of him, with his intimidating size and stature, but the child didn't care about this in the slightest.

He continued, 'There must be a better way to go, than going through a forest to the market?'

The kid just shrugged and said, 'Nittil says this is the only way. Don't worry Sir, he knows the forest like the back of his hand. He has plenty of experience of it.'

Otax's men started to giggle at the child telling Otax not to worry. That was short-lived, when they saw the glare in Otax's eyes. He was seething now.

He looked down at the child and said, 'I'm in charge here kid, and I will say where we go.'

The child seemed unphased and said back, 'Well you will have to take that up with Nittil, but you'll have to go into the forest to do so. As Nittil says, the forest will give us cover from the aliens if they come after us in that ship.'

Otax appeared to concede to that, but he would catch up with this Nittil and tell him exactly who was in charge!

He begrudgingly looked at the child and said, 'Lead the way then kid, if you know what you're doing?'

At that comment and attitude the kid took offense.

'I've been in the forest loads of times, Sir,' he said through gritted teeth. 'You and your men will be safe with me. My name is Innex. Remember that.'

Innex then waved his hand, gesturing for them to follow him through the door. As they manoeuvred out of the door together and up a small incline, the sights and sounds were things that Otax had never encountered before. Trees were enormous. You couldn't see the tops. It looked like they went up into the clouds. On the ground there was fauna everywhere. There was no obvious path in amongst this green fauna ahead of them. There were so many bright and beautiful colours that Otax was taken aback. Why had he not gone this far in the past? He would have loved this. It was glorious. He came out of his daydream, when the last man came out of the door and slammed it shut behind him. The man was going to jam the door shut, so no aliens or beasts could follow if they came down the tunnel, but Otax wouldn't let him in case there were any stragglers from the city who had followed them. He also didn't think it was worth jamming the door, as those huge beasts would get through that old rusty door with ease.

Innex turned to them, 'Now follow me in single file men and don't touch anything. It might be beautiful in here, but it's extremely dangerous nowadays. Most things will kill you,' looking purposely towards Otax.

Otax just glared back thinking, 'What a little know it all! Who does he think he is!' They walked through the forest with no problems, but Otax had a sense that something was following them.

He said this to Innex, who just shrugged and smiled at the big man and said, 'Possibly a lion or tiger. They won't attack us. We are a large group making a lot of noise. I would not want to be at the back though,' Innex said with a smirk on his face.

They came to a slight clearing. Only slight, as everything in here seemed overgrown. Some of the city people, in the groups that were ahead, were sat talking and having a rest. Otax went over to them and asked what was going on.

One person said, 'This is where Nittil said we will stop and camp for the night. He has taken some men with him to get wood and things for the camp, while the other kids go and get food, as they know the safe things to eat in this forest.'
Otax took out his bow and said, 'I will go too.'
He grabbed some of his own men and was about to leave, when Innex said, 'I best come too to keep you safe.'
Otax said, 'Ok,' but disliked Innex.
Innex, to be fair, was great. He found some animals quicker than Otax and his men did. Otax had to shoot and kill them though, as Innex did not carry a weapon. They returned to this make shift camp area in the forest, and it was looking more like a camp now. There was a fire lit, and some branches and large leaves had been positioned to make some covered areas. The covered areas would protect them from rain and also hide the light from the fires. Innex said how it rained a lot in the forest. Thankfully they were back in time, before it got dark. The kids, who had gone for the food, had excelled themselves with their hoard of supplies, all sorts of fruits and berries, but no meat. Otax took delight in the fact they couldn't hunt and he was the one who had got the meat. He threw his kill down in front of the fire.
'Does anyone know how to cook this?' Otax asked, as he had never actually cooked before. He always had someone do it for him.
A kid stepped forward and said, 'I do, Sir.'
Innex looked over and said, 'Hey Nittil. It's great to see you again.'
Nittil looked over and nodded towards Innex. Otax was surprised, as he thought Nittil would be an older teen, but must have been about thirteen, the same as Innex. This did not make him happy when he realised this. He went over to Nittil, aggressively standing as close as he could to his face.
'Who put you in charge, boy?' he said, disregarding the looks he was getting from people.
To his shock this child was not scared of him either, which was similar to how Innex had responded. They were not scared of

Otax at all. This just aggravated Otax further, as in the city Otax was feared by everyone, or so he thought.

'No one, Sir. I'm not looking to be in charge, but I know the forest better than any of you. I thought I could help people escape the beasts and flying aliens. You can be in charge if you like? I'll just lead us all through, as I know the forest so well,' Nittil said.

'That's good kid. You can do that,' Otax uttered.

Otax pointed back into the forest and said, 'Me and my men will camp over there.'

Nittil looked and said to Otax that he should stay with the main group, as it was safer. Otax chose to ignore this and wanted to be alone with his men.

Nittil said, 'That's up to you. I think it's a bad idea,' and walked away.

Innex interjected and said, 'You should really listen to him. He knows what he's talking about.'

Otax had had enough of being told what to do and walked off into the forest, summoning his men to follow. Otax took his men a few hundred metres further into the forest away from the camp. They set up an area next to some colourful trees. Bright blues, reds and oranges. So many colours you could not even imagine it. He told his men to get to work, and start making fires and covered areas for them to sleep under. He also got them cooking his meat too, that he had hunted earlier! They did not take any fruit and berries from the kids in the main camp area. Instead he had noticed some berries in the trees they were under and took them to add to his meat. They sat there having a laugh and a joke around the fire. After an intense day, they just wanted to relax. They ate all the food and sat back. After a while, some of the men started making strange comments about the crazy tree colours.

'They're so bright and glowing,' one said.

They started to hallucinate and see things that weren't there. Otax suddenly could see this too. The colours were ten times brighter and he started seeing people from his past in the trees. These people had died years ago, but he could see them. He wanted to party with them. He had never been this happy in his entire life. He started swaying from side to side with a huge grin on his face. He could hear a few screams, but he didn't care. To him they seemed to be in the distance. Nothing to do with him. Then something grabbed him and tried to pull him up. He was delirious. All part of his hallucination trip. He was slowly being lifted to a crazy bright heavenly looking place. In his mind, he really wanted to go to this place. So bright and appealing. It was so high off the ground, about ten feet. When all of a sudden, he came crashing to the ground. He got back to his feet and tried to climb back up, but he was being stopped by something. He wanted to fight, but in his drug addled state, was unable too. He was sure he could hear someone say, 'Quick, get him back to camp.'

He was being dragged away then, and half way back to the camp he blacked out. Otax woke the next day to the worst headache. He was under a sheet that wasn't his and below a cover he did not recognise. He sat up slowly. He ached all over. He stuck his head outside and to his amazement he was in the main camp now. Innex spotted him and came rushing over.

'You were lucky last night,' he said. 'Nittil went looking for you after you left the camp and found you below the hydro trees. Not a good place to be. He rushed back to get help straight away, as he saw the berries you had been eating. The tendrils of the tree had grabbed you. He knew you wouldn't want to come back to reality!'

Otax said, 'Why wouldn't we?'

Innex continued, 'Well you ate the berries, and they're extremely intoxicating and cause hallucinations, which is what the tree wants. The tree can then grab you without a fight, as the tree feeds on meat you see. It can then ingest you. Luckily Nittil and the others got to you in time. The tendrils of the tree are strong. Hard to chop off, and that tree is nasty. Looks beautiful, but will put up a fight for its prey. You only lost a couple of men. Could have been all of you.'

Otax sat there feeling stupid. He could not believe he had lost men to a tree, but actually he thought he was glad he found the tree. He thought he could make a fortune from those berries.

83

What a drug they were! Otax asked Innex where Nittil was, so he could thank him for last night.

Innex said, 'Just sit. I will get him, as I don't think you can stand up and get anywhere.'

Innex strode off and Otax tried to get up. Innex was right again. He did not have the strength. So, he sat there considering this new drug and all the possible new riches he could get from it. They just had to get out of the forest and back to the city, and hope the aliens had gone. He had regained his strength back by around midday, and it was time for the group to leave this area and move on. Otax found Nittil at the front of group on the walk, and the big man thanked him for what he had done for him and his men. The youngster was very humble and courteous. He did not know how to deal with compliments. Otax started talking to him. Nittil did not want to open up, even though Otax kept trying.

'How do you know so much about the forest?'

Nittil fell silent and Otax did not think he was going to say anything, but then Nittil started to explain, 'I stumbled upon it really.'

Otax was surprised by this and was going to say something when Nittil continued, "I found the tunnels years ago and I went into them to explore. I went further and further each time, before I found the door. It took a few days before I had the courage to open the door and see what was on the other side. When I did, all those fragrant smells flooded into the tunnel. I wasn't sure what this was, so I went up to explore and out of the tunnel, and like you I got caught up with all the vibrant colours. I had never seen trees this big before either. Before I could go any further I heard a weird sounding voice, which told me to stop and not go any further, as it was a dangerous place. I think he or she was saying that for my safety, as they could see I was just a child. All of sudden, the voice then told me to go back to the city, where it was safer. It said the forest was not a place for a city child to be. I just stood there not knowing what to do. The voice then said again, 'Go back kid.' To this I replied, 'What for?' It seemed to flummox the voice and it said, 'What do you mean what for? Do you have a family?' I said,

'Yes, but my Mum and Dad are addicts and I have a brother I have to look after. We are starving and living off scraps from the streets. It just said, 'Not my problem kid. Go back.' I stood there and probably looked a bit pathetic. I saw a movement in the trees and it looked like something was moving away from me, but then it stopped. The voice said, 'I know where you could go kid. The market. It's safe and they look after orphans.' I was tempted by this, but I replied, 'They are my family. I can't leave my brother.' The figure seemed to move away again and said, 'Your choice.' At that point I sat down and after a couple of minutes from right behind me this time I heard, 'Are you going or not?' I said, 'I thought you didn't care?' I looked up and it was a hooded figure, average height, dressed all in black. The hooded figured replied, 'I don't really, but I didn't want to see you become some animals snack. You're too small to be a meal for animals in here.' The figure must have taken pity on me, as its tone of voice had changed. It was not so menacing, but I could never clearly see its face. It was always distorted. It said, 'There's plenty of food in the forest for you and your brother. I will show you what is safe and not, but you will have to listen to me as a lot of this can kill you as well.' I looked up and smiled. It said, 'Your training starts tomorrow.' I trained with it for months. Then when it thought I knew enough, the figure was gone. It left a message that if I or any of the kids had enough of the hard city life, then we were safe to go through the pass to the market."

Otax listened to this story intently and had to ask, 'Who was this stranger?'

Nittil said, 'I have no idea, but hopefully I meet the stranger again. I owe it a great deal. I took it upon myself to train the others after that, and here we are. Glad I bumped into the stranger.'

Otax said, 'I'm glad too.'

On the rest of the journey through the forest they had a few run-ins with the animals. The animals were huge and in groups. Thankfully the people had some weapons and were able to fight them off, and there were no casualties. With Nittil leading the way there were no problems with the trees or fauna. The aliens didn't seem to have tracked them. Perhaps they hadn't found the entrance or were too busy with the remaining people in the city. Otax thought on a few occasions he saw the flying aliens, but Nittil reassured him that they were just birds. The aliens would continue to play on his mind.

They came to the edge of the forest, and looking from the treeline they could see the pass. It was about half a mile away and up in the mountains. In-between this was a grassy prairie area with no cover. The pass would be quicker than going to the main entrance, which was around the mountain face and a good few miles away. They could not afford to be in this open exposed area for too long, in case they were spotted. Otax just hoped they could get through this pass, given what happened to his men the last time they tried that way! With Nittil and his team, they knew it was their only chance. They were going to try and go through the pass that night, but Nittil said that they would be crazy to do that, as the mountain lions would cut them down. So, they set up camp just inside the edge of the forest and waited for early morning.

They were up and ready at the crack of dawn. They ate well for breakfast, as they knew they needed all the energy they could muster. There were thousands of them and they all needed to get across the clearing as quick as they could. They got to the last tree of the tree line. Otax was about to give an order, when Nittil and the kids started running for the pass. Otax thought, 'Oh. That's his plan!' and started sprinting himself towards the pass with everyone, who then just copied. It was not ideal, but hopefully it would be effective. Thankfully this was effective and they reached the mountains edge without incident. Only a few cuts and bruises from people falling over on the uneven grassy soil of the prairie. They all started to climb the mountain face. It was a little way up to the pass. Otax sent Nittil up first with a few hundred others. Thereafter, a child went up with each group. Otax went with the last group. He was with Innex. He smiled within, as he was grateful to be with Innex. They climbed up and started walking along the pass. It was tight, with sheer rock faces either side. For Innex this was no problem, but for Otax this was a little snug! It was about two metres wide, but still a bit tight for him. Innex took it in his stride along the pass, talking all the time without a care in the world. Otax, on the other hand, had a strange feeling the whole way that they were being watched. A couple of times, he thought he saw rocks fall not far from them, like something was there. To his relief, nothing seemed to happen. They got to the end of the pass, with Nittil waiting for them. He pointed down and a few miles in the distance they could see the market. There was a line of people making their way down to the market.

Nittil stayed until the last person came out of the pass, and Otax thought he heard the kid say, 'Thank you.' A voice coming down the pass then said, 'That's not a problem, Nittil.'

It took a while to get to the market, because there were so many people. When Otax got there, they did not seem very happy to see them. It was Cirius who was there, and it wasn't the warmest welcome from him. More of a wonder, as to why they were here.

Otax was about to explain when he heard from behind, 'Vaughn's back again, let him past.'

Otax saw a horse drawn wagon pull up with a man on it. He nodded to Cirius and Otax, but just kept going past them. Cirius smiled at Vaughn, but then turned to Otax and glared. 'What you doing here, Otax? We nearly didn't open the gates. We only opened them, because of all the kids with you. We told your men when they tried to attack us the last time, you are not welcome here.'

Otax started to explain, 'We were attacked by aliens and we lost the city. This was the safest place we could think of for all our people and their families.'

Cirius just snorted, 'You only think of profit. You don't care about families. Aliens? You could have thought of a better lie than that couldn't you? If this is your only way to get into the market, that is low even for you.'

Otax was going to refute this when Nittil came up behind and said, 'It's actually true, believe it or not.' As soon as he said it he heard someone scream, 'Run for the caves. Get cover.' They looked over in shock and saw people running through the market to get to the cave system. Then suddenly something zipped overhead and started blasting the mountain near the cave entrance, trying to bring it down. The mountain was strong and took the barrage without crumbling. However, they had never seen the mountain tested like this before, so had no idea what powerful blasts it could withstand or for how long. Otax looked up and pointed to the ship, and gave an 'I told you so' look to Cirius. Cirius didn't care. He just turned and ran for the cave. The ship turned back sharply and started blasting the market. Not the people, but just the stalls and market fronts. It had another attempt on the mountain, as it passed over. A few pieces of rock sheared off the face, rolling down the face, but most of it held firm. Just a small trickle of rock pieces. Most of the people had reached the cave system, including those that had escaped the city. Others had scattered to safety, as they thought the ship could do no more damage. The ship must have realised it was not causing the desired damage and went towards a clearing and set itself down. The clearing was a few miles from the main gate, so some people quickly went back and closed the gate. Otax told Cirius that closing the gate might not be a deterrent, as these beasts were strong and had powerful weapons as well.

Cirius said, 'If they get past the main gate, they won't get past the door to the cave system.'

Otax did not share this optimism and said, 'We should have people in the rocks hiding and ready to put up a fight. Does the city cave system have a way out other than the market entrance?'

Cirius said that it didn't, but they would be safe in this cave city, as it was deceivingly large and plenty of places to hide.

Vaughn had come up behind them now and said, 'That's no plan. You have to put up some fight.'

Cirius replied, 'Are you going to help us?'

'I can't help you fight, but I can help you set up for one,' Vaughn said.

Cirius, Otax and Vaughn considered strategies, but knew the best thing they could do was to slow the aliens attack on the market. They just had to hope the cave system would hide them and keep the large majority safe from the aliens.

They set a few traps and hid a few people in the rocks with bows ready to use, to try at least to slow their progress. It didn't look too good for them though. The colourful aliens flew over first seeing who they could blast, but would not go near the cave, as they seemed to know they would be trapped and the people would overpower them. It took a while for the larger beasts to arrive. Otax knew they were very slow with their little legs. As Otax expected, the gate was not much of an obstacle, and they blasted it with their weapons and pushed through the remains. Some of the men pushed a vat of boiling oil down onto the beasts from a broken section of mountain above, and then ran back towards the cave. The beasts just walked through the oil like it was a warm shower. The beasts actually seemed to really enjoy it. The people had all retreated to the cave now, and in the square where the market once was, the beast formed up. They were huge, menacing and in their hundreds. Cirius was going to close the door to the cave system, but Otax and Vaughn thought this was pointless having seen what the beasts had done to the gate. The beasts started moving slowly forward, so all the people in the rocks let their arrows fly at them. They seemed to bounce off them, but never really slowed them. The flying aliens swooped in to try and get the people in the rocks, but the people ducked down and ran quickly towards the cave. The flying aliens flew up and away, so Cirius went to close the door shut.

Then someone shouted, 'What's she doing?'

Cirius and Vaughn looked out, assuming everyone was inside the cave, but they could see Annette walking into the square. They stopped pulling the door.

Vaughn nipped out and shouted, 'Annette, what are you doing?'

She had a quick glance in his direction, but kept walking. She stopped right in the centre of the square, straight in front of the beasts. It looked like they would not even notice her and would keep walking. She held her ground, as they carried on marching towards her. Then suddenly the beast at the front put his hand up and they all came to an immediate halt. The beasts made some chilling noises and the flying aliens kept swooping around. This must have been a scare tactic. They did not shoot though. Annette just stood there like she had no care in the world. Vaughn thought they would tear her apart, and was seriously thinking of going to help, but didn't know if he would reach her in time. In the distance, he thought he could see something moving fast and screaming something. He thought it was coming from the pass.

The beasts kept doing the chilling screams, but with no effect. Annette thought she could hear something coming from the earpiece of the lead beast closest to her. Were these orders from somewhere? The beast was shaking its huge head. They stopped screaming and went eerily quiet. The crowd of beast separated down the middle, and an even bigger alien species came out of the crowd towards Annette. This species was around ten-foot-tall with four arms. It was coming directly for her. She would not be moved though. To her amazement, as it got to her it bent down. It's one red eye looked down at her, as she looked up. It spoke to her in English surprisingly.

'Get out of the way little girl. We will not be stopped today.' She looked straight at it and shook her head. This infuriated the alien and it grabbed her arm very gently, for a creature of its size. It dragged her to one side and pushed her to the ground out of the way, and then turned back to the beasts. In an alien language it shouted what must have been a command to carry on the attack. Within seconds Annette was stood back up in front of them. The beasts would not march over her. The one-eyed alien tried again, but the same thing happened. She could feel the alien was strong, but it did not seem to be using its strength to hold her, so she kept jumping up and running back in front of them. It was like a game.

The voice from the distance was getting closer. Vaughn was being distracted by the flying aliens trying to stun him and so he could not help. The others were too frightened to come out of the cave. The one-eyed alien was in Annette's face now.

'Look little girl, you are trying my patience. Get out of the way,' it said. 'I will not keep playing these games.'

She kept shaking her head. The alien growled and pulled a small bar from behind its back. The bar morphed into a razor-sharp looking spear, that glowed from side to side. He put it close to Annette. She pulled her face back a little, as this spear was red hot.

'Just think what I could do to you with this, little girl.'

To this Annette stood her ground and said, 'My name is Annette, and do with that what you will, but I'm not moving. I am not letting you hurt or kill anyone today.'

The alien pulled the spear away from her and looked back towards the crowd of beast, but they did not seem to know what to do. So, it turned, lifted the spear and drove it down. As it did this, there was an almighty scream from the voice approaching.

Chapter Seven

Four years on and Archer was loving life. He was now one rank under the General, a Lieutenant General, that annoyed the General greatly. The General hated Archer and was never afraid to show it, which never bothered Archer in the slightest. To add further to the General's annoyance, Archer always brought Cundill with him. Cundill was now a Captain. The General thought Archer was crazy, as he just thought Cundill was Archer's bodyguard. The General had been trying to keep Archer back for years. The first year was hard for Archer trying to get to know everyone, and who ran in whose circles. For a year and half the General would promote anyone, but not Archer. Archer was smart and learned quickly. He learned who to ingratiate himself with, and who he could bully when it came to promotions. People dropped out of promotions due to intimidation, or some of the officers started rallying the General believing Archer was the right man for promotion. In the end the General had no choice, but to promote him. Archer thought it was great that he had risen up the ranks, as quick as he did. The General would still not attack the aliens, even though this was Archer's main goal still after all these years. That's what he lived for. The revenge on those aliens. This consumed him daily. So his plan was to wait until the General was gone, or come to an unfortunate end. While he waited he had been starting projects to set this in motion, so when the General had gone Archer would be ready. Archer had kept his men from Mars together, and according to other soldiers on the base Archer et al had come from a base in the northern area of Scotland. They had kept the secret that they were actually based on Mars, and it was only him and a few of his men that knew they still had the little alien in their possession. After years of torture, the little alien had started to cooperate. Archer could not get the weapons technology from it yet, but he would. Patience had been needed. It seemed the alien would help with the engine technology though. So, Archer went to see the science department. They put him in touch with a younger member of the team called Dr Chantelle Che. She was not very co-operative and came across as a little sharp. She said she would never work for him and it's not her section. Archer had a feeling about this girl and thought he recognised her. There was something about the way she acted. Someone of her age must have been ambitious and very intelligent to have got to her position within the science department. So, to turn him down without even thinking about it did not seem right to Archer. Archer thanked her for her time, but with a scowl he walked out of the room. How could he get close to this girl or find out who she was? Why was she so reluctant to investigate this new technology? As a scientist, surely this would intrigue her?

Walking down the corridor, Archer bumped into Chantelle's superior, Dr Simmons. Simmons was not happy that Archer had gone to Chantelle before going to him. Simmons was saying that he was the best scientist in the whole place, and he found it disrespectful that Archer would go and see Chantelle first. Archer remembered someone saying there was someone on the base who was egotistical in the science department. Simmon's definitely lived up to this reputation and then some more. Captain Cundill had now joined them in the corridor, silently walking up mid conversation. Archer was considering having Cundill intimidate Simmons, when he thought perhaps he could use Simmon's ego to his advantage. So, he calmed Simmons down and told him what he wanted. Simmons just looked at Archer and laughed, which did not amuse Archer. Simmons stopped laughing when he noticed Archer's body language change. He said that it was not possible for that technology to integrate into the engine technology, even though it was cutting edge for the time. The engine technology on the base had only been needed for cars, and nothing high speed. He questioned why Archer would need such fast engines inside the shield. Archer looked Simmons straight in the eyes, and Simmons noticeably shrunk a little.

Archer said, 'Don't worry about the technology, as we have someone to help you with it. The shield won't last forever.'

Simmons said, 'Theoretically the shield can last forever, but if you want the engines making then we can do it. However, the General will have to know and sign off on them.'

Archer just put his hands on Simmon's shoulder and said, 'Does he?'

Simmons looked at him and grinned, 'Not if you don't want him to! I don't like the old man anyway.'

Archer had started to warm to Simmons.

'The problem you have is that what you want to do is going to cost, and cost a lot. You are going to need money. A backer from somewhere,' Simmons said.

Archer looked at him and was annoyed, but knew Simmons was right. He told Simmons that this would not be a problem and he would sort it. Archer told Simmons to get a little team together, who he trusted, and to be ready as he would be shipped off to work on it very soon. Simmons walked away with a massive grin on his face and a hop in his step.

Over his shoulder Simmons said, 'I will. You can trust me.'

Cundill turned to Archer and said, 'Do you trust him?'

Archer replied to Cundill and said, 'You're the only one I trust! If Simmons says anything no-one would ever believe him, so I don't think he'll say anything.'

Cundill looked at Archer and questioned where he would get all this money from that he would be needing for this venture. Archer said he was unsure, but he would use some of his military power and influence with the government to try and get the funding. Archer hated politics, but knew he would have to dabble sometimes, as he had seen the General doing on many occasions. Basically, the General ran the country and nothing could happen without his say so, but he had to try and make it look like the people had some say. Therefore, he had kept parliament and they dealt with money issues that he did not want to deal with. Archer was not looking to the top of the government, as any conversation with the prime minister or top ministers would get back to the General. So, he would look for someone who was young, upcoming and possibly slightly naive, so he could use and mould them to his advantage. He had asked around and found out about a young twenty-four-year-old called Rupert Smith-Jones, who seemed like a possible candidate. He had been a minister for six months and had made a name for himself. Previously he had worked in the city before this. Archer decided he was the one for him. He set up a meeting with him, in what he had been told was the nicest restaurant in London, to make him feel comfortable. Archer had never been to London before in the four years, as they had remained on the base during this time to keep them away from too many people asking questions and less conspicuous.

The time came to go to the meeting. Archer wore a smart suit, instead of his uniform, which he actually quite liked. He did not want to stick out like he would in his army gear. Archer got to the restaurant and he was first there. He spoke to the concierge and slipped him some money to seat them in a quiet, secluded spot. Smith-Jones turned up a quarter of an hour late, which made Archer unhappy. They went to their table. Archer had noticed there were some other officers in the restaurant, so was happy to get to the table where the concierge had put them, where nobody would see them. Smith-Jones got straight to it.

'Thank you for asking me here, Archer. I have been trying to get in here for ages. I've heard the food and drink in here is excellent.'

Archer replied, 'Oh it is.'

He was lying, as he had never left the base. This was the first time he had been to London and on the amazing train to get there. Who invented that train he wondered to himself? The young minister ordered some wine, checking that Archer did not mind. Archer didn't. The wine came and Archer poured it. When Smith-Jones asked Archer why he had set up this meeting, Archer liked this. It seemed this minister was straight to the point.

'I'm glad you asked that, Rupert. I'm looking for cash for a project and I thought you were the right man for the job.'

Smith-Jones looked at him and appeared interested in this.

'And what job would that be?'

So, Archer ran him through what he had planned and Smith-Jones just sat back in his chair.

'That's ambitious,' he said, 'But I'm not that high in government yet to help you with that.'

Archer knew he had peaked his interest though and played on his naivety.

'Well if it's too big for you, can you put me in touch with someone who can help?' Archer said.

Smith-Jones held his hands up and said, 'Hold on there. I didn't say I'm not up for it. If you can wait a while, then I can lobby a few people to get what you want.'

Archer smiled inside and was thinking how he liked this young man.

'Yes, but not long. I want it up and running in three months.'

Smith-Jones smiled and said, 'I'll have the money in two.'

The two men continued to chat cordially and ate, before finishing their meeting and going their separate ways.

Chapter Eight

Chantelle just sat there shaking after that meeting with Archer. She could not believe how brazen the man was. She had kept her distance ever since the large right-hand man of Archer's had bumped her in that corridor, and she had sent him flying across the floor. She had changed her style completely after that, to go off radar on the base. Miss Che had wanted to her to quit her job after hearing of this event, but Chantelle loved what she did, and was not going to run away because of one man. Chantelle had heard of Archer's meteoric rise in the ranks, and all of the bullying tactics he had used over the years. His men seemed to act like thugs, and she always wondered where they had come from. They must have been the people she had seen in the hangar that day, but everyone had been told on the base that these new people had come from Northern Scotland. They were told these people had been in Scotland for years and had been forgotten about. The story was that Archer had got restless and had wanted to move his troops to better themselves, but that story did not sit true with Chantelle, or Miss Che when she told her. The meeting kept playing around in Chantelle's head over and over again. She must have been thinking out loud as 5.8 come out of sleep mode, and changed from phone mode to robot. He shocked Chantelle when he stood behind her beeping. Even with his enhancements, she could not afford the voice box for him. She apologised to 5.8.

'I don't need you at the minute. I was just thinking out loud.' The robot changed back to the phone and went into sleep mode. Chantelle sat there wondering why Archer needed these engines. The speeds he was suggesting would not be needed inside the shield for this country. The train was more than fast enough to move around the country. She surmised it was for interstellar travel to different worlds, as a possible use for these high speed engines. To her, this still did not feel right though. The shield was up and would not be coming down anytime soon. The ozone layer was still too fragile. They would all fry if the shield was lowered. None of this made sense. The way Archer was going around was not subtle either, and the General would find out as he was highly observant. She would not be telling the General though. She continued her work for the rest of the day, but could not wait to get back home to Miss Che and tell her all about this meeting. As always, with information like this to share, the train and hover skates never seemed quick enough to get her back home. Her journey home seemed a blur, with the meeting on repeat in her head. She burst through the door and 10.16 was not too pleased about her aggressive entrance. Chantelle just dropped her work things at the door. 10.16 went to admonish her, but she was in the living room in seconds, standing in front of Miss Che. Words were coming out of her mouth before she could think. 10.16 come up moaning too!

Che said, 'Quiet, the both of you.'

They both stopped talking.

'Right,' Che said looking at Chantelle. 'You came back all worked up and before you start speaking, just calm yourself.' Chantelle took a deep breath and explained about the meeting with Archer. She told her the new information about the engines he wanted. She had already told Che about his rise in the ranks and everything she knew about Archer. Che just sat and chewed the side of her lip.

Then she said to Chantelle, 'Can this engine he is talking about be made?'

Chantelle replied, 'Theoretically yes, but not quite yet. Our technology is very good, but we have never needed this sort of travel before.'

Chantelle continued, 'He seemed very confident. Probably too confident it could be done.'

Che said, 'Would this take a lot of money, if possible though?'

'Oh, yes,' Chantelle said, 'Nothing like this has ever been tried.' Che sat there again for a while contemplating his intentions. Then she got to her feet and turned around to look out of the window.

From over her shoulder she said, 'I don't like it that you work anywhere near this man. He seems dangerous.'

98

Chantelle said, 'I'm not quitting for one self-obsessed man.'
Che turned, 'I thought you would say that. Well if you are going to stay, you will have to keep an eye out and listen to whispers. Find out what you can. Archer seems to have an agenda and I think it's far more than these engines. It feels like he wants something more outside the shield.'

Chantelle was amazed and slightly taken aback by this comment, and said, 'I thought there was nothing left outside the shield? I thought the loss of the ozone layer took care of that?'

Che looked at her and just said, 'Well, there is something more he is after. I'm sure of it. I will look into it myself. I will seek out some of my old contacts.'

She grabbed Chantelle by the shoulders and looked her straight in the eyes.

'You have to be careful though. He can never find out your talents or he will try to use you. You are special, as I've always said. A man like this will use everything and everybody to his advantage to meet his desires.' Then whispering, 'I have heard of men like him before in the past.'

Chantelle stood looking at her wondering what all this was really about and who she knew from the past. It felt like there were now even more questions in Chantelle's head after this conversation with Che. What was the 'past' reference about?

Chapter Nine

Archer was ecstatic with everything that was happening. Smith-Jones had come through with his boast that he would get the cash he needed within the two months. Archer didn't know how he got the money and to be honest he didn't really care. Smith-Jones had taken his cut and there was still enough, and probably much more than was needed for this project. The little alien, they had kidnapped back on Mars, had done the schematic drawings they needed for these engines. Dr Simmons and his team had got to work making the engines and designing a ship for them to fit on. Archer did not care what the ship looked like, just that it worked. However, Simmons and his large ego wanted it to look sleek and aerodynamic. He would not show Archer the drawings though. Simmons kept asking Archer where he got these technical drawings from, as they were so advanced and beyond the team's knowledge. Archer said that he would never tell him and to stop asking, but asked Simmons if he could get the parts required.

With a smile, Simmons said, 'With all this money, yes and more!'

Archer asked how long it would take to build. Simmons thought about one year, but he could see the anger in Archer's face to this comment, and changed it to being more likely to be a few months. The smile on Archer's face was huge hearing this smaller length of time, and he then turned to the Cundill.

'All my plans are coming together, Captain,' Archer said gleefully.

Cundill still struggled with being called Captain.

Archer continued, 'Even if the General goes and I get command of all the forces, I still don't know if I will have enough forces for me to destroy all of them.'

From behind him he heard, 'Destroy who?'

Archer closed his eyes and turned around to see Dr Simmons was still there, and had heard what he had said.

'You don't need to know that,' Archer said.

To that Simmons then said, 'If you need more men, I might be able to help you there.'

Archer scoffed at this, 'How could you? Our strength and shields are part of our DNA, unless you know how to get thousands of women pregnant and age the children to fighting age?'

From behind him, he heard Cundill chuckle.

'Maybe that's the case or not,' Simmons said. 'When the General put me in charge of the whole science department he gave me access to all of the files. He took me down to the vault. The files in there showed what jobs people were currently working on, but there were also millions of archived files. I wasn't going to go through all of them, so I locked the files away. When we got new junior science officers that I couldn't be bothered to deal with, I would send them down to the vault with these files in to see if they could find anything interesting. They never seemed to find anything useful in these files, as the science was out of date and useless now, but there was this one file. Someone had tried to destroy this file. It said 'enhanced humans' on it. I told the officer at the time that this was good work and I would take this file myself and look into it. I have never had time to do this.'

Archer was suddenly very interested by this file and said, 'Do you still have this, Simmons?'

He replied, 'I hope so,' but wondered whether he should have committed to this, as Archer did not like failure.

Archer said, 'You had better go look for it then.'

Simmons scurried off to his office first, with Archer and Cundill behind him. They then headed towards the hangar, which this vault was in. There was a horrible, musty smell and there just looked like old pieces of paper scattered around the place in piles. Archer had never seen so much paper before, as the base had computers from what he had seen in the years he had been there. Who knew this hidden vault could contain so much past knowledge and information.

Archer and Simmons started grabbing piles and swiping folders off the top, intently looking for this file. After a number of hours of going down the piles, they found what they were looking for.

101

The folder read 'enhanced humans,' scruffily written on the front by what looked like a fountain pen. In the folder, there were many papers. Archer and Simmons sat there reading them all, and it appeared there was a complete chemical formula, but with Archer not being a scientist he did not understand this chemical concoction.

He turned to Simmons and said, 'Do you understand this?' Simmons shrugged and said, 'Of course I do, but I'll get a specialist in this field to look at it.'

He knew that really this was out of his chemical knowledge range, but did not want to admit to Archer that he did not fully understand how this mixture would enhance bodies.

Archer said, 'Please not Dr Che, as she will not help.' Simmons smirked, 'Oh god no! I would never ask her! I don't trust or like her,' which pricked Archer's interest even more. He would probe Simmons later about this comment about Chantelle.

Archer said, 'Who is this specialist you are asking advice from, and can they be trusted?'

Simmons said, 'Yes, they can be trusted,' but Archer was a little sceptical, as Simmons was being so vague about this person's credentials.

They walked out of the vault, leaving the folder on the top of a pile on the table, and went back to their respective areas on the base.

In the laboratory, Simmons started to flick through his contact list of top scientists in the field of genetics and mutations. One of them stood out. He contacted Dr Dring to come and look at these papers they had found with this human data and testing on. He was very keen on hearing about this from Simmons, and said he could get to the base in a couple of days.

Dr Dring arrived and Simmons greeted him. On the way to the vault Simmons was gloating about what he had found down there on these papers. It was like he had written them himself and discovered this formulation. They reached the stair case and carefully walked down the stone steps to the vault. They went in and Simmons guided Dr Dring to a huge wooden table with piles of folders and scattered papers. Simmons sat down at the table and pulled a pile of folders towards him, knowing that he left the folder on the top of this pile the other day.

'No, no, no! It's gone!' Simmons exclaimed.

Simmons sounded panicked and Dr Dring could hear this in his voice.

'Is there a problem?' Dr Dring asked.

Simmons turned around and looked very pale.

He whispered with shaking in his voice, 'The folder. It's gone! No-one else should have been down here.'

Frantically he started moving folders and throwing them onto the floor. This was to no avail.

'He will kill me,' Simmons said.

At that point, there were footsteps coming down the stair case and the door opened.

In walked Archer who said, 'I saw you heading this way with your friend, so I thought I would come and join you.'

Simmons looked nervously at him.

'It's gone, Sir. It's gone!'

Archer said, 'What's gone?'

Simmons looked down and said, 'The folder. It's been taken.'

Archer was furious.

'Look at me, Simmons. Who could have done this? Who else has access to here? What have you done?'

Simmons just stared at the table in disbelief and said, 'Perhaps a junior science officer has been back down here, that looked at the files for me before. I'm really not sure. No-one should have been down here since we were down here. Perhaps they still have access?'

Simmons was highly confused, and was so unsure how this could have happened. Where had this folder gone and who had taken it?

Archer angrily shouted, 'You need to stop the officer's access into here. You better find that folder and quickly.'

Simmons looked petrified by Archer's demeanour.

Archer turned to Dr Dring and said, 'I'm really sorry for the inconvenience. I'll escort you off the base now.'

As they walked back to the vault door Archer slammed it shut, leaving Simmons in the vault, who was already moving folders and papers in the hope of finding this missing one.

Chapter Ten

Chantelle took Miss Che's advice and had been trying to keep track of Archer on the base, who had been suddenly spending more time over at the science department. Chantelle had become less conspicuous, as she had stopped colouring her hair after her encounter with Cundill in the corridor. Chantelle had been socialising less with the other scientists in recent weeks, so she was also less obvious to others too. She had even stopped going to talk to Joan at lunch. She hadn't wanted to do this, but thought it was what was needed. Chantelle saw Archer walk into the laboratory with Cundill by his side as usual. He never noticed her, so she thought she could follow him easily. Archer and Cundill went to another section of the science department. They were not in there very long. They now had Simmons with them, who appeared to be leading the way to somewhere. Chantelle thought, 'Oh no, not Simmons!' The three men hurriedly walked through the base. Chantelle was in the shadows, following closely behind them. The three men then went to an older part of the base, where Chantelle had never been before. There was much more security here, so she could not follow them into this building. She stayed and waited. Half an hour later, all three men came back out. They looked ecstatic, with huge grins on their faces. They walked back to Simmon's office. They were not in there long this time. As Archer left the office she heard him comment, 'Good work, Doctor.'

Simmons smug voice replied, 'Thank you, Sir.'

Chantelle went back to her laboratory area to contemplate what she had just witnessed. That evening she told Miss Che about the day's events. Miss Che thought that Archer and Simmons together was not good and very suspicious. She suggested Chantelle needed to work late the following night, implying that they needed to know what was in that building Simmons had gone to. Her and Che developed a plan for the following day. It would be a long day tomorrow, if all they had planned came to fruition.

The following day came around quickly. Chantelle did her usual work shift and stayed under the radar. She stayed longer claiming overtime as she needed to finish off an experiment, was the excuse she used. As most staff left the base that evening at the end of the shifts, Chantelle was the only one left in the lab. She allowed the base to go quiet, before heading towards the building she had tracked Simmons to the previous day. Knowing she could not enter this building, she stayed in a small building opposite watching the guard's movements. She looked like she was working, but really was spying out of the little window. She was hoping the guards would change shift and the change would distract them. She was there for half an hour, and was at a point where she thought the plan would not happen. Then suddenly the two guards began to move. She heard, 'You're late,' and then a muffled noise. The two guards left the door and she decided that this was her opportunity to get into this building. She opened the door and popped her head out. The two guards were talking to whom she assumed were the new shift guards. They had their backs to her. So, she crept out quickly, keeping low and against the wall. She had dark mode on, camouflaging her in the low light of the evening, and she reached the door of this building. She quickly looked back and no one had noticed her. They were all still in deep conversation. Given their lack of concentration, she could only assume this building did not have that much to guard, but why have guards then? She opened the door and slid in, as quiet as she could, pulling the door shut behind her. In front of her was a long corridor. It was unremarkable. Grey walls with rooms off it on both sides. No obvious cameras though in the area. It just felt like all of the buildings on the base. Chantelle did not have time to dwell, as the guards could be back at any time. She thought divide and conquer is needed. She got 5.8 out of her pocket, woke him up and got his medbot out too. She put her hover skates on, so no one could hear her walking around on these concrete floors. She started at the room nearest to her and 5.8 began in the rooms on the other side of the corridor. Chantelle's first room was a dusty laboratory with what looked like chemical formulae and diagrams on the old chalkboards, which were outdated nowadays. With a quick look around, there was nothing important in there that she could see. She headed out and at the same time 5.8 came out of the room opposite.

'Anything?' she asked.

5.8 just responded with a negative beep. The same negative response came from the medbot too. It was the same for all of the rooms down the corridor. There just didn't seem to be anything important in there. So, why was Simmons in here? There must be something. Had they missed it? They were towards the end of the corridor now, and off to the right Chantelle noticed a staircase going down to presumably a lower floor or basement. She checked the rest of the rooms on this floor, but neither her or 5.8 found anything of interest. She walked towards the staircase and peered down, and could see a little red-light flashing. She carefully walked down the staircase towards it. Halfway down she noticed it was a camera angled towards something at the bottom. Strange that it was not looking up the staircase she thought. She paused and sent the medbot down to look from behind the camera. The medbot images showed what looked like quite an old bit of kit, that clearly had not been upgraded in decades. Beyond the camera the medbot showed a door a few yards ahead, which the camera was being focussed on. It looked like a large metal safe door with a digital pad alongside it, for accessing whatever was behind the door. She got the medbot to do a hologram of this area at the bottom of the staircase, and place it in front of the security camera lens. This meant Chantelle would be able to hover up to the door without being spotted by the camera. Once the hologram was in place, she made her way down quickly to the door. It was so old that she thought she could have just ripped it off its hinges, but she could not be detected, so instead looked at the keypad. There must have been millions of combinations of codes for this, but this would be no problem for 5.8, who plugged in and within seconds the door was opening in front of them. As they went in, it resembled an old vault with papers and books stacked everywhere on old wooden shelves, enclosed by old dusty concrete walls.

Chantelle wondered where to start. What was she actually looking for in amongst all of this? How long did she have before someone might come down here? This amount of papers was huge and would take years to go through. She started to panic, but pulled herself together quickly. Time to get started, as there was no time to lose. In corners of the room there were a few old looking computers covered in cobwebs, alongside shelves of papers. She got 5.8 to start accessing any of the computers it could, while she started sifting through the papers. She pushed the vault door closed and turned the lights off, so if any guards came they would not suspect anything. The medbot would be able to open the door from the outside. She used the infra-red on her visor to scan the papers. Most of the papers had out-dated research on them from many years before. This must have been the place where Simmons was sending the junior science officers a while back, as Simmons did not like to use robots to do jobs. What was Simmons trying to get them to find down here to take credit for himself? The man had never had a new idea for years, but would always try and take credit for others ideas. Chantelle was getting worried. She had been down there for a while and nothing. 5.8 was not getting anywhere quick either. How long do these computers take to boot?! She thought this was useless and she would never find anything on her own. She sat back in her chair and she sensed something, which made her look towards her left. There was a light flickering on the edge of a computer screen. The motion of the light had caught her visor. The only other screen turned on was the computer that 5.8 was on, on the other side of the room. She wandered across towards this big desk, where this annoying flicker was coming from. The desk had a small computer on one side of it, and the rest of the desk had numerous piles of folders and papers all over it. On top of one of the piles, she noticed a folder with its flap slightly up and open. The folder had some writing on the outside, which was dated about two hundred years ago. She thought the papers inside would probably be outdated, and this would be another folder to be discarded. However, to her surprise, the first paper in the folder was titled 'Enhanced humans.' Chantelle started reading it and could not believe the genetics in just the first few paragraphs. The genetics specialist of today in the year 2200 would struggle to understand this, let alone the twentieth century when this was dated. Chantelle read for a bit longer, and then noticed she had been down there for an hour. She thought she had better get out of there, otherwise she would look suspicious leaving the base so late. She was not meant to do so much overtime. She told 5.8 to download any files that seemed useful and shut the system down. She tidied the other papers back up on the desk, so it did not look like anyone had been in there. She closed the folder making sure the 'enhanced humans' papers were in there and held it under her arm, as both her and 5.8 went out of the vault. Thankfully the medbot reopened the door for them. She was not leaving that folder behind, as she knew Simmons and Archer would use it in the wrong way. She did not know what she was going to do with it, but Miss Che would know what to do. Going up the stairs, 5.8 was converted back into phone mode. As she did, she heard the door at the end of the corridor above start to creak open. She knew the guards would be in doing their rounds checking rooms and buildings. She shot across the corridor to the nearest room. She just got inside the room, as both guards entered the corridor. Chantelle had a quick scan around the room. It was basically empty apart from a desk. She knew she would be found if they came in, but hid under the desk anyway. She went into dark mode, but if they put the light on or shone a torch then she would be detected. Chantelle could hear the guards checking room after room, and it would not be long until they reached this one. She started to sweat a little. She did not want to be found. She knew in a fight she could beat them, but this was not part of the plan, otherwise her strength could get noticed yet again. From the closeness of the steps, one of the guards was just outside the door now, so she readied herself. Hopefully it would not come to this, but perhaps she had no choice. The door slowly opened and the guard was talking to the other guard on duty with him. The torch light shone across the room.

Chantelle nearly bolted out from under the desk to confront him, when suddenly the guard said, 'Did you hear that?'
The other guard replied, 'Hear what?'
'Shhhh', he said as they both listened.
It was deadly quiet. Chantelle had a quick peak, and the guard was actually looking out into the corridor. There it was again. A pinging noise from down the stairs, where the vault was.
The guard's attention had been raised and he said, 'Quick. Let's get down there.'
He ran from the doorway with the other guard just behind him, and they ran as quick as they could down the staircase. At first Chantelle panicked and worried she had left 5.8 down there. She checked her pocket and to her relief he was still safely in there in the form of a phone. In the haste of everything, she had forgotten she had put 5.8 in phone mode on the way up the stairs earlier. With the guards preoccupied with the noise from the vault she thought, 'This is my chance.' She leapt from under the desk and was out of the door and back into the corridor in seconds. In the corridor, she realised what had been making the pinging noise. There waiting for her was her medbot. She felt guilty that she had forgotten about it. It must have flown into the vault door a few times to have made the pinging metal on metal noise. Then it must have flown up past the guards undetected, as it was so small, and in their haste, they would not have seen it on the ceiling above them. No time to dwell on it, she had to get out the building as she heard the guards say, 'There's nothing down here. Quick, let's get back up there.'
She put the medbot back in 5.8, skated to the door and out of the building, before they could even get back to the top of the stairs. That was far too close. She could feel herself shaking, as she walked back to her laboratory to collect her belongings and go home. She was going to tell Che she could not do this anymore. She was not made for these espionage activities. As she went to leave the base she hovered up to the security post, which seemed to catch the guard off guard.
He jumped up and said, 'Can I see your ID, please,' as he always did.

Tonight, Chantelle was extra stressed. She passed it to him. The guard looked at it and then back at her.

'Are you ok?' he said.

Chantelle said, 'Yes, fine thank you. It's a little chilly tonight.' She tried to look calm and excuse her visible shaking for being cold. He looked her up and down again, and Chantelle thought she would have to explain some more.

He passed her identification back and said, 'Goodnight Dr Che,' and opened the barrier. She was out and on her way home on the train. Time to contemplate what she was going to tell Miss Che when she got back home about the experience and findings. As soon as she got through the door she started talking, but no-one was there. No 10.16 or Miss Che in the apartment. She sat in her room and started reading the paper again. Where was Miss Che? Chantelle fell asleep that night and Miss Che did not return.

Earlier that day Drake had rang Miss Che and said, 'Get to Lincoln quickly.'

She had sent Drake to check on the base. Drake was someone she had known and trusted from the underworld for a long time. A short little man with mousy brown hair, and indistinguishable features. She had sent him to follow Archer for days now. Drake had been watching from outside the base, as Archer never left the base. He had seen Archer from a distance from time to time, but the last few days he had been seen with the scientist and accompanied by his men. Miss Che had now joined Drake, and they thought this was strange behaviour from Archer. They continued to watched them that day, and remained overnight taking turns to survey Archer's and his men's activity around the base.

Earlier the next morning, a car arrived outside the base and Drake and Miss Che saw Dr Simmons meet this person at the entrance. Simmons and this unknown person walked across the base to a building hidden behind the others, which was out of sight. After a little while Archer then appeared with Cundill by his side, and they walked in the same direction that Simmons and this other person had gone in. It was not long before an animated Archer re-appeared with Cundill and this unknown person, escorting this person off the base. Where was the scientist? Simmons had not re-appeared with them. This raised suspicions. What was happening? Archer stood with Cundill by his side talking furiously with each other, but Che and Drake could not determine what was being said. Something had clearly aggravated him. They then set off across the base together. Overnight there had been some activity. Men were loading vans and lorries with wooden crates, and Archer was supervising this. One of the vans seemed of great interest to Archer, as he had gone to it and was surveying the inside himself. Che and Drake stood in their hidden spot together. She was exhilarated, having not done this for a long time. She had stopped working when she had needed to look after Chantelle. She had forgotten the adrenaline rush she used to get from such jobs. Drake had already informed her of the past few days goings on, and how unusual it was for the base to be so active. The convoy of vans and lorries suddenly started moving and heading for the barrier exit. As the laser barrier deactivated, they drove out of the base. They were moving quickly for such big vehicles. Drake was prepared for this. As they moved above him on the road system, he had his rifle out and planted a homing beacon on the side of one of the lorries. Miss Che had transformed 10.16 from being a phone, and it was now a car. They both jumped in. Drake told Che to hold back, as the beacon had a fifty-mile transmitter on it. They were travelling north in pursuit of this convoy. Within half an hour, they had reached Scotland and were driving quickly even further north. Miss Che thought she knew where they were heading and she was right. They had gone over the isles towards the Outer Hebrides. It was such a remote area. She put her car into spy mode, as she thought she might get seen too easily. It would be nearly invisible now. There were not many places to hide up here. The convoy flew to a base, which was definitely in the middle of nowhere. Che and Drake stored some of their gear under a slight overhang on a small hill a few miles from the base, which was the best they could do for now to remain undetected. They left the gear and carefully crept towards the base, as close as they dare. The security looked very high, as they watched from afar. Drake and Che were both carrying spybots on them, but were not even sure if they could get through this sort of high technology security. So, old school espionage it was. They sat hidden with binoculars. The base had a few hangars on it, which the convoy of vans and lorries had gone into. Che and Drake just sat it out. They knew that Archer and his men would have to come outside with whatever was in these vehicles.

Out of the distance, suddenly there was another vehicle above them. It went straight for the base entrance. It was Dr Simmons! What was this scientist doing up here now too?

Chapter Eleven

Inside the hangar, Archer was overly excited and enthused about what he was about to start. He wanted these engines made, and soon. He had seen Simmon's designs for the ships and Simmons was not wrong. The designs looked amazing to Archer and just what he wanted. The designs would be useless though if the engines did not work.

The little alien was in the secure van, and Archer was in and out of the van making sure the alien had done all of its drawings and measurements for the engines. Archer took them off him, without even a thank you, and passed them straight to Simmons and his team. They were looking at them for hours. Simmons looked at Archer and asked him where he had got these from.

Archer replied, 'That's not your concern, Doctor. Can you build them or do I need to get another team?'

Simmons looked at him, feeling a little betrayed by this comment.

'We can build it, Sir. We are just getting to grips with the drawings. It's very technical and nothing we have seen before. We have never needed space travel.'

The team got to work and Archer's men travelled all over the UK to get the parts. He was sure they had everything they needed, but he was wrong. It was lucky Smith-Jones had got him more money than he asked for, as he would likely need all of it now.

It was months in now and Archer was getting impatient. He also had the General pestering him to return to the base, as soon as he could. Archer suspected the General knew what was going on, but he realised he could not touch him now as Archer had built up too many allies. Archer and Cundill went to Simmons. It was good to see Simmons and his team still hard at work. Archer shouted up to Simmons, who was on the top of an engine, and Simmons came scurrying down. He had dirt all over his face, and goggle marks round his eyes and on the top of his head. He had a huge smile on his face.

'Good timing, Sir. We were just about to fire up the engine to see if it works.'

Archer was ecstatic by this news.

'By all means, Doctor. Go ahead. We are watching.'

The whole team came off the engine and went into a control room in the hangar. They did a countdown. More for symbolism really, as they could have just pressed a button. The engine ignited, but it did not seem to do anything at first. Archer's impatience with Simmons was about to reappear, when there was an almighty whoosh sound. The engine came to life. A large plume of blue flames fired out the back of it. Archer thought it was beautiful. It stayed on and they did some checks, and then they turned it off once they were happy with it. Simmons went to Archer, and Archer shook his hand. Archer said, 'It's not over yet. I need another one of them making.'

Simmons looked drained, but up for the next challenge. With a smile he said, 'I can't wait.'

'Next we will need to test it in the air,' Archer announced. 'I hope your ship design will enable this, Simmons?'

Simmons looked wounded, 'It will, and will look good doing it.'

Archer loved his confidence.

More time passed by and more engines were built and finished. Two were fitted to the ship, that had also now been finished by the rest of the team. They wheeled the ship outside ready for the test flight. They were going to use their best pilot that piloted the ships from Mars. Simmons was unaware of why this person was chosen for the pilot job. The pilot was worried, as he had never flown anything this fast before, so Archer had to reassure him that all would be fine. The pilot fired up the engines and the ship shot vertically up into the air. The thrusters were fired up and he was gone. Archer could not believe the raw power and the amazing sounds the engines made. There was no time to admire this invention, as the ship was back again. Why had the ship returned so quickly? Was there a problem with the ship? As soon as the ship landed, Archer went straight to the cockpit. The pilot looked in shock.

'What happened up there?'

'Nothing, Sir. Everything was great. The fastest thing I've ever flown.'

Archer looked confused by this answer and said, 'Where did you get to, Flight Captain?'

'To the bottom of England. The computer then picked up the shield, so knew we couldn't go any further, so I flew back.'

'That must have only taken a few minutes round trip?' Archer questioned.

The Flight Captain replied, 'It took fifty seconds round trip, Sir.'

Archer turned to Simmons with the biggest grin ever and said, 'Get your team to work. I want a fleet of these ships. Me and you are going back to the base.'

Simmons really wanted to stay and help, but saw the look in Archer's face, so did not even question the order. He gave his next highest-ranking team member the order to finish the project, as Archer had requested.

Chapter Twelve

Miss Che rang Chantelle to make sure she was ok. Chantelle seemed very excitable and told her that she needed to show her something urgently. She would not tell Che on the phone. Che told her she would return in a week or two. Chantelle seemed disappointed and asked Che not to be too long, as this was important.

Chantelle finished the call with, 'I love you.'

Che was not usually sentimental, but she welled up at that, responding, 'I love you too. See you soon.'

This was the longest she had ever left Chantelle before and she missed her. Chantelle had clearly softened Che over the years. She loved taking care of Chantelle and wanted the best for her.

Che walked back over to Drake and he said, 'Here comes another one.'

Men had been coming and going for days now with parts.

'God knows what they're building in there,' he said.

At that moment the hangar bay doors opened and Che said, 'Looks like we're about to find out!'

They both looked at each other. Out of the doors came a ship. They were about to say something, when the ship took off. The thrusters were powerful and ablaze. As the ship flew over them, the sheer force from it knocked Drake and Che off their feet. They landed flat in the grassy area they had been stood on, and this completely shocked them. They were just trying to get to their feet and feeling very light-headed, when the ship came back in. The roar of the ship was deafening and they could not hear each other. They just looked at each other and both knew it was time to head back towards the safety of the hill, where they had originally positioned all of their gear. They still had ringing in their ears, as they walked back to the hill. The ringing slowly subsided and they could hear each other again.

Drake said, 'What do they need that for? It won't be able to go out of the shield.'

Che said, 'Well whatever it's for, there must be something outside of the shield they're after. They are clearly preparing to go out there sometime soon. I'll tell the bosses that this could be used to get troops around the country quicker, and possibly to try and snare their gangs.' She paused and looked at Drake and said, 'Could you stay a few more days and watch, just in case something else happens we need to be aware of. I'll come back and get you.'

He did not really want to, but for Che he would. She thanked him and got in her car, and went back to London.

She met with the bosses and told them what she had seen. They were concerned and would ready themselves, in case these soldiers come. After this meeting, Che made her way home.

As soon as she walked in Chantelle was hugging her and telling her how much she had missed her. You could feel the warmth and emotion between them, and they looked so happy to be together again. Chantelle sat her down at the table and made her a cup of tea, and then could not contain herself any longer and began to tell Che everything she had found. She told Che how she had found the vault and then the paper titled 'Enhanced humans.'

At that point, Che stopped Chantelle and said, 'Enhanced humans. You have found it?'

Chantelle looked at her slightly puzzled.

'You know about this?' she said.

'Only rumours,' Che said. 'What does it say?'

'I have just finished reading it. So hard to follow and I'm not sure that I fully understand it. There is a chemical formulation in there, which says that people go into a chamber and are injected with this formulation to get the right reaction or enhancement. The chemicals in this formulation are very complex, and it looks like it was developed and tested on subjects over many years. What a great mind must have come up with this. The science is so advanced and is beyond its time. From the paper it looks like various animals have been tested with it, but then....' she paused, 'then a human was injected with it. The details of this man suggested it could have been a soldier. The paper said this went well, and then more men went through this procedure. It never gave names in this paper, which is strange for a scientific experiment.'

Che sat back in her chair, 'I can't believe you found this. I thought it had been lost.'

'It's not that good,' Chantelle said.

Che looked at her, but Chantelle continued. Chantelle had so much to say about this find.

'Three years later, the paper's author added that the test was flawed and the formula needed to be adapted.'

Che's face lit up at this. She looked at Chantelle.

'You have found the first formula. The one that made him.'

'Who's him?' Chantelle asked.

'It doesn't matter,' Che said. 'We must keep this safe.'

'But it's flawed according to the paper,' Chantelle said looking more puzzled.

Che said, 'Who was the author?'

'It was signed by Errett Palethorpe,' Chantelle said.

'Yes, I thought so,' Che said. 'That man was a liar and the scum of the earth.'

'How do you know this? It was so long ago,' Chantelle asked.

'It was passed down through the ages is all I will say,' Che replied.

Miss Che started to walk away from the table, when she turned and asked, 'Did you find the second paper?'

'No. What second paper?' Chantelle said.

'Oh god. I hope Archer doesn't find that. I hope that was destroyed. What I know for sure, is that your DNA comes from the first formula.'

Chantelle was taken aback. She had the flawed formula in her. Che reassured her that it was not flawed, but it did not suit what Palethorpe had wanted to gain from such a formula input into humans. Miss Che showered and returned to the table to eat. She then told Chantelle where she had been the last few days and what she had seen in Scotland. Chantelle had no idea why Archer was making the ships either. Both said that they couldn't get out of the shield, so it must have been needed for something in the country. Their only thoughts were that it would be used to curb the gangs in the cities. Miss Che asked Chantelle if she could get back into the vault. Chantelle said that security had been heightened after Simmons had found the paper had been stolen. Chantelle was reluctant to carry on spying anymore, as it felt like this was a very unknown situation she was getting herself involved with. Che did not want to push her, but they needed to keep a surveillance on Archer, as there was something more to all of these goings on. Miss Che sat at the table thinking about the events she had witnessed in Scotland. What was she missing?

The morning soon came around. Both Chantelle and Che were pre-occupied by everything they had read and witnessed recently. Chantelle went to work leaving Che at the table, who was still clearly bothered by what her and Drake had seen. As she sat staring towards the wall, Che suddenly jumped. Why was it only Archer going into that van? He always came out with something in his hands. It must have been very important to Archer and perhaps very secretive. Miss Che got in touch with Drake, who was still watching the base up there.

'Drake,' she said into his earpiece. 'Is that security van, Archer was so intent on protecting, still on the base?'

Drake replied quickly, 'Yes, why?'

'Has anyone been in it?' Che asked.

'No,' he said. 'Not since Archer left. They bring resources like food and water to the van occasionally, but all I can see is a flap on the side of this, so no-one actually enters the van. There seems to be security around that van at all times.'

Che said, 'I think there is something alive in there.'

'I suppose so,' Drake said.

'Drake, I want you to stay there. I'm going to come back and join you.'

'I can stay,' Drake replied.

'We're going to break into that van and see what's in there,' Che said.

'That's crazy,' Drake replied. 'There's security everywhere.'

'And that's why they won't expect it,' Che said.

Later that day, Che re-joined Drake in the hidden spot. They watched the base for a few more days. The two of them had been putting a plan together, watching the movements of the base each day. On a dark night, they put their plan into action. Getting through the fence surrounding the base was not a problem. They just hoped the soldiers were pre-occupied in those hangars and not in dark mode around the camp, otherwise Che and Drake would not see them. While they had been observing the base for days, they had noticed the security guards did not appear to be professional soldiers. The soldiers seemed to have other tasks on the base. At their target van, there were two guards at the back door. That would not be a problem for Che and Drake. There was a shift change due in an hour, in the early hours of the morning, and they hoped the security would be less attentive to their duties. So, from their hidden spot just behind one of the hangars, they sneaked out. There was a courtyard to get across and they had to be careful of a light that shone across, as it swept round from time to time. They got to the front of the van safely without being seen. They could hear the security guards talking about what they were going to have for breakfast, in an attempt to keep themselves awake for the final part of their shift. Che and Drake crept around the van and incapacitated the two guards quickly. They did not have much time. They tried to hide the bodies, but there were not many places to hide them. They searched the guards for keys for the van, but they did not have any keys on them. It looked like Archer was the only one with keys to this van. They would have to blow the hinges on the van to get in. They put some small explosives on the hinges, so as not too make too much sound, but enable them to blow them off. There was a small bang, as they triggered the explosives. It did not have quite the desired effect though. One of the hinges was gone, but the other was just hanging on. They pulled the door to the side, so Che could slide in. This was not easy as Che was a tall woman, and there was not much of a gap to get between.

Drake said, 'We have to be quick. Someone might have heard that.'

Inside the van, it was dark and now filled with smoke from the hinge's explosion. She could just make out a tiny desk in the

121

middle of the van. That was all that they could see, realising Drake had also slid through into the van with her. They knew something or someone was in here, but it was so dark they could not see properly. As the smoke slowly subsided, they turned their phone lights on. They had no choice. They needed to see what was in there, so they hoped no-one would see the lights from outside. They scanned the van and there was nothing. Che was frustrated.

'This can't be,' she exclaimed. 'There has to be something in here.'

Then suddenly they heard men outside coming in their direction.

Drake said, 'Damn, they must have heard. We need to get out of here.'

Che looked at him disappointedly, nodded and they both turned to slide out the van and run. At that moment, they heard a rattle noise in the van. They paused and turned around. Drake had pulled his knife out ready, and in the light in the corner of the van there it was. As the smoke had subsided, they could see into this corner. It was chained to the wall with what looked like a cable tie. It was the tiniest little thing they had ever seen. What was this 'thing'? They have never seen anything like this before on this planet, so did not even know what species it was or how it had got here through the shield. It looked bruised and battered. There were cuts on its body, with a yellow substance creeping out. Was this its blood? Drake went to kill it, but Che grabbed him.

Drake looked at her and said, 'This must be dangerous, if Archer wanted so much security for it.'

Che looked at him, 'Look at it, Drake. It's clearly endured a great deal under Archer, and perhaps we could learn a great deal from it.'

Drake wasn't happy and went to attack it again.

Che disarmed him and said, 'I say, we take it with us.'

'On your head be it,' Drake said.

Che bent down to the little creature and it pulled away. It seemed petrified of humans. She did not know if it understood, so she held her hands up.

'Don't be scared, little thing.'

She cut the ties off and it tried to bolt, so Che grabbed it. She put it in her backpack and sealed it, leaving a small gap in the zip so it could breath. She headed to Drake, who had made his way to the back door. They pulled it open again and jumped down and out. They landed and as soon as they did they heard, 'Stop there.' They looked over and security guards were running towards them. Che knew she could not convert her phone to a car, as the base would have had blockers to stop her doing this. They had to get to the fence line and beyond to enable the car mode. Luckily there were no soldiers around, just these security guards. Che gave the bag to Drake.

'Go to the fence where we came in and wait for me. I'll take care of the security.'

Drake ran off and Che met the security head on. There were six of them all with stun batons. Little did they know they would not stand a chance with Che. With karate kicks, she took the first two men out. Somersaulting then into the next two, kicking and punching as she went. Spinning higher off the two of them, she then landed on the next man's shoulders. He went to stun her, but she knocked the baton out of his hands with her heel. She crushed him with her thighs and he collapsed. He fell forwards and Che landed on her feet. She spun around, kicked out and took the last man out. She stood in the centre of the carnage, but not for long as more security and possibly soldiers could be heard. It was time to get out there, so she ran for it. Che got to Drake at the point they entered earlier. Two guards on the floor were knocked out at Drake's feet.

He looked at her, shrugged, giggled and said, 'They got in my way.'

Che and Drake clambered through the hole. As soon as they got through, Che pressed the button on her phone and threw it in the air. There in front of them was her car. They jumped in and they were on their way.

'We have company,' Drake said.

The security was after them on their hoverbikes. Che had to lose them somehow. Out here it was so remote it would be hard to lose them. Very few places to hide. They sped over

123

little dikes and hillocks, and security was closing in. The only weapons the security had were the stun batons. Other weapons were destroyed centuries ago. The country did not think they would need weapons at all, as they had the enhanced humans nowadays. Che and Drake's main concern was that the security could throw and attach tracking devices onto their car, if they were to get close enough. Che needed to dodge these, as they tried to escape. The car flew up the highest hill they could get up. Although the cars could fly, they could never reach the heights of mountains. They did not have the power for these gradients. On the other side of the hill, they had gained some speed and more of gap between them and the approaching security. Che had noticed a small jut on this hill, they had just come over where possibly they could hide. This would mean reversing back on themselves. As Che and Drake approached the next hill, this was the time to attempt to lose the security. They raced around the hill with security still following them, closer behind them than they liked. They circled back towards the previous hill and landed the car into the jut, which was a small cave. The security was still catching up and circling the second hill. Che powered down the car and they hid out of sight in this little cavern. They waited and they heard the security fly by. This was tense. They gave it a minute before crawling out to survey where the security had gone. She could not see where they had gone. She could still hear the echo of their bikes in the distance somewhere. She was not waiting around, they needed to get away from here. Powering the car back up they accelerated back out of the cave, and towards the east of Scotland. Security had tracked them again and were in pursuit. Che and Drake had a good enough lead on them. They reached the east of Scotland. They knew where they needed to get to. They needed to get to the train station in Edinburgh. They got there just in time, changed the car to phone mode, and boarded the train at the station a few seconds before it was due to depart. As the train left, the security pulled up. The security had no way to stop the train, as it had now reached full speed. They knew Archer could not get police involved, as he could not tell anyone about what he was up to. The train reached Kings Cross in ten minutes, and Che and Drake were off the train and disappeared.

Che got back to the apartment and set the bag on the table. She opened it as wide as possible and left it. She then went and got some cookies and milk and placed it next to the bag, to try and coax this creature out. She wandered across to the other side of the room and waited and watched the bag. It took about an hour and then the bag moved a little. A little head popped out of the bag and looked around. It had not noticed Che, but had seen the cookies. It moved quickly across the table and started eating them. To Che, it seemed happy. She couldn't but feel sorry for this poor thing. Years ago, she might not have felt this way. Chantelle had softened her over the years. For good or bad she couldn't decide, as she smiled to herself. The little thing finished the cookies in no time and was lapping up the milk. It was just finishing, when Miss Che moved towards it. She startled it and it shot back into the bag. It must have felt safer in there. Miss Che sat down at the end of the table and waited again. This time it did not take so long for the little thing to pop its head up. It looked straight at her. She smiled and said hello to it. It cowered back into the bag, and then slowly climbed back out.

'That's it,' Miss Che said, 'I won't hurt you.'

It seemed to her that it actually understood her. Did Archer have a way to communicate with it? She thought it must have been a brutal way by the amount of injuries on its body. She would never do that. She just talked softly to it, telling it who she was and who Drake was who it had seen earlier. She told it how Drake had gone home and it was only her here. To her amazement, the tiny little being spoke back to her. It was in its own language, but tried to communicate with her. Miss Che thought there must be a way to speak to it. All of a sudden Chantelle came walking into the room. The tiny-being ran back into the bag. Chantelle looked at Miss Che and asked her what that was, and what she had been up to in the days she had been missing.

Miss Che said, 'What, me? Nothing,' with a sly smirk on her face. 'Come over, Chantelle. See if it will come out again.'

Chantelle sat next to Che and the bag moved. Out came the tiny-being. No bigger than a large man's hand. It looked at Che and she reassured it that all was ok, and that Chantelle was a friend. It walked down the table and stopped in front of the two women. It started to talk, but they couldn't understand it. Miss Che was disappointed by this, and the being noticed and stopped. It looked at Che and pointed. Che did not understand, but then realised it was pointing at her earpiece. She had forgotten she was still wearing it, after the adventures of the last few days.

She pulled it out and said, 'Do you want this?' and the being nodded.

Che knew it understood her. She set it on the table and the being started to work on it. It must have had tiny tools on it, but as it was so small she could not see them with the naked eye. It stopped and gestured to Che to take it back. Chantelle sat quietly alongside, completely amazed by this being. She could not register what this being even was, or how it could have come here through the shield. It was non-sensical to her. Che carefully picked the earpiece up and put it back in her ear. The being started speaking again, and to Che's surprise her earpiece was translating the little being's speech. Chantelle moved slowly from the table to retrieve her earpiece, and the being did the same thing on it, so both Chantelle and Che could decipher what the being was saying. It told them what Archer had done to it and what it had been working on for Archer and his men. It did not tell them where it had come from and how it came to be on this planet. Miss Che would have to come back to that question. Che asked what the ships were for, but the being said that it did not know. She felt like it did know, but perhaps did not trust her enough yet. It said it had given Archer designs and details for fast ships, but not hyperlight speed ships to get out of the galaxy. Both women looked at each other.

'Why would he want that anyway?' Che asked.

The being just shrugged.

Che did say, 'You're not telling us everything are you?'

126

The being just looked and said, 'I don't trust humans. I have only met evil ones.'

To Che, this answer did not seem to just relate to Archer and his men. Clearly the being had had other bad experiences with humans in the past, but when and where remained the question. The being continued to speak and declared that it knew Archer was really after their weapons technology, and it had been very close to giving away this information. He thanked Che for rescuing him when she did, before he broke and gave away the information with all the torture he had been subjected to by Archer and his men.

Chantelle said, 'Why would our soldiers need technology when they have their strength and shields accessible to them?'

To that the being asked for something to write on. They gave him a little notepad and he started writing and drawing the parts he would need. They were everyday items, so they got them easily for him. The two women carefully placed the parts he had asked for on the table. The little-being began to work again moving the parts into position. After an hour or so, it was ready. The being asked for a target to be set up across the room, which Che had walked across and set up. The being had made the tiniest gun they had ever seen. It took aim, but to their shock, it took aim at what looked like Che. It was physically shaking. Che thought it was going to fire and was about to move, when she saw a small muzzle fire. The bolt gained in size, as it moved through the air. The bolt was huge, as it passed her and missed the target, hitting the wall with a huge bang.

Chantelle said, 'That thing aimed that at you.'

Che nodded and went over to the table. She was about to disarm it, when she noticed the being had dropped the gun and was crying uncontrollably and rocking from side to side.

It was saying, 'I'm sorry. I couldn't do it. I'm not a killer like humans are.'

That night Chantelle lay in bed just staring at the ceiling. All her beliefs that the shield was there for protection, as the ozone layer been destroyed, were now in tatters. A little alien-like being on the table in the kitchen was now making her question everything she knew. How could that get to Earth? Where had it come from? How did it have such advanced skills, especially in weaponry? The biggest question though was still, 'How did it get through the shield?'

Chapter Thirteen

Archer had got the news from the base that security had been breached again. His anger at this was uncontrollable and he smashed his office to pieces. This was another thing lost in his quest for vengeance. First the 'enhanced human' paper and now his little alien. Archer had loved living on Earth, as he thought it was superior to Mars in many ways, but he hated these weak humans that were on Earth. These humans seemed weak and demanding, and did not seem to have much commitment to their duties. He would never dream of using these sorts of people as security normally, but on this planet, he did not have enough men to do that job. He couldn't use the General's men, as they didn't really trust him or like him at all. They were just loyal to the General and no-one else. He liked loyalty, but this was no use to Archer right now. Perhaps when he becomes General, they would have no choice but to follow his orders, he surmised with a wry smile. He marched out of his office with a purpose. He thought and hoped these Earth humans would become useful to him soon, as he walked to the vault. As he was walking to the vault he met Simmons on the way, who was just starting his shift.

'Hello, Doctor,' Archer said.

Simmons reply was short, but Archer didn't care. Simmons was still in a mood about being taken off the team working in Scotland. He knew he was missing out on something important, and felt like he had been demoted by being back at this base working in the vault. Archer asked if anything useful had been found in the vault yet, especially anything as good as the 'enhanced human' project paper. Simmons winced, as he knew Archer still blamed him for losing that.

'No not yet, Sir,' he said. 'There are so many papers down there to go through, and so much is out dated science it has no use to us anymore.'

Archer just looked at him, 'Well keep looking, Doctor. There must be something of use down there.'

Archer walked off, leaving Simmons to go to the vault. Down in the vault Simmons sat back in his chair. He was so humiliated doing this junior officer work. He was meant to be in charge and not doing this menial work. How could he show authority when he was seen doing this soul destroying job? The robots were milling around him logging on the old screens, whilst he was reading through papers on the tables and shelves. He came to a paper about weapons. The weapons were crude to him. They were not sophisticated. They were weapons which had some type of projectile coming out of them. Perhaps he could fit them to the ships Archer was building. If he could not find anything better in the papers, then perhaps he could make these to cause a lot of damage. Maybe this would please Archer. Archer would never tell Simmons though what he wanted all of this for. Only Archer and his men seemed to know why.

One of the robots shouted, 'Sir, Sir.'

Simmons had to think about that one, as no-one else had ever called him 'Sir,' but he quite liked it. Simmons went over and said, 'What is it? I'm busy,' trying to sound like he was busy when he wasn't doing much.

The robot said, 'I think you best read this, Sir.'

Simmons sat at the screen and started to read. It did not take long until a smile came across his face. 'You best go get Archer,' he said.

He thought smug old Archer will not like this. Archer walked into the vault, and there was Simmons with his feet up on the table and hands behind his head. Archer cleared his throat and Simmons jumped into the air, which made Archer giggle. Simmons still had a weird smile on his face.

'What did you call me down here for, Doctor? I hope something important,' Archer said.

Simmons just smiled and said, 'Oh yes, Sir. I think you'll find this very interesting. It's over here on this computer.'

Simmons started to read, with Archer stood behind him. The paper on the screen was all about how the shields that surround the soldiers actually worked. It actually wasn't in their DNA at first. It was generated by a little device just inside the skin at the arch of the neck, and connected straight to the brain. The user could simply think it needed the shield, and then the device in the body's system would generate it, as and when needed. It would take milliseconds from the thought to it then forming all the way around the body.

Archer just stood there shocked and said to Simmons, 'I thought it was part of our DNA?'

Simmons liked the fact he had annoyed Archer and smugly replied, 'I'm no nanobot scientist, but it's definitely not produced in the genetics of a human being.'

Archer just shrugged it off and said, 'This is good news, Doctor.'

This was to Simmons dismay, as he thought Archer would be bothered by the news that he wasn't unique.

Archer said, 'We better get a nanotech scientist down here. I want to speak to a specialist immediately about this device. Good work, Simmons. Keep looking.'

Simmons faced dropped, as he thought finding this information would get him out of here.

Archer met Dr Huk from the nanotech department and showed him the paper. Huk was impressed. It was ahead of their technology by a long way.

'Where did you get this paper from, Sir?' he asked.

Archer replied, 'It's old data that we have just found. Can it be produced?'

Huk looked at him, 'Now I have this paper, then yes. Not quickly though. It will take time to produce these device units.'

'I need millions, Doctor,' Arched said.

Huk replied, 'That will take years, Sir. We could do about five thousand units a year I think.'

Archer was not pleased, but told him to get started making the device units as soon as possible, as they would need them.

Archer now needed to find people to implant the units into. Archer turned to Smith-Jones back in London for this, to see how they could recruit more people and get them interested in joining the army. Smith-Jones was not positive about this, as he said people had got lazy, and did not think they needed an army anymore under the shield. Although the people had been told many years before that the shield was there to protect them, as the ozone layer had been destroyed, some people had also ignorantly thought the shield would protect them from attack from other outside forces.

Archer looked at him and said, 'There must be some people who would join up?'

Smith-Jones said that the only ones he could think of were those that were in poverty, and some of which he suspected lived in old tube stations and other abandoned buildings in London. Smith-Jones had never seen these people, but had heard of them. They were not a class of society he would associate with.

'No-one would miss them then?' Archer devilishly said.

'I suppose not,' Smith-Jones said cautiously, as Archer's eyes lit up at the thought of them being used for his plan.

Archer returned to the base and told his men of the plan to recruit more people. He told them to head to London and round up all the able-bodied they could find, whether they liked it or not. They found thousands living in these squalid conditions. They did not like being told they were leaving London, but were rounded up and sent back to the base, where they would be trained. Who could stop Archer now? He put Cundill in charge and would have him whip these useless humans, he thought they were, into soldiers. That's how Archer worked. Bullying and intimidation to get what he wanted. These new 'soldiers' did not like taking orders or physical work at all. Some of the better soldiers had been fitted with these device units that Huk had made. They struggled with them and the units did not seem to work at first in their bodies. They could not use their minds in a powerful enough way to get the shields to surround them. They needed more training to use their mind to control the device unit. In time, some of them mastered this. These new soldiers did not have Archer's soldier's immense strength, but at least they were bodies who could fight with them.

Archer had been communicating with Dr Huk about the force shields, and why they did not have to put units in their children. The children would have them when they came of age. Huk surmised that the first technology was used so much that these units had just integrated into the DNA. It must have taken decades for this to have happened, and the technology must have adapted with the subjects over the years.

Simmons seemed to have gone quiet and not been heard from for a while, so Archer visited the vault. Simmons was still there and sulking. He had had enough, but would never say that to Archer.

Archer went up to Simmons and said, 'Anything new? I haven't heard from you for a while.'

'Nothing I would say of importance, Sir,' Simmons replied.

'You have found something then?' Archer said.

'Nothing of scientific importance or what you have been asking for, so didn't think it would be of interest to you,' Simmons said.

'What is it?' Archer replied slightly irritated.

'Well the last entry on the computer was about a paper, whose author became the prime minster. That same author was the one who wrote about the enhanced humans and the shield device unit. At the time, before the shield went up to protect us from the sun's rays, he had wanted to explore outer space. He had written that he would colonise Mars and use it as a base, in case him and his men did not reach the Kuiper belt and beyond. They would use Mars as a stop for supplies of food and resources, if they needed to come back from this outer region of the galaxy.'

Archer's faced dropped, as he thought he descended from an ancient colony on Mars, but realised he was possibly a descendant from these people from Earth.

Simmons continued, 'He planned to leave three ships on Mars to colonise it, and the other thousands of soldiers would carry on towards the Kuiper belt. As before, someone had tried to delete this information on this computer, but they had not done it very well and I got all of the information back. I was so disappointed when I read it. It's useless information for us, as no-one has ever left our Earth like that or could ever leave.'

Archer looked at him and said, 'That's right Doctor, but I would like to read the file myself.'

Simmons looked at him puzzled, 'Ok, but it's a waste of your time.'

'Just humour me, Doctor. Outer space intrigues me,' Archer said, as Simmons downloaded the file. Archer returned to his fresh new office with the file. He could not wait to read it. He had always been told the Mars colony was a mission from Earth to see if Mars had life on it, and whether Earth could source any energy materials from it. When they had found there were no materials, the colony of people had remained there and the people back on Earth had just forgotten about them. So, the colony carried on working and the soldiers were there to protect this colony. Now reading this paper changed everything he thought he knew about his past. There must be thousands of humans still out there somewhere if they made it past the Kuiper belt, but they had made no contact and none had returned. Archer had thought they were the only humans out there on Mars, and then it dawned on him. The aliens who attacked him might have also killed those humans destined for the outer regions of the galaxy. His anger towards the aliens that attacked him on Mars had just got greater. He intended to destroy the aliens soon enough, with his grand plan slowly coming together.

Archer received a message from Joan that the General wanted to see him immediately. Archer stored the file and shut down his computer. He would have to come back to this and did not want anyone else accessing it. Archer got to the General's office, and as usual was made to wait. After an hour, he was ready to walk out as he had things to do. He went to get to his feet to leave, when Joan's phone beeped.

'You can go in now Archer,' she said.

Archer went in and the General was behind his big desk as always. Archer realised just how much he disliked the man, and noticed he had definitely aged recently. Archer had not seen him much, as he had been so busy.

'Sit down, Archer,' he said abruptly, 'This will probably take a while.'

Archer sat and the General began.

'Did you not think I would find out what you've been up to, Archer? Getting all the scientists re-assigned. All the people you have taken from the city streets and the slums.'

134

The General was furious and Archer had never seen him so mad.

'I told you to leave it, Archer. Those aliens that attacked you are no longer your problem. They cannot and will never get through this shield.'

Archer replied, 'They found a way through our shield.'

The General scoffed, 'That was an air shield. It's much thinner than ours and older. They have been trying to get through ours for years now and still not penetrated it. You are still determined to get revenge. You need to let it go. My men will never follow you while I'm alive.'

Archer remarked, 'For how much longer?'

The General looked Archer straight in the eyes, his face was red raw with anger, 'Is that a threat, Archer? If it is I will throw you in the cells.'

'No, no, no threat Sir. Just an observation,' Archer said.

'Don't worry about me, Archer. I have many years left, and while I'm alive we will never attack the aliens. Remember I can see everything, so stop what you are doing now.'

At that point the General dismissed Archer. On his way out, Archer was already thinking that he needed to double operations, and would deal with that senile old man!

Archer got back to his office and was making calls immediately. He was on the phone to Scotland to see how many ships they had built so far. Fifteen was the answer. He wanted more, but this was better than nothing. Were the weapons attached to the ships was another question for the team. Apparently the last one was being fitted with them.

Archer then spoke to Cundill to see if the new soldiers would be ready in the next few days. He did not seem certain. Only half had their device units for the shields fitted, and about a quarter knew how to use them and actually fight with them.

Archer said, 'We need them Cundill, otherwise we will be short of men. We are going in two or three days. Any longer and the General will shut us down.'

Cundill said that they would be ready, but in his own mind he was uncertain. He would take them anyway. He speculated some would be casualties of war.

Archer did not want to deal with the General, but he was in good health and would not be going of natural causes anytime soon. So, Archer would have no choice and would have to deal with the General himself. The General's men would only follow the General, so Archer needed to think of something fast. He spoke to Dr Huk about getting a medbot. Huk said that this would take a day or two. Archer knew this was cutting it fine, but told him that this would be ok.

The next day was hectic for Archer. He had to make it look like nothing was going on, so the General did not think he was going ahead with the attack. Archer was on the phone all day, checking on the troops, making sure they all had their shield devices fitted. Cundill would make sure they could use them. He did not tolerate failure.

Dr Huk had the medbot for Archer. He showed Archer how to use it. Archer set his plan into motion. It was 4.15pm and he went to the General's office for his normal meeting, when they were both on the base. When he was leaving, he left the medbot just under the lip of the General's desk. Archer nearly ran back to his office. The medbot was linked to his phone. Archer knew he did not have much time. The General would be leaving to go home very soon. So, Archer got the medbot up and flying. It came from under the lip of the desk, and there was the image of the General sitting signing some forms. So, Archer sent the medbot towards the General. With the bot being about the size of an ant and the General's eye sight not being so good, this would mean he would not see it coming. The General removed his glasses and Archer flew it straight at the General's eye. The medbot pierced through his retina. The General quickly rubbed his eye. He must have thought he had an eyelash go in his eye. Archer was not waiting around, so he sent the bot into the General's brain. The medbot's laser was then used to sever the inside of the brain. It did not take long. The General went limp in his chair and he was dead. Archer manoeuvred the bot out of the General, and activated the self-destruct mode on the bot. With a tiny pop sound, which no-one would have heard, the bot was gone.

Archer knew he needed the night to get everything ready. He could stall the General's secretary for most of the day tomorrow, so no-one would find the General too soon. Later that evening Archer went to see Simmons. He had a proposition for him. He wanted Simmons to make a hologram of the General to address everyone on the base. Simmons was not sure at first. He knew how much his men loved the General, and if they ever found out it was Archer who killed him it would be the end of both of them. Archer enticed Simmons by saying that he would never have to work in the vault ever again. He would be happy with this. Simmons wanted more though, so he offered him the lead scientist role on all projects, which would be authorised by him and only him. Wherever Archer went, Simmons would go too. Simmons did not know what Archer meant by the last comment about going everywhere with him. He would love being in charge with someone younger like Archer rather than the old General, who never really liked him that much.

Simmons got to work on the hologram. Well sort of, as he got someone else to do it as he couldn't. All he told his worker was that the General needed it, so he could convey information quicker and all would know it was coming from him. A few hours later, Simmons logged in the speech Archer had written for the General's hologram. They were ready. Archer took the device into the parade ground. There were soldiers everywhere. This pleased him, as most would see the hologram here. The hologram would be patched through the whole base though so everyone would see it, and those offsite would be notified of the speech too. The hologram was about twenty foot tall. Simmons had outdone himself this time. The hologram of the General cleared its throat. Most soldiers had stopped to admire the hologram, but when he started to talk it made them all stop and listen.

'Soldiers, this is a dark day. I hoped I would not have to say this, but we have been under attack for months by alien ships. The shield has been withstanding their attack, and I was hoping it would thwart them enough that they would leave. However, the analysis received from the shield supervisors show that the shield is weakening. We can't afford for the shield to completely collapse, and let anyone in or let the sun's radiation in. So, we must attack ourselves. I ordered Archer to construct a fleet of ships, which is now complete. With a heavy heart, I tell you soldiers to gear up for a war. We are going to have to attack them head on.'

He continued, 'With my age, and lately ill health, Archer will be in charge of all forces in this attack. I pray you will all be safe in this war.'

The hologram went dim and disappeared. The soldiers stood there for a few seconds, and there were murmurings about Archer being in charge.

Then a sergeant stepped forward and shouted, 'You all heard the General. Back to your barracks all of you and prepare for battle.'

In Archer's haste to get the attack ships ready, he forgot about transport to get the men to battle. Then he remembered the beat-up old ships still in the hangar, they had used to come from Mars. The engines were damaged, but the ships would be big enough to hold enough troops. They got them from Mars, so they should be able to transport the men around Earth ok.

So, the first mission for Simmons was to get the engines on these old ships up and running again. As usual, Simmons recruited others to do this manual work for him. They got the engines going. They were not as bad as they originally expected. They did have a few questions about how old the engines were, and why the engines were covered in star dust. Simmons just avoided these questions with none specific answers.

Now, Archer knew the time was right. He had to go to the control room and deal with the young officer, Habersham. He had not dealt with him much since that day when they needed to get through the shield, and be rescued by Earth. The officer was still being obnoxious and had a poor attitude towards Archer. Under duress, and as it was a direct order from the General on the hologram, he would do as Archer told him. All the time Archer was thinking that this 'kid,' as he called Habersham, could be a problem in the future. He did not have time to deal with him now though. He had three transport ships to sort out and orders to be given to send one of them West and two of them East. They would also all be ordered to attack at night, and at the same time, to catch the countries off guard and stop them informing each other.

Chapter Fourteen

General Blasius just stood on the main deck of the alien ship, the Valcareren, looking out. It was a bright and beautiful day. He just stared at the UK's shield, or what he thought was a shield as he could not actually see it. When you're bored you will do anything to occupy your mind. There were not that many people to talk to now either. Blasius had dropped the last of the Mbalame off about four months ago, and had come back to hover up here ever since. He did not want to leave the Tilluke too long. The Tilluke were tenacious little beings and were still trying to get into the shield. They had been at it for years, but would not give up. Blasius looked around the ship. It was baron. Only a skeleton crew left now. He thought probably a few thousand left on the ship, but for a ship the size of the Valcareren it was scarce. They had dropped thousands off all over this planet. He wished he could be doing his duties with the others all over the world, but he had promised the Tilluke he would not abandon them. He was a man of his word, so he never would. They had their little skiff ship, but if anything did come out of the shield and spotted them they would not stand a chance. He started to daydream about his own planet then. Very similar to this one. Beautiful oceans, lots of forests and jungles, and a great metropolis of millions of people. There was always a hive of activity. He loved it until the dark days when 'they' turned up. Then all of a sudden, he was pulled out of his daydream.

'General, General,' one of his lieutenants was shouting at him. 'The communications have been jammed. We cannot contact our people.'

The General's mind was racing. He knew there was going to a be an attack.

The lieutenant said, 'What shall we do?'

Before the General could give an order to put the shields up, a huge pipe came out of the water to the side of them. Lots of ships flew out of the pipe and into the air. They were extremely fast. Their weapons were crude, but effective. They took out the communications all together and knocked out the shield generator. All the General felt was sadness. He knew these attackers had cracked that single Tilluke they had captured years before. Only a Tilluke could have designed these engines on these attacking ships. The Tilluke must have done schematics to show them where the shield generator was on the Valcareren ship as well. These attacking ships were now swarming around the Valcareren, and battering it with these crude weapons. Blasius's crew tried to fire back with lasers, but with the lack of crew and the attacking ships being so fast, Blasius's Valcareren ship was just a sitting duck. The ship was shaking from all of the incoming fire. Blasius thought the armour plating should be able to withstand the fire for a while, but not for forever. There were people running everywhere, but Blasius stood where he was. He had to keep a clear head. He could see the Tilluke skiff ship just from where we he was, and he was determined to protect the them. He hoped the attackers had not seen them. He noticed the Tilluke were moving off west. Although land was further away to the west than the east, he knew Captain Cecilio was there and the Tilluke trusted him. Blasius ordered his ship to follow the them and stay above the Tilluke's ship for cover. The attackers got more agitated when they saw the Valcareren ship start moving, and started firing towards the engines.

His lieutenant said, 'We have to go, Sir. We need to break orbit and hopefully they won't follow us into space.'

Blasius stood there stricken for a few seconds, but realised the lieutenant was right. There were too many lives on this ship to risk, and if the Tilluke got to Cecilio he would do his best to keep them safe. So, he gave the order. They were just peeling off to go to space, when General Blasius noticed the pipe from the water was still out. As they started to climb, three transport ships sped out of the pipe. He recognised they were the old ships from Mars. He wanted to turn back and engage, but this was not a wise idea with the attackers trying to destroy the engines of the Valcareren. If they did any more damage, they would not make it into space. The three transport ships split up, one headed west and the other two to the east.

The lieutenant pulled Blasius's arm and said, 'There's nothing we can do for them now. We need to get out of the atmosphere and hopefully fix the ship. We can come back and help them later.'

Blasius turned with a tear in his eye, 'You're right. Keep going. Get us out of here.'

The Valcareren made it into space, but not without being badly damaged. The lieutenant was right. The ships stopped chasing them, as soon as they got to the upper atmosphere.

In space, Blasius could see the armada that had followed them all this way from his galaxy. These ships would try to get down to Earth to help their people, but they all had skeleton crews and not enough fire power. They could see the attackers in the clouds below. He expected they would ambush them if they tried to go down and help.

Blasius sat in his chair sobbing, thinking that this was his fault and that thousands would die. As he quickly regained his composure, Blasius decided to send a ship over to one of the Mbalame ships. With their communications down, he could not communicate that he needed what was left of his fleet. The fleet needed to keep flying into the atmosphere to make it look like their ships were trying to avoid Archer's ships in the clouds, but also reach their alien counterparts on the planet below. This was only a ploy, as he knew his ships could not fight. They did not have enough people on board to man the guns. Blasius just wanted to keep Archer's human fighters occupied and distracted, as he knew if they joined these battles on the ground then his troops and their new human friends would not stand a chance. At least doing this, it would give them a chance of survival. Blasius's crew were working night and day to try and fix his ship, but they were not sure they had all the parts they needed, and he could not find the Tilluke to help them. Blasius worked on fixing the communications, along with fixing the ship.

Chapter Fifteen

The alien children lived within the caves now. They run out of the cave system, through the newly constructed door, and into the market. The market was quiet apart from these children of the alien races of Omorfi Stvar, Mbalame and Gogortasana, who liked to play hide and seek around the market while it was quiet. It was early, so the market wasn't open yet. The children could use it as playground, and had chance to play in it before it opened. Their parents, who were the market stall holders, were just beginning to arrive from the caves. They told the children to go and play outside the gates, while they set up the stalls. The children did as they were told. They ran out of the gates and into the open space outside. They were heading towards the mountains. They struggled to get around the teenagers of the Omorfi Stvar and Gogortasana, who were in training in hand to hand combat. There were also a few of the Gogortasana training to use guns, and some of the Omorfi Stvar training to use their newly acquired spears. The Omorfi Stvar children received spears when they became teenagers. At the head of the rows, shouting out orders, was the huge figure of Captain Cecilio. He liked to take the new recruits and was a good teacher. Cecilio was about to shout at the younger children to get off his parade ring, but they kept running. He called it his parade ring, but it was actually a bit of wasteland. When the children ran past a figure, that was sat on a boulder watching the training, they waved at the figure. Cecilio thought it waved back and he had to go and check out who this was. He thought he better be safe than sorry. Cecilio got one of his sergeants to take over the training and he slowly walked over to the figure. The figure was small and had a cloak and hood on. From this distance Cecilio could not see who it was. As Cecilio walked over, the figure just sat there and did not move. Cecilio put his hand behind his back to grab the bar in case it attacked him. About fifty feet away from it now, Cecilio dropped his hand to his side and relaxed. He went over and sat next to the figure. It rested its head into Cecilio's side, and he put one of his arms around it.

In his own language Cecilio asked, 'Why are you here again? There's nothing else I can train you in. You know all you need to know.'

The figure replied in Omorfi Stvar, his language, 'I know, but I just like to watch the kids train.'

Cecilio looked down and said,' You're still a kid too.'

The figure pulled back its hood and it was Annette.

She looked up at Cecilio and in human language said, 'I know. It's nice just to sit here and daydream about THAT day.'

Cecilio sighed and said, 'I wish you wouldn't.'

Too late as Annette was already daydreaming again:

Just standing in front of the huge creature she was scared out of her mind, but defiant no-one would die that day. It drew it's spear up high. Annette closed her eyes waiting for the end. She heard the thud of the spear in the ground millimetres from her. The heat off it felt like it was going to burn her. The huge alien dropped to its knees in front of her. Sobbing she thought, but wasn't sure. It pulled it's helmet off then and looked straight at her. It was the most beautiful creature she had ever seen. For its huge size, it had soft looking features. Light purple skin with dark purple, long, pulled back hair. Perfect nose and cheek bones. It was its eyes Annette was drawn too. Its eyes were pure white like human eyes, but the iris was amazing. It was silver looking with gold flecks in it, and the blackest cornea. It had a single shiny tear running down it's cheek. It continued to speak in English, so she could understand it.

It said to her, 'I can't do this. I won't kill children, even if they are human.'

Annette did not know what that comment meant. The beasts behind this alien were getting restless and started to move. Annette did not know what to do, but the beautiful alien just held one of its four arms up and gave the halt signal. The beasts all stopped and looked at one another. One shouted something she could not understand, and then all started to shout and scream and started moving again. It looked like their weapons were ready, but the weight of the weapons and their short broad legs made them move quite slowly. The beautiful alien was still in front of them. It looked at Annette and then stood up to its full height. She did not know what it was about to do. Had it changed its mind? It pulled its spear out of the ground and then spun around to face the beasts. It screamed at the beasts, clearly in their own language, with its spear in the air. This time the beasts listened and stopped immediately. The beautiful alien seemed to changed its stance and it was like it was getting ready for battle. The beasts seem confused, but one by one dropped their weapons to the ground. To Annette, the beasts seemed to look relieved. The beautiful alien turned back around again to Annette.

'What did you say to them?' she said to it.

The alien looked directly at her and for the first time smiled at her. It was glorious.

'I just said that there will be no bloodshed today, and if there was it would be mine. I said that we are not going to attack.'

Annette was so relieved, but did not know what to do, as she stood in the front of the alien.

The alien said, 'I best talk to your leaders. We have a lot to discuss.'

Annette looked at it and then ran off leaving the aliens behind. She went to find Cirius, her leader. The big one in charge turned around talking to the beasts. The meeting was set to be in the main hall in the cave system. Cirius felt safer in there, just in case this was a deception to get into the market. Then they could run and hide in the caves. Everyone was in the main hall ready for the meeting, Cirius's wife, Otax and Nittil from the city. Hundreds of others had gathered to get a glimpse of these beasts. Vaughn seemed to be in the background. There was a knock on the door and some of the men opened it and quickly stepped back. Annette was at the front and then was followed by the beautiful alien, as she had named it. It had to stoop in behind her, as it was so tall. Another huge beast was with it. Cirius thought this must have been the bodyguard! You could feel everyone go tense in the room and the anger was palpable. The people started screaming and throwing things towards the alien and the beast. The creatures just stood there and did not even try to block anything. One cup hit the purple beautiful alien in the face and it started to bleed silver blood, but all it did was wipe it off. This infuriated Annette and she screamed for the people to stop, but they carried on. It took Cirius's intervention to calm it down.

He put his hands in the air and shouted, 'People, people. We said we would meet and that's what we'll do.'

The chaos slowly subsided and they all sat down. Though the purple alien looked a little uncomfortable, as they did not have a chair big enough for something of its size. Before Cirius could speak, the beautiful alien stepped in.

'I and we, the Gogortasana,' gesturing to the beast like alien stood next to him, 'Would profoundly like to apologise for our actions. We attacked with malice and not thought. Thinking we would have no choice running into humans, after our escape from them again.'

Cirius butted in and said, 'What do you mean 'again'? No human has ever left this planet.'

The alien looked at him exhausted and said, 'That's for another day. We are here to try and right a considerable wrong.'

The crowd murmured and Otax spoke up, 'You killed some, and injured many people in the city. How are we meant to believe or trust you?'

The alien looked like it dipped it's head in shame and said, 'I understand that. All we can do is try and make up for our mistakes. We can't bring people back, but we will try our best to help you with whatever we can. Our technology is far more advanced than yours, and we are willing to share and help you back to where you were.'

The people stirred again, but in conversation.

The alien went on, 'The Gogortasana are not really warriors. They are great builders and want to help re-build your city.'

Otax sat upright, seeming to like this idea.

Cirius sat back in his chair thoughtfully and said, 'But we still can't trust you.'

The alien said, 'Let our actions show you we can be trusted.'

'We will have to have a private meeting about this. Could you leave, so we can?' Cirius replied.

146

The beautiful purple alien nodded, stood up and left with the beast and Annette.

Outside it said to Annette, 'Should you not stay with your people?'

She shook her head and said, 'I like to be with you,' which shocked him.

It said, 'Well, my name is Cecilio.'

Once outside Cecilio contacted his General, via the communication systems, to tell him that they had had a meeting, and he wanted to call off the attack around the world. Blasius was not happy about this decision, and even more so the fact they had been talking to these humans. Blasius did not like or trust humans, but Cecilio talked him round with the help of this little girl Annette. So, Blasius agreed with Cecilio to call the world attack off, and to Blasius's amazement all the alien races wanted to help the humans too. They were all sick of war.

The first year was tough. No-one seemed to trust anyone, the aliens or the humans. There were often small fights here and there, and signs popping up saying 'aliens leave'. Otax had gone back to the city, and true to their word nearly all able bodied Gogortasana had gone with him. They left their families at the market for safety though. The rest of the Mbalame and Cecilio stayed at the market to fix what they had destroyed. The next three years was the best of Annette's life, and for everyone. Cecilio and the Mbalame, along with a few Gogortasana, fixed the market and more. They showed them how to grow crops better than they did before. They removed the radiation out of the soil with their machines. They even had machines that made food out of nothing, or so Annette thought! They installed an old shield generator from one of their ships for the market too. It encompassed the entire market, along with a new gate. However, Cecilio was not convinced it would last very long if attacked, as the generator was so old. Cecilio took it upon himself to train anyone who wanted to learn their ways of combat as well, so they could protect themselves from aliens like him he would joke. Most were not ready for combat yet. Annette took him up on his offer though. She was good as she was very quick, listened and learned quickly. More and more kids heard of Annette doing this, and more kids joined her. Nittil was the first to train with her and Cecilio. Jimbo was about a lot too, but seemed to disappear when Nittil turned up. Vaughn just seemed to go missing after that meeting and out of the way of the aliens. No-one knew why. After a few years of training for Nittil, he went back to the city. He felt he had to go back for his family to help them out. A year later, Annette was fully trained in Cecilio's warrior ways. They gave her her own spear. It was a kid's size, as Cecilio's type of spear was far too big for her. Also, you could not wield another spear, as it was set to your DNA and no others in the universe. After all of this, Annette and Cecilio had become very good friends. They went back and forth to the city. The city nowadays was a mixture of various alien races, along with humans. They all called themselves 'people' of the city, no matter where they had come from. Cecilio was not lying when he said that the Gogortasana would do a great job. They were re-building the skyscrapers back to their original glory and then some. They were enormous. The more time spent around the Gogortasana, the more Annette liked them. Despite their beast-like looks, they were gentle creatures. When they stopped work, small kids would climb up them and they would play with them. Tossing them up in the air and catching them. If any of the Mbalame went on these city trips, they would play with the kids too. The Gogortasana would toss the kids in the air and the Mbalame would catch them in mid-air and fly them around for a while, before dropping them back down for the Gogortasana to catch. The kids loved this. The Gogortasana were always laughing and joking. When Annette really got to know them, she wondered how such gentle creatures could start attacking people. She thought she would have to push Cecilio for answers. Otax was always trying to persuade the Gogortasana to become his security, due to their size and strength, but they were not interested. They did not like him, but Otax was the leader of the city, as the people had voted him in. They had to deal with him now.

Back at the market was the happiest place it had ever been. Everyone was happy.

At this point, she was snapped out of this daydream by Cecilio. 'Well,' he said, 'I'm going back to train them. Would you like to come and show them how it's done?'

Annette smiled and said, 'I best do, I suppose. If you're training them, they need all the help they can.'

Cecilio tried to look hurt, but just giggled at this comment.

Chapter Sixteen

Now in the West, under the cover of darkness they came. The low hum of the engines were the only sounds. Cundill was hoping they couldn't be heard or seen. He had got most of his original soldiers that had come from Mars with him, about a thousand or so from Earth and a few hundred of the new recruits. All three attacks were planned to start at the same time at night, to give an element of surprise in the dark. All of the soldiers turned their dark mode on. They were nearly on the city. Cundill thought the skyscrapers looked glorious, and all that work the aliens had put in would be destroyed. They got the red light from the pilot to get ready and the whole ship went dark. The ramp at the front started to drop and the men shuffled forward.

Cundill stood up and said, 'We want none alive, men. You have your orders. No stopping for the traitors either. Just keep going.'

The first units dropped out above the first skyscraper. With their shields up, they would not be using their parachutes. They would use themselves as human torpedoes, and run straight into the towers and take them down. They hit the first skyscraper and it rocked, but did not collapse. Cundill could see his men with their huge strength sliding down the side of the building, punching holes in the building to weaken it. He could hear screams, but the expected laser fire did not come. His men reached the bottom and started attacking the foundations. It did not take long to bring down the skyscraper after that. Cundill was ecstatic.

'Onto the next one,' he screamed to the flight captain. 'We need to bring them all down and get to the aliens.'

The Gogortasana did not have great eyesight, but could not believe what they had just seen. The humans were so obsessed with revenge that they were willing to kill their own too. The Gogortasana rushed to where the first building had collapsed, and they could hear the ship just further down above them. They moved as quick as they could. They used their long huge arms, so that they could move quicker. Their legs were too short and broad to move them quickly, and if they had their weapons on them too their heaviness would have slowed them. The weapons had been locked away in a weapon shed a few blocks back. They did not have time to go and get them, as they wanted to help the city 'people'. They reached the next building being targeted by Cundill and his men. The men were attacking the foundations again. They could hear, but not see, smashing up above them on the building. Dust from the collapsed building was starting to fill the air and affect their vision. They did not have time to go into the building, so some started to climb the outside. They were strong themselves and excellent climbers. As they were going up, they were dodging soldiers on their way down. The soldiers tried to grab the Gogortasana and bring them down. The Gogortasana were grabbing people out of the windows, throwing them down to other Gogortasana on the ground and gesturing to them to run. They were trying to rescue as many people as they could. They were directing them to run back to the skiff ships, that they had bought with them to the city from the market originally. They successfully saved a few people from the building before its collapse. The Gogortasana were trying to rescue people from the next building now, as Cundill and his men moved building to building. The Gogortasana reached higher levels on this building. They could not throw the people between them, so some people clambered on the backs of the Gogortasana. The soldiers were smashing the foundations yet again, so the Gogortasana just kept climbing and more people were hanging onto them. They were starting to tire and slip a little, with the weight of the people on them. The building was beginning to shake, and then it started to fall. The Gogortasana thought they had lost this one and everyone would die. When, from around the adjacent building, one of the skiff ships flew in with Nittil flying it. The building was collapsing, and the soldiers on the ground started hurling huge chunks of debris up at the skiff and them. The Gogortasana started throwing people onto the skiff. One of the Gogortasana lost his grip and fell. The others kept grabbing people and throwing them onto the skiff.

151

In the end, they had no choice but to jump on the skiff themselves too. Nittil stayed a while longer, dodging the falling building and seeing if he could rescue any others. There was one more. A kid just fell out of one of the windows. Nittil just caught him on the way down. He had to get out of there then. He pointed to the floor of the skiff, where there were two Gogortasana guns. That's all six people could carry. So, the Gogortasana picked them up and immediately starting blasting at Cundill's ship overhead. That stopped the soldiers dropping out the ship, and the ship stopped and backed off. This left the soldiers on the ground in a bit of a quandary. They did not have enough on the ground to keep attacking the buildings, so they just attacked anyone trying to escape. Nittil set down the skiff, and two Gogortasana with the guns were off and blasting at the soldiers. They couldn't kill the soldiers, because of the soldier's shields, but the laser fire from these powerful guns would slow them immensely. Archer could see these images back at the base headquarters and was not happy.

'Get that ship down, Captain,' he said, 'And help them soldiers.' Cundill found the nearest open space and got the ship's captain to land it. As soon as they hit the ground, the soldiers were running out of the ship. They were like packs of wild dogs. They did not let anything get in their way. Of course, Cundill was the last off the ship. There was a unit of soldiers coming down the block, as people were trying to flee. A group of around four Gogortasana saw this and thought they had no choice. The Gogortasana let the fleeing humans go past them, and then they stood right in front of the oncoming soldiers. The Gogortasana held their hands in the air, as if to indicate surrender. The soldiers did not care. They attacked and killed all four. People that did manage to escape reported what had happened to the surrendering Gogortasana. The remaining Gogortasana thought they only had one option left, and that was to fight.

Nittil took some Gogortasana back to the weapon storage shed, and they loaded enough weapons for hundreds of them to use. They got the weapons back to the remaining Gogortasana in this part of the city who were still left, and in the vicinity of the soldiers. They took the weapons and were firing at the soldiers, as quick as they could. This would be their last stand against these soldiers. Nittil wanted to stay and help. They would not allow him though. He knew they wanted him to go and save as many people and Gogortasana as he could with the skiff. Nittil flew off, with green blaster fire everywhere. Soldiers were jumping around and dodging the weapon fire. The soldiers kept coming though. Nittil kept going and picking up Gogortasana that were left. Many were injured, and sadly some had died trying to save people from the buildings. He also managed to pick up a few hundred more aliens and humans. He returned to where the other skiffs were, which was where he had taken the first skiff earlier. There were about thirty of them and they were all full of all the alien races and humans from the city. The skiffs were up and leaving and now flying to the market, a slightly safer place. When in the air, they could hear the firing still in the city below, but then everything went quiet. Nittil accelerated his skiff, as he knew the skiffs would be the next target. Cundill, seeing the skiffs leaving stopped the attack. All over the city, there were dead and injured Gogortasana, and people strewn everywhere. Cundill did not care. He ordered the men back to the ship. They were going to follow the skiffs. He wanted every last one of the Gogortasana and people dead. They would return later to the city to make sure there were none left.

Chapter Seventeen

Captain Evan Habersham just managed to get off one of Archer's ships in time. He had jumped off the ramp without anyone noticing. This was easy enough, as all the soldiers were pumped with adrenaline ready for action. He had disobeyed an order doing this, which he had found very difficult, as following orders seemed to have been something he always did unconsciously without question, but never knew why even when it seemed wrong. There was something about the General's last order that did not quite sound right to him. One, it came from Archer, the man he hated; and two, it did not appear to be how the General usually operated. He should know, as he was one of the General's sons. No-one knew that, as the General was a very private man, who thought his children should not get special treatment. He wanted his children to rise through the ranks on merit and not because of who they were related to. That last order, 'Kill everyone and humans as well, as they are traitors, as they are working with and friends with the aliens,' was supposed to have come from the General. This did not sound like his father at all. His father had been watching all these people for most of his life from afar. He had never left the UK to go outside the shield, and had never wanted to. He had plenty of spybots all over the world watching, just in case. This was not to help these people, as he said they were self-sufficient, but just to make sure they never found out what truly happened to them. If they did, they would probably have attacked the UK. His father, over the years, had come to respect the people that were left in these countries for their resilience. To call them traitors just wasn't right. Evan could not go to his Dad's office to see him, as if he had been seen he would have been court marshalled for derelict of duty. He would have to bind his time, and go in under the cover of darkness. He waited in the hangar, where the ships had departed, with a few soldiers from Archer's old Mars unit still around. He hid from them and watched them. It was strange they had not gone on the mission he thought. They seemed to be acting as security. He waited for hours, and then later on he sprang into action. He went into dark mode and exited the hangar. He had been on the base most of his life, so had no problems getting to Hangar One containing the General's office, and without being seen. The office just before his father's was Joan's, his father's secretary's office. Surprisingly, she was still there. Archer came out the office and Evan hid down the corridor. He heard Archer say, 'Sorry for your loss.' Archer walked past Evan, without noticing him. He noticed Archer had left the door open. He would have to get past Joan, but couldn't wait any longer. He edged up towards the office and could hear Joan sobbing. At this point, he could now see into the office. She had her back to him and was getting her things together. This was his chance to get to his Dad's office. He was almost at the office, sliding past Joan below her desk when he heard, 'There's no point going in there Evan, your father's gone.'

He stopped in his tracks. No-one had called him that, and he did not think people knew his actual name. He turned around, and Joan over her shoulder still sobbing said, 'Your father is dead.'

She turned to face him, 'You can come out of dark mode now.' He had forgotten he was still in that. He looked her in the eyes. The devastation in her was visible.

She went on, 'After I saw that order, I thought I best come to see your father. It did not seem right and I found him slumped in his chair. I rang for help, but knew he was gone. Archer and his medical team that he brought with him arrived surprisingly quickly, and took his body away even quicker. Archer just said there would be a thorough autopsy.'

Evan was still trying to take this all in.

He said, 'How did you know I was here?'

Joan looked at him and said, 'I had an idea you would come to see your father. I knew you were his son. Your father confided in me years ago. I also know you have a brother too. I would never tell anyone, especially Archer. You will have to stay at mine tonight, as I don't know if Archer will have your house under surveillance.'

Evan just nodded and thanked her. He was a bit confused and did not know how to grieve yet. They got back to Joan's house. She made Evan something to eat and then he just went straight to bed. The day had caught up with him and he felt exhausted. He just laid in bed with his eyes open, and tears were streaming out the sides of his eyes. He wasn't an emotional person, so at first, he thought he had something in his eye and tried to rub it, but they were still streaming. Then he realised he was thinking of his father. He really wasn't that close to him, but it must have upset him more than he thought. Evan was just falling asleep, when there was a knock on the door. He bolted upright with his shield up, and went straight into dark mode. He heard Joan say, 'Who is it?' but could not hear the response. He went and stood at the top of her stairs. He could not see the front door, as Joan had another door before it. He could only just hear them and it sounded quite heated. He was sure he heard, 'Who are you talking about?' and thought that response came from woman's voice. They seemed to continue speaking in a lower volume and not so heated. He was about to come down the stairs, when Joan walked back in the house. She looked up the stairs and Evan came out of dark mode.

She started with, 'Someone is here to see you, Evan. I told her you were not here, but she would not take no for an answer. Will you see her?'

He thought about it and couldn't remember if Archer had any women in his ranks.

He looked at Joan and said, 'Can we trust her?'

'I think so,' she said, 'I know she has no love of Archer.'

Evan nodded and said, 'Ok. Let her in.'

She was only short and he was sure he had seen her before, but could not put a name to her face. Joan gestured towards her and said, 'This is Chantelle.'

Evan came down the stairs and they all sat in the lounge.

'Well', Evan said, 'How did you know I was here?'

Chantelle looked at him at little shyly, then looked away and said, 'By coincidence really.'

Evan looked and said again, 'How?'

'Well after getting to the base, it was in chaos. I watched the hologram message from the General. It did not sound right to me, so I spoke to someone who told me to follow Archer. I followed him as much as I could throughout that day. His movements were all over and he was seeing and talking to everyone he could. Then he seemed to get an urgent message, which is when he went to Joan's office. He made some calls on the way. He met some people outside the hangar and I hid. Then about twenty minutes later they came out with a body bag. I stayed where I was and then that's when I saw you in dark mode.'

Evan wondered how Chantelle knew about dark mode, but did not question this and allowed Chantelle to continue.

'I saw Archer leave, but you sneaking into the hangar was more interesting. I wanted to check Joan was safe. She is my friend.'

Joan smiled at this.

Evan looked at Chantelle straight in the eyes, 'I don't know you, so I don't know if I can trust you.'

Chantelle said, 'I took a risk following you here and I have no love for Archer. Definitely not his little pet Simmons either. We are going to have to start trusting each other, as we need to know what Archer is up to.'

Evan sat and took this all in for a few seconds and then said, 'That's easy. He wants all the power and all of the aliens dead.'

Chantelle was confused and asked, 'Why is he so hellbent on killing aliens?'

Evan answered, 'Because they attacked him and he lost his home planet.'

Chantelle just looked at Evan, shocked at this statement.

Evan laughed, 'I forgot you won't know that Archer and his men are basically Martians. They lived on Mars all of their lives. He likes it on Earth, and he's been after the General's job ever since he's been here. He just can't stand the fact the aliens beat him and he just wants revenge. Now the General's gone, he's going to get his chance.'

'Wait a minute,' Chantelle said, 'What do you mean the General has gone?'

Joan softly spoke up at that point, 'The General is dead, Chantelle.'

Chantelle could not believe this. She knew the General was old, but seemed quite well the last time she saw him.

'That's why Archer was in my office,' Joan said. 'It felt strange, as he seemed to already know the General was dead. He got a Doctor there very quickly. They whisked the body off to the morgue.'

'Was it the base Doctor?' Chantelle asked.

Joan replied, 'No. That's the strange thing. I had never seen this Doctor before. Definitely not the base Doctor or one of ours.'

Evan said, 'He obviously doesn't want our Doctor to do the post mortem then. Very interesting.'

Chantelle said, 'We need to find out where the body went. It's a bit morbid, but we have no choice. Joan, do you think you could find out?'

She nodded, 'I think so.'

'See if you can, and we'll meet tomorrow and decide on our next step,' Chantelle said.

Chantelle got up and said her goodbyes.

The next day Joan went to work as usual. She went to see Archer. Being the General's secretary, he knew she would be in to see him. She could not believe it when she saw him. Archer told her that they had already done the post mortem and the General died of natural causes. This shocked her, but what he said next was worse.

He said, 'The General is to be cremated in two days at the crematorium in Lincoln. His body lays there ready.'

Joan was disgusted. Everything that man had done, he should have been getting a state burial, but she did not say anything else to Archer.

'Is there anything you would like me to do?' she said.

She was barely holding her emotions together in the room with Archer.

'No, that's ok. I have everything under control,' he said with a smirk.

Joan muttered to herself, 'I bet you do!'

The rest of Joan's day was a blur. She did not believe a word of what Archer had said. The end of the day could not come quick enough. She raced back home and Chantelle was already there, with Evan looking a little uneasy around her. Joan did not delay in letting Evan and Chantelle know what had happened that day. She was so furious about what Archer had told her, and his mannerisms towards her. He clearly did not care. She stopped talking and the room went deadly silent. Evan jumped out of his chair, startling both the women in the room.

'I don't believe a word of what that man said,' and stormed into the kitchen.

The two women looked at each other, and Joan just said, 'Let him be. He'll calm down in a while.'

Chantelle nodded, 'I think we're going to need help in this one. I know exactly the person who could help us. Are you and Evan willing to come to London and meet her?'

Joan did not know how to respond and then Evan returned to the room. His eyes were sore and red. Chantelle suspected he had been crying. He apologised for storming out of the room. Chantelle said, 'I have someone that can help, if you are willing to meet her in London?'

Evan did not want to leave Lincoln, but knew that they needed more help, so they all set off for London. Within an hour they had reached Miss Che's apartment.

Miss Che listened to everything they had to say and she decided very quickly to help. She thought Archer wanted more than just revenge, and she did not want him to get what he wanted.

Che said, 'I hope we can get our little friend to help us too.' Evan and Joan looked at her wondering what she was talking about. Chantelle went over to the corner of the room for a while, and then came back and set the bag on the table. She unzipped it open. They all just sat there frozen. Joan glanced at Evan and he shrugged his shoulders. They did not know what they were meant to be looking at. Then all of a sudden, a little head popped up out of the bag. Joan nearly fainted, but Evan seemed to recognise it.

He said, 'I've seen your people before. They've been trying to get through the shield for years.'

Hearing this, the little alien nearly jumped out of the bag. It seemed to understand that and then it spoke.

'They're still trying to help me escape then,' it said.

Joan sat there with her mouth open. She had never seen anything like this before.

Evan said, 'Yes, they were trying to get in. They had to flee, when the attack started.'

That sent the room deadly quiet again.

'Archer's attacking?' Miss Che said.

Evan just nodded to indicate he agreed.

Miss Che said, 'We need to get in and see the General's body and hope we can find something, or there will be a lot of dead. Not just aliens, but humans too.'

They all agreed, even the little alien friend. So, they formulated a plan.

Chapter Eighteen

In the East, Lutherine was the head of the guard for the Jasny Stern forces and took the responsibility seriously. He took control of the mid-European sector, when General Blasius ordered the attack to end. They did a treaty with the humans to protect the humans and re-build. He was in charge, but liked to come on duty at night sometimes. He noticed after four years of nothing happening, the guard were getting a little complacent and lax in their duties. They were falling asleep and not keeping their concentration. Lutherine knew this was not good, as he had studied recordings, and been told by the Omorfi Stvar about these human soldiers. It was his life's work, and he was now sixty-two years of age. He thought he knew the human's tactics and what they were like in battle. Lutherine was outside the hut they called the Guard Tower. The aliens and humans together had re-built parts of the city, after the aliens attacked four years ago. The Omorfi Stvar and Jasny Stern were not the greatest builders, unlike the Gogortasana, but with the help of their new human friends they were getting there. Lutherine never thought he would say that humans were his friends. He started his routine checks out on duty, and then looked up into the night sky. With his amazing eyesight, he thought he could see something moving at high speed towards the city. The object came into his view very quickly, and he knew what it was. It was one of those ships that had escaped Mars. He knew this was an attack. Lutherine ran as quick as he could over to the main gun, which was always ready for such situations. Many had not thought this gun was necessary, but Lutherine had always insisted it was. Now he was glad he had. The object was still far away, but he could see the ramp was down on it. He suspected these soldiers would hurtle down the ramp, bring down the buildings and kill many. Lutherine would not let that happen. He felt guilty for attacking these humans in the first place. He was not going to let these humans on the ship attack them as well, just because the aliens were there. He got to the gun and jumped into the chair. The gun came to

161

life, as Lutherine was nearly pure energy. He powered the machine. Since landing on Earth, he had become stronger from the sun's rays. He sat there a few seconds to allow the ship to get closer. He could now see the soldiers on the ramp readying themselves. Lutherine flicked a switch and the city just seemed to come alive. It was as bright as a summer's day, as what the Jasny Stern lacked in building, they made up for in energy. They had built massive new powerplants for the humans, that would last for decades. Maybe forever, using the sun's energy. Lutherine fired the gun and started pounding the ship, especially the ramp, which knocked the soldiers back up into the ship. He noticed the ramp start to close rapidly, but he kept firing.

Over his ear pierce the Omorfi Stvar commander came on, and in his own language said, 'What's going on, Lutherine?'

'We're under attack, Sir. Still firing at the ship. You best get the forces ready and start to evacuate the people. We need to save as many as possible,' Lutherine replied.

'Thank you, Lutherine. I'll get on with it. Keep me posted where the ship lands or hopefully crashes,' the commander said.

'Yes, Sir,' Lutherine replied.

The ship had considerable damage. Flames coming up from it. So Lutherine paused the fire for now, as he was worried the ship could come down onto the people and the city. The ship flew over the city, and appeared to come down twenty miles in the distance from what they could see. He heard a crash and knew that they would not have long. These soldiers on the ship would want to attack all of them, and even more so now, given they had just been blown out of the sky. This would make them even more determined to succeed. Lutherine's forces joined him quickly. There were around a few thousand of the Jasny Stern alien bikers now, glowing with their new-found energy. A few skiffs also flew in with around fifty to sixty Omorfi Stvar soldiers on. Others would stay to help the evacuation, along with the humans. Lutherine got to his bike and sped away in the lead. They all followed, and would wait at the edge of the city. They sat and waited. Lutherine did not expect these soldiers from the ship to attack from the forest. It would give them the element of surprise, but Lutherine knew from his studies that the human soldiers would attack from the open fields, as they would arrogantly think they would not lose and feared no-one. Four hours later, they did just that. The soldiers from the ship came bounding across the fields. These soldiers could jump quite large distances, because of their sheer strength. They got to Lutherine and his forces very quickly. There were around two thousand of these soldiers leading the way. There were possibly about another thousand more behind these, coming more slowly, and these were the soldiers Archer had recruited from the city and trained to use the shields. Lutherine had never seen soldiers that were slow like this before. Lutherine decided his best plan was to attack the leading soldiers first to catch them unaware. So, Lutherine and his forces attacked by flying in on their bikes and blasting. They hit the bulk of the soldiers, who were taken aback, as the Jasny Stern were a lot more powerful and so were their blasters. This scattered the soldiers and knocked many to the ground. The Jasny Stern had not witnessed their blasters being able to knock soldiers off their feet before, and it looked like they had actually hurt the soldiers by doing this. Lutherine thought that finally they had been able to hurt them a little. The soldiers slowly started to get back on their feet. Lutherine, with more confidence in his plans, was going to attack again as the soldiers got up. The Omorfi Stvar commander ran across to try and stop Lutherine from attacking them, as he thought the soldiers would be more prepared. The soldiers dodged and blocked shots this time from Lutherine and his forces. Lutherine lost some of his forces this time round. More Omorfi Stvar forces came from the skiffs to join the attack. They charged at the human soldiers. They wanted to give Lutherine and his forces chance to regroup, so covered them. The Omorfi Stvar had their spears out, glowing and ready. They had learned their lessons from Mars, along with training from Cecilio. They would not go to match the human soldiers for strength, as they knew the human soldiers were more powerful than them. Instead the Omorfi Stvar would use their spears to put the soldiers off balance. They would use the tactic, slice and retreat. They would slow them and try to tire the human soldiers. The Omorfi Stvar did this and it worked well for them. Lutherine and his men re-engaged with the attack, but they were less successful this time. He was losing his forces quickly. The slower human soldiers from behind had also started to join in the attack now. These soldiers had shields, but were not as strong as Lutherine's forces. They could be blasted off their feet, and appeared to be knocked out for quite a while. The Omorfi Stvar were starting to struggle with the huge numbers of Archer's soldiers. With Lutherine having lost many as well, the order came. Lutherine ordered them all to retreat, both his forces and the Omorfi Stvar. He had no option. He did not want to take the fight into the city, but this might be their only chance. He just hoped enough people had been evacuated from the city by now, as he did not want them to get involved in this battle. The Omorfi Stvar filled their skiffs and flew back into the city. Lutherine and his men were just behind them. Lutherine kept turning back now and again to slow the soldiers advances towards the city. It slowed them a little, but Archer's soldiers were determined to follow them. As they reached the edge of the city, they could see the large buildings. They would have to fight, using the buildings as cover.

Archer's soldiers reached the city and started to bring down the buildings everywhere. You could hear cries from some of the buildings.

'They haven't got everyone out!' Lutherine exclaimed with dread.

Archer's soldiers did not care if they killed aliens or humans. They were going to kill everyone there in front of them. Lutherine and some of his forces, along with some of the Omorfi Stvar had reached the centre of the city. They were going towards the largest building. He noticed people still in there, and then realised some of Archer's soldiers had outmanoeuvred them and were attacking the foundations of this building. Lutherine fired on them, which stopped them, and they turned on him. Two of the Omorfi Stvar were not waiting. They bound past the soldiers and into the building. Lutherine evaded the oncoming soldiers, who were running at him. He just got into the building. The Omorfi Stvar were very quick, bounded up to the first levels and smashed the windows out. The windows were low enough for aliens and people to jump out and run. Lutherine gave them cover and then returned. The Omorfi Stvar got higher up into the building, but there were no skiffs about. They smashed windows out again and they were now surrounded by many aliens and people wanting to escape, but it was too high for them to jump out. Archer's soldiers were back attacking the foundations again and the building was beginning to shake. Lutherine flew his bike upwards, grabbed as many people onto his bike as he could carry and then he was off. Not as many as he would have liked to have rescued though. He took them out of the building and dropped them off outside. He told them to run and find cover, and hopefully find the skiffs. He then went back. He had to avoid debris being thrown by other soldiers arriving at the building. He got into the building and went up. He started loading more people, when the building suddenly shuddered. It started collapsing around him. He grabbed one more child, but that was all. He just got out in time, but tragically no-one else did. He would tell everyone about the heroism of the Omorfi Stvar giving up their lives for others. The city seemed lost to him. Archer's soldiers were destroying homes and buildings. Lutherine's forces did not seem able to stop them. The death toll was getting higher. He received a message that the skiffs were on the other side of the city, so he told his forces to do what they could to reach the skiffs, taking anyone with them they found along the way. The commander was filling the skiffs as soon as people arrived. Lutherine and his remaining forces needed to reach the skiffs, as quick as possible. He estimated he had lost three quarters of his forces and most of the city had been destroyed. It was sad, but they had no option but to flee. The plan was to go and join Captain Cecilio, if they could escape on the skiffs. Nineham stood in the carnage they had just caused in the city. The men around him were jubilant. They had not had the best start to the battle when their ship came down, but in the end, they had completed the mission Archer had given them. They had destroyed the settlement. They had destroyed as many aliens as they could, and also the human traitors. Archer viewed these humans that had been friendly with the aliens and working together with them as traitors. Nineham was not as happy with the situation, but hoped Archer would view him better now after his failure back on Mars. Nineham contacted Archer on his device. There was Archer in front of him, as a miniature hologram, and Archer could see everything. He was telling Archer all the good news about what they had accomplished and Archer was delighted. He told Nineham there was a chance of promotion when he returned from this Europe mission. Half way through the conversation there were whirring noises. Nineham saw in the distance about ten skiffs and hundreds of biker aliens. The skiffs looked like they were full of aliens and people. They disappeared before Nineham could do anything.

Archer's delight was short-lived as he said, 'Was that what I thought it was, Nineham?'

Dejectedly Nineham nodded and said, 'Some have escaped, Sir.'

'You know the orders, Nineham. I want all of them gone. This is very disappointing. I will send a ship to help mend your carrier ship, but I want all of them dead Nineham,' at which point Archer signed off.

The message was clear to Nineham. Nineham was so mad, that he tore down the last home with his bare hands. He hoped there were people in there, as he was so incensed.

Chapter Nineteen

In the Far East, Commander Danelaw got the pilot to bring the ship in low. It was dark, so they didn't alert the aliens that they were coming in to attack. He was not sure what technology or sensors the aliens had. The briefing from Archer before they left was limited, because they were not sure of the alien's capabilities or which race of aliens they would be coming up against. In the briefing, Archer had said they should attack from the sky first. Danelaw did not agree with this. So, Danelaw set the ship down about twenty miles from the city. They would march in from there. Danelaw got the men to go into dark mode, and they set off. At their speed, it did not take them long to arrive on edge of this city. He worried they might have been seen on the way there, but nothing happened. He realised he was over thinking. They kept to the outskirts of the city. The city looked broken. The aliens had been clearly trying to mend the buildings, but it looked like the buildings had been like this for decades. There was moss and rust all over the lower parts, along with debris in the streets. This was not fresh debris, so it had been attacked decades ago. It had been sat there for a long time.

Danelaw had his men surround as many buildings as they could, but Beijing was a huge city. They could not surround as many as they would have liked. As soon as they started the attack they knew this would be a volatile situation. In position, he gave the order. They took down ten buildings extremely quickly, as the foundations of them were crumbling through dereliction and age. It did not feel like these aliens were very good at construction. He heard screams in the crashing buildings and he just tried to ignore it. He tried to tell himself he was doing his duty and following orders, as he had been trained to do. As his men reached the next building, suddenly about thirty glowing balls bounced in-between them all. The balls exploded blowing him and his men off their feet, as they were caught by surprise. The balls reformed and were glowing on the ground next to them. Then they seemed to be retracted back to wherever they had come from, as they just disappeared from in front of them. Danelaw ordered a unit of his men to go after whoever did this. He brought reinforcement soldiers forward from behind. 'So, it begins,' Danelaw thought. Danelaw re-focussed his men and they started to try and destroy the buildings again. From above, huge flying aliens had joined the attack. They were flying into the buildings, and pulling out aliens and humans from within them. They were trying to rescue them and evacuate the buildings. The flying aliens were emptying the buildings quicker than Danelaw's men could pull them down. Danelaw was getting frustrated by this, after having success at first. He then got a message in his earpiece from the unit that had gone to find who had attacked them earlier with the glowing balls. Apparently, they had cornered a few of the aliens, and Danelaw was asked what they should do with them. Danelaw ordered them to kill all, but one. They were to bring this one back, along with the technology they had used for the balls. Danelaw had had a thought and wanted to use the glowing ball weapon to their advantage, as throwing debris at these huge flying aliens was proving useless. The aliens were about eight foot tall and could fly very gracefully. Danelaw's men were not getting close to hitting them at all. The unit brought the one alien back. It looked like a child to Danelaw on first glance, as it was only about three foot tall. It had enormous green eyes on quite a small face. This looked out of proportion. It had blotchy orange skin with braided flaming red hair, and was quite a portly shaped creature. It was wearing baggy clothes, and had something hanging from its strangely shaped nose. Danelaw hadn't noticed this at first. What could this be hanging from its nose? Perhaps the alien couldn't breathe the air? Danelaw was not sure on the gender. He had never seen this species of alien before. The alien was shaking in the presence of Danelaw and the men. Danelaw was about to find out if the alien was helpful and forthcoming.

Danelaw turned to the sergeant of the unit that had captured the alien and said, 'Where's all the tech I wanted?'

The sergeant just threw orange alien severed arms down on the ground in front of him. Danelaw was disgusted by this, but it was him who had ordered them to get the technology off the aliens.

'They wouldn't give us the tech, so we just took it and more!' the sergeant laughed.

Danelaw thought the captured alien was going to be sick at the sight of this. Then he noticed the alien had a strap over his hand.

'Is that what I want?' pointing to the alien's hand.

The alien seemed to understand what he said and nodded, quickly removing the strap and trying to hand it over to Danelaw. It obviously did not want to end up like its friends. Danelaw put his hands up and said, 'Wait a minute. You need to show us how it works first.'

It nodded again, pulling the strap back over its hand. It seemed to understand, but could not speak. Or did it not want to speak? It turned it's skinny three finger hand around and there was a tiny device in the palm of it. The device was glowing. He pressed into the strap, which triggered the device to create a large glowing ball, larger than its hand. A large glowing ball was now greeting Danelaw and the men.

Danelaw said, 'Show me what it does, but don't throw that thing at me otherwise it's the last thing you'll do.'

The alien raised its arm and the ball did not move. However, as soon as he did a throwing motion the ball travelled about ten feet away from them all. The alien did not try and throw it too far. The ball just sat on the ground not doing anything.

Danelaw said, 'I thought they exploded? They did on us.'

The alien tapped the device on the side and the ball exploded. There were glowing pieces everywhere. The pieces then started to reform immediately, and the alien put his hand out and pulled it back. The ball shot back to his hand and sat there glowing. Danelaw was ecstatic. He got the men to take all the devices from the hands of the severed arms. Eight or so devices. More than enough he thought. He looked at the alien and told it not to worry, as it would be going with them. He told it that it could be useful. Danelaw did not think it would be, but he didn't want to kill the pathetic little thing.

His men started using these devices and could throw them over large distances. They started bombarding buildings with them. It was great to see the destruction with these balls, and the flying aliens not knowing what to do. They did not like to see their own weaponry being used against them. If the flying aliens flew too close to the men on the ground, the men would then hurl these balls at them. The men took a couple of flying aliens down when they did this, while other men were still targeting and bringing buildings down at the foundations. The flying aliens were desperately trying to rescue people from crumbling buildings, whilst also trying to evacuate other buildings being bombarded with these balls. Danelaw was so happy that the battle was going their way. The flying aliens had summoned some skiffs from somewhere and were loading them with those rescued. Little orange aliens on the skiffs were now throwing glowing balls down onto Danelaw's men below. It didn't do much, as the men met fire with fire. They were throwing balls back at them causing collisions of the balls in mid-air, resulting in explosions and a stalemate. Danelaw could see the skiffs filling up quickly. He looked down at his little alien and it just cowered. He just thought that there was no point taking his anger out on it and left it alone. His men had destroyed many buildings in the city.

There must have been fifteen skiffs now, with what looked like hundreds on them. The skiffs whirred off and flew out of the city, towards mountains visible in the distance. Danelaw knew that this mission was going to take longer than they first anticipated, or Archer said it would. He ordered his men to follow the skiffs and head for the mountains. He was determined to finish this attack. They left the city with structures destroyed, and dead or injured everywhere. It looked chaotic behind them. The chase was now on to get to the mountains. His men were quick, but the skiffs were quicker. The huge flying aliens were swooping down towards them with some sort of energy weapon, now they were out of the city. The aliens only had the men to aim at. The blasts were starting to hurt Danelaw and his men, as their energy levels were depleting. The men were weakening, along with the fact they were running to the mountain area, where the weather conditions were becoming poorer. They had never experienced this cold weather, having been under the ozone shield all their lives, and it was starting to show. The men were also getting anxious, an emotion they had never felt before. Danelaw could see that this was going to get worse. Using the glowing balls his men managed to bring down a few skiffs, but with the huge aliens attacking continuously from above they could not bring anymore skiffs down. The skiffs all seemed to be heading for the same mountain range. Danelaw believed they would be able to corner them, as he thought the skiffs would not make it over the top of these high, white covered mountains. He expected the gradient would be too high for the skiffs. As they got closer to the mountains, to Danelaw's surprise, he could see the skiffs were landing at the base of it. The aliens and humans were jumping off the skiffs. He noticed some sort of tube all the way up the side of the mountain. As Danelaw and his men got closer, the men took aim at the tube. Their aims felt random and far from the intended target. Danelaw knew they needed get closer and quickly, and wanted his men to up their pace. As they got within around half of a mile, they could see clearly now that the tube contained a track system with some sort of train at the bottom of the mountain. This must have been set up by the aliens in the past. As they got even closer, the train looked full and was starting to move. They took aim again, but missed miserably. The train shot along the track and accelerated at astonishing speed into the tube and up the mountain. It reminded them of the trains back home in the United Kingdom. As Danelaw and his men reached the base of the tube he had an idea. They would climb and follow the last train that went up the tube. Unexpectedly, the huge flying aliens swooped down and destroyed their own tube. The men looked up in terror and defeat. They would have to climb these mountains to get to the top now, with the assumption this is where the trains had gone to. Danelaw, knowing the men were utterly spent, told them to break out their tents and rest. They would start again in the morning.

Chapter Twenty

The skiffs from New York city were now reaching the market. Everyone was rushing out to them to see if they could help. There were injured in every one of the skiffs, and they rushed them into the market area. The doctors they had were trying to do their best for the injured, and Vaughn's medicines were helping immensely. Cecilio, Annette and a few others jumped into an empty skiff. They were going to go and help the Gogortasana that were left in the city. They were just about to leave, when Nittil flew his skiff into view and set it right down in front of them. The skiff was full to the brim with aliens and people alike.

Nittil jumped down and raced over, waving his arms screaming, 'Don't go. The Gogortasana commander said that they would hold them back as long as they could, and that Cecilio should get ready for what is coming…..and it's definitely coming! Protect their families and all the people that are left.'

Cecilo shook his head, 'We must do something,' he said.

He nearly got to the controls of the skiff, but Nittil jumped up on the skiff and put his hands on Cecilio's back.

'Let them go,' he said, 'And honour what they have done to save many lives.'

Cecilio looked down with a tear in his eye.

'They are my friends,' he said, 'And I will do as they wish.'

He then powered down the skiff.

'We will be ready,' Cecilio said.

Cecilio got to work immediately. He got everyone into the market that were unable to fight and got them to put the shield up. They put it up, and he told them only if there was an order to retreat should they lower part of the shield and let them back in. He also had a heated exchange with Annette and all the humans that wanted to help them.

Cecilio said, 'It was us who started this fight, and it should be only us that have to fight it.'

Annette and the others disagreed with this and said that the soldiers from the UK were now attacking them now too, and not just attacking the aliens. In the centuries after the nuclear attack the UK had never even bothered to come to their assistance or offer them aid. The aliens had done more for them over the past four years, and so they felt they had no allegiance to these soldiers from the UK. Cecilio only agreed for them to be a back up to his troops. Cecilio's troops would be front and centre, even though his troops had been depleted. Cecilio and his troops got their spears together. Driving them into the rock face, with spears linked together, they formed a twelve-foot-high shield of protection. It was at the foot of two adjoining cliffs, across the gap between the cliffs, that led into a prairie. The shield and the troops were about a quarter of a mile away from the entrance to the market. Then, with another two sets of spears driven into the rock face, they created an even larger shield, that must have been around twenty foot high. It was very impressive. Any attacking soldiers might be able to jump this with their strength, but it would be a struggle, as Cecilio also planned to get the Mbalame to attack from the air. If they did jump the shield, they would have used a large amount of energy, which would slow them down. Cecilio just stood there looking at the shield, with his hands on his hips, thinking if there was anything else they could do to withstand this upcoming attack. Annette joined him.

'We are ready,' she said, 'Let them bring whatever they have got for us.'

Cecilio looked down on the small girl and smiled. Annette always impressed him.

She looked up at him and said, 'Are you ready, Cecilio?'

'I think so,' he said, but did not sound as certain as she was. 'I wish we had more people. If they find the pass behind us, as the other way in, then we are finished. We can't afford to send any other troops to protect it. We need all we have.'

Annette, in her own positive way just said, 'You worry too much, Cecilio. No-one apart from Nittil's group have ever got through there, and I doubt if these idiots will.'

Cecilio laughed and walked back with Annette to his troops.

Chapter Twenty One

From back at the base, Archer told the flight captain to fly the transport ship as low as they could over the market to frighten the people. He wanted the men to drop in behind the shield that the aliens had put up, but there was no chance of that. As soon as they lowered the ramp, the multi-coloured Mbalame flying aliens bombarded them. It did nothing to hurt the men. These aliens just seemed to have stun weapons. The blasts were powerful, and the sheer amount of blasts going up the ramp meant the men could not leave the ship. They would have no chance of evacuating the ship that way. They would have to land and come in on foot. They wanted to land in the prairie below the market, but the other alien troops had set up camp there. These aliens were firing up at the ship from the prairie. The ship needed to go to the next biggest area of open land it could find. It landed on the other side of the shield, in a clearing that all could see. Archer told the men on the ship to make camp. He decided that this tactic would make the aliens and humans in the market area terrified of what was to come. Archer told them that they would then attack on the following morning. The night would be long for the aliens and humans, as they knew what the soldiers had done to most of their friends back in New York City.

Cundill got the elite unit together and Archer gave them their orders. This unit was to move overnight. They set off for the pass in the mountains and planned to attack the aliens from behind. Abbott, Sherlock and the other six in the unit were making good progress in the dark. They had to go around the mountains, which surrounded the market area. They could not go over the mountains, as this would take them days. With the sheer face of the mountains, there was no way to climb them. The whole unit was in dark mode, and lucky they were. There was a huge number of flying aliens out tonight. They did not know what the alien's eyesight was like. In the dark, the unit was nearly invisible. The unit had been moving for hours now, and they could see in the distance that the sun was beginning to rise. They still had nearly a quarter of the distance to go. So, Abbott being in charge now, after Nineham was put in charge of the mission in the East, got the unit to increase their pace. They reached the foot of the mountain and could see the entrance to the pass. The entrance was above them and around a hundred foot up.

The sun started to rise, as it was now early morning. Abbott contacted Cundill and told him they were nearly there, and had not been detected. Cundill was pleased and informed Abbott that he was going to start the attack. Abbott acknowledged this and told Cundill that him and his men would head into the pass, and if there was a big enough area then him and his men would take a break, eat and sleep to try and regain their strength. Cundill was not happy with this, but understood. He said, 'Don't be too long. We need your surprise attack, as soon as possible.'

Abbott signed off and they all started to climb. It did not take them long to get to the entrance of the pass. They went into the entrance. It was quite narrow, but they could move quick enough. In the distance, they could hear the battle begin. Maybe half way down the pass, they came upon an open area which would allow all of them to spread out and rest. Abbott told the men to take out their sleeping bags, as they would be resting here for a few hours.

Cundill got all the men in order. In front of the men, they had set up four of the guns they had stolen from the dead aliens back in the city fight. They were going to use the alien's guns against them to frighten and anger them. These weapons were powerful. By using these weapons, it was hoped it would save them having to pound down the shield and exhaust them. Unfortunately for the men the guns were so heavy that although they could carry them, they would not be able to jump over that twenty-foot shield with them. The men made some trestles to sit them on and would let the weaker men fire on the shield, while the enhanced soldiers jumped the shield and engaged on the other side. Cundill took out the little bot Archer had given him, and Archer's holographic image came up.

Archer told them all, 'Good luck. You have your orders. Leave no-one alive,' and then he was gone.

Cundill stored the bot and confidently marched out to the front of the men. He stood there for a few seconds, and then raised his arm and dropped it crying out, 'Attack.' The guns started blazing and were bouncing off the shield. Laser blasts were going everywhere and dust was flying. The men charged past Cundill, speeding towards the shield at full pace, while the others kept firing. Cundill just stayed where he was. He would join in when the battle had raged for a few hours. Perhaps, after Abbott and his unit had attacked. Cundill was not going to risk his own life! He was a coward really unbeknown to many. He never did join the battle!

Cecilio stood back from the shield, but at the front of his soldiers. He could tell they were apprehensive, as he was also, but did not want to show it. He had to be strong for them. The night had been long and they were all anxious. Most were very young, especially Annette's group of humans. Cecilio just hoped they had all had enough training and they stayed close together. Cecilio was shocked into reality, when the outrageous soldiers started firing at the shield with the Gogortasana's weapons. This nearly made Cecilio sick. He could not believe the egregious behaviour of these soldiers, as they used dead being's weapons back on their own beings. Cecilio turned around to see his own soldiers, some were crying and all looked petrified. He thought they were going to turn and run. Annette and her unit stepped forward. Cecilio seeing this smiled at their heroism, but put his hands up to pause them. Cecilio cleared his throat and shouted over the blasts hitting the shield, 'Friends, stand firm. The attack has started and they are using our weapons against us. We have to remember they took these from our dead friends. We have to honour them by fighting these things with all we have got, and probably more. I will stand and fight. Who is with me?'

It went quiet, apart from the blasts in the background. Cecilio thought he might be on his own, then all together a great roar went up and they all stepped forward. Weapons were at the ready, and the Mbalame took to the skies. Cecilio knew this would be a long drawn out fight, but he would keep his people and his new human friends safe, as long as he was alive.

Annette, at the back with her unit, grabbed hold of Innex.

'I have a mission for you,' she said. 'I want you to go to the forest and try to find Vaughn. We are going to need his help and hopefully his people.'

Innex was not happy with this, as he wanted to stay and fight.

So Annette said, 'Don't worry. There will still be a fight when you return.'

Cundill's soldiers were flinging themselves at the shield, that Cecilio and his men had erected with their spears earlier between the rock faces. Some soldiers got over, but the Mbalame's firing knocked many of the soldiers backwards with the power of the Mbalame's weapons. The handful that had got over were causing chaos though. They were scattering Cecilio's men, using their strength. Cecilio ran over and engaged two of them himself. The soldiers were a lot stronger than Cecilio, but Cecilio was not going to use strength to deal with them. He spun two spears between his four arms with mesmerising speed. The soldiers kept going straight at Cecilio, but he just kept blocking their blows and putting them off balance. It meant they could not use that amazing strength of theirs. His plan was to wear them out, and lessen the power of the soldier's shields. Then he could do some damage to them with his spears. The two soldiers he had been engaging were slowing now and starting to breathe more heavily. This is my chance Cecilio thought. As he went to thrust his spear into one of them they seemed to know his intentions, and leapt back over the shield. Cecilio took this as a small victory though, but this would not be for long. His men had also been fighting courageously and sent all the soldiers back over the shield. Cecilio suspected this was going to be a very long day.

Abbott awakened and all he could hear was the cries of the battle. He laid there smiling to himself. It must be going well he surmised. His earpiece was buzzing and he answered it. It was Cundill in a panic.

178

'Where are you, Abbott? We have been going at it for six hours now and we are not getting anywhere fast. Get here immediately,' he commanded.

Abbott replied, 'Yes, Sir,' straight away and signed off.

He smiled. They had slept a lot longer than he had expected. They must have been more exhausted than he realised. They would be well rested and ready for the battle ahead. Abbott was not about to rush though, for a person like Cundill.

He woke the others and they had some breakfast from their supplies. They sat in the clearing, laughing and joking. All along they listened to the hollows of despair coming from the battle. It was like a joke to them. All the men got their gear together and were getting ready to leave to join in the battle. At the opening to the next section of the pass ahead of them, that they needed to go through to get to the battle, they heard a weird muffled voice.

The voice said, 'Can I help you, gentlemen?'

Abbott did not turn around, but just said, 'We don't need any help.'

The voice came back, 'I hope you're not going to try and go through the last stretch of this pass.'

Abbott, still not turning, said 'We are going straight through.'

The voice came calmly back and said, 'Let me put it another way. You are not going through the pass.'

Abbott, who was now very annoyed, turned and looked at where the voice was coming from. It looked like an average size human with a cape and hood on, so you could not see it's face. It could have been an alien, but the shape perceived from the cape outline did not fit any of the descriptions of aliens he had been told about before.

Abbott said, 'We are going through, unless you have an army back there. If you do, we are still going through!'

His men laughed at this comment. The life form just stood there unmoved.

Confidently it said, 'You will have to go through me to get into the remainder of the pass.'

The men laughed again, except for Abbott.

He turned to the men and said, 'Looks like our first casualty of this war.'

The men now started moving towards the life form, not really bothering to get ready to fight. In their heads, eight men against one body ahead of them was not going to be an issue, and they did not think they were going to need to fight it. This was a serious misjudgement. A few hours later after this confrontation, Abbott woke in the most pain he had ever been in. His jaw had been broken. He looked over to the men, who were in even worse states. They were all writhing in pain on the floor of the clearing. Abbott got to Sherlock, who had a broken arm and possibly ribs. He was struggling to breathe. He gestured towards Sherlock, questioning what had happened. Sherlock was holding back tears and speaking slowly through gritted teeth, because of the pain.

'Well Sir, that thing did not wait. It came at us. You had just got your shield up, but it did no good. It moved like lightning. The power it possessed was nothing like we have ever seen before. It hit you and your shield slowed the blow, but it got through and you were launched across this clearing. We all dropped the gear off our backs ready to fight it. It was useless though. I have never seen anything that fast and strong. It just tore through all of us. We tried to fight it, but we were scattered from side to side all over the place. We were on the floor and it stood in the centre of us. It felt like it was admiring its success. It must have been checking us out, as it then pushed its hand through our shields, pulled our earpieces out, and crushed them under foot. It then calmly just walked away back down the pass, like nothing had happened.'

After Sherlock had explained all of this, he passed out with the pain. Abbott could not believe that this had happened to them. They had never been bested like this by one single being. He just stood there wondering how they were going to get out of here in the injured states they were all in. They all had serious injuries. Abbott just hoped that Archer would want to know where his men were and send some help. Then Abbott sloped down to the floor and passed out again.

Chapter Twenty Two

Back in the UK, Miss Che had Chantelle, Evan and Joan in her London apartment. They were discussing the tactics to get to the General's body. They worried that Evan was too close to the General to go, and could be a liability to the mission. Chantelle and Joan were not good at espionage, so they would remain behind too. On the other hand, this was where Miss Che shined, and so they decided Miss Che should go. She took the little alien with her as he would be useful, because of his size and ingenuity. Chantelle had given Miss Che her medbot as well, which Miss Che would ask her where she got that from at some point, but one problem at a time Miss Che thought. The medbot would be highly useful. Miss Che and the alien went back to Lincoln. The alien stayed hidden in her backpack. She kept getting weird looks from people, as her bag occasionally moved when the alien moved within it. She had to tell people it was her dog in there. They reached Lincoln and she got her car out. She drove past the crematorium. The amount of security was breath-taking. This peeked her interest even more. Why would a dead body need this amount of security, no matter who you were? She turned around and went back again to see if there were any soldiers there too. There was to her dismay. She would not be able to take the direct route she had wanted to. She stayed in a local hotel nearby and waited until dark. Later that night, she headed back towards the crematorium. Earlier she had noticed an old abandoned church, not far from the crematorium. So, she drove up as far as she dare to the church, hoping there were no soldiers around in dark mode. Miss Che broke into the church, and then made sure her phone was linked to the medbot. She gave the medbot to the alien. The alien and medbot set out towards the crematorium. The alien was so small that it could hide under hedges and behind objects, that Miss Che simply couldn't. It avoided security without issues and made its way towards the vents in the building's walls. There were lasers and security bots everywhere in these vents.

Miss Che thought that was it and it would have no chance of getting through, but the clever little alien had made a device that turned off lasers without being detected. When the device went near a security bot, it caused the security bot to reverse its direction and turn around. Miss Che was really liking this little alien. How did it do these things? It got to the vent above the General's body, and dropped the medbot into the room. The alien waited there. Miss Che started moving the medbot towards the General's body immediately. To her surprise, there was no actual security in this room. Perhaps they thought there was enough security outside, that little to none was required inside. She flew the medbot up to the General, as she wanted to see his heart first. She flew the medbot up to his chest, and the medbot cut into the body with its little laser. She drove it along veins and arteries, and into his heart. The medbot scanned the heart and found no trauma to it. So, Miss Che knew that this was not the way he had died, despite what Archer had reported. She then sent the medbot around the General's organs. Everything she could think of, as the main organs that could have caused death. Being an assassin, she did however have quite a good knowledge of ways to die. So, the next organ to look at would be his brain, as there was nothing obvious in the kidneys, liver and stomach. Moving up inside the body, towards his brain, was when security bots were detected inside the General's body. She could not believe it. She had never seen these bots inside a body before. She would have to be careful to get her medbot past them. She hid the medbot behind a bone and watched the security bots movements. There must have been around a dozen security bots in his body. She waited, and after a while there was a gap, so she took it. Without detection she passed them, and reached the brain with her bot. The medbot's sensors activated almost as soon as it entered the brain. The scans were off the chart. The trauma in the brain was immense. The medbot flew in closer, and even with her untrained eye she could see little laser blast marks in his brain. She was convinced now that, as she had suspected, it was Archer who had killed the man and now she had the proof of it. As she was beginning to remove the medbot from the General, one of the security bots spotted it. The chase was on. She hoped the security bots did not communicate with security outside, but she found out quickly that they could. She could hear the alarms and men running everywhere. She flew the medbot towards the nose, with the security bots following immediately behind it. She had to swerve the medbot and hide behind bones and muscles, as she tried to outmanoeuvre them and get to the nose to get out of the body. Security bots were blocking the way to the nose, so she directed it towards the ear and out instead. She flew the medbot up to the vent. The security bots were still chasing, and despite their small size they made a huge noise. To Miss Che's relief, as soon as the medbot got close to her little alien friend, all the security bots turned around and went back to the body. The medbot just got into the vent, when the rest of the security personnel burst into the room. The alien retrieved the bot and went back along the vent system, whilst the security personnel were removing the security bots from the body to see what had occurred. This gave the alien time to make his way back, which to Miss Che seemed to take a long time. She stayed hidden in the church, as she could hear security everywhere outside. They seemed to be moving in her direction. The alien came running into the church.

'We need to be going,' it said.

She grabbed the little thing and threw it in her backpack. She would say sorry for that later. No time now, as she ran out the back into the darkness. She could hear security a little way off, so she kept running. All the while she was thinking, if there are soldiers in dark mode she would be captured and that would be it. Thankfully she did not come across any. Perhaps, they were at the crematorium. She got her car out and they were away. They stayed in the hotel for the rest of the night and then set off back to London at sunrise.

They told the others what they had found. Evan was devastated, but not shocked. He always suspected there was foul play, and Archer would have had something to do with it. Chantelle knew who they had to get hold of too. It had to be Simmons who had something to do with this. Archer would not have been able to do this by himself. They planned to go and find Dr Simmons and go to the communications room on the base, so they could inform the rest of the men. Hopefully that should stop the attack Archer was co-ordinating. The men had the utmost respect for the General before his death, and the General had been the only one they took orders from. They only ever saw the General as their commanding officer, and this would make them want to hold Archer accountable for his actions.

Chapter Twenty Three

Back in America, the Gogortasana and Mbalame had done well. They had kept the number of soldiers getting over the shield to a minimum. There were hundreds trying to get over, but only a handful had managed it, as the alien's powerful weapons had kept knocking them back. However, as it got later in the day, then both alien races were starting to tire. As they tired, more soldiers were getting over and causing a lot of damage. The number of injuries were rising. Cecilio was busy battling two soldiers again, and hadn't noticed another six had also got over. He hadn't, and wouldn't give the order to Annette and her unit to engage, so they stood there and watched from about hundred yards away. Annette just paced around in front of her unit. They saw some of the Gogortasana get scattered by these six. The Mbalame had swooped in again to help. This, at least, slowed the soldiers. The Gogortasana seemed to be slow to get up, and Annette knew they would not stand a chance. She had had enough of watching her friends get hurt. It was time to act. She did not want to see them die.
Annette turned to her group, 'Get your weapons ready. We are going in.'
There were a few murmurings that Cecilio had not given the order, but Annette said, 'We have no time to wait. Do you want your friends to get hurt anymore?'
They all screamed, 'No.'
Annette turned and said, 'Let's get to the fight then.'
She quickly told Nittil and three others to go and help Cecilio, and shouted, 'Charge.'
She was off and running, with the others in hot pursuit. Annette was lightening quick. She was always fast as a kid, but got faster and faster with age. No-one could keep up with her, not even the men. She could see one of the soldiers approaching one of the Gogortasana's that was lying on the ground still. It was obvious what was about to happen, so Annette went straight for the soldier with all the speed she could. She was about ten feet away, with the soldier stood over the fallen alien,

so she launched herself. She spun through the air, pulling the bar out from behind her back and extending it into her spear. She went over the top of the solider and cracked him across the head on the way past. She landed on her feet about ten feet away on the other side. She slid to a crouched position, with one hand on the floor for balance and the other hand behind her back holding the glowing spear. Annette looked up to see the solider just standing there. That blow would normally have split a human's head clear open, but he just stood there. The soldier rolled his head, and then turned and looked at Annette with a wink and a smile.

Annette stood upright and waved him over and said, 'Let's dance then, big boy,' doing her best to antagonize him. This comment did the trick and infuriated the soldier, who then charged at Annette. She was happy about this, as it gave the fallen Gogortasana time to get up and run. The soldier was fast for such a big man, but Annette side stepped him with ease and smashed his leg with her spear. This knocked him flying to the ground. The solider flipped himself up onto his feet immediately, taking Annette by surprise. She was still too quick for him, as she side stepped and dodged his next volley, leaving him strewn on the ground.

The soldier was slower getting up this time, but was determined to with Annette's continuous goading. 'I thought you guys were meant to be good fighters? Yet you can't even hit a little girl,' she said mocking him.

He charged her again, this time even quicker and throwing even more powerful punches. Yet again she just kept dodging and weaving. The big soldier was starting to puff and pant. Annette, on the other hand, was not even sweating. She put the soldier on the ground for the third time and he sat there breathing very heavily. She gave him a tap on his shoulder with her spear and this time he winced. She knew she had finally hurt him. In her naivety, she let the soldier get back to his feet. As soon as he did, he leapt back over the shield, just making it. He was totally drained. When he landed on the other side of the shield he shouted something back at Annette. She had gone to help more of her friends, so did not hear what he said.

They all fought, until it was going dark. Then even the soldiers needed to rest. A couple of times, they tried to be sneaky and attack using their dark mode, but gave up eventually once they realised they could not get over the shield. Cecilio had been clever and placed motion sensors on top of the shield, so knew they were coming and they forced them back immediately.

Cecilio walked through his men, thanking everyone he could for their efforts today. He then went to the medical hut they had set up to talk to the injured and keep their spirits up. They were all grateful he went to see them in person. On the way out of the medical hut, he spotted Annette's group. He marched directly for them. He hated the fact that kids had to get involved in this fight. The group were sat around five or six little campfires, along with the Mbalame. The Mbalame got on really well with the kids, but he had no idea how they communicated with each other. They just laughed and joked with each other. Cecilio loved that.

'Where's Annette?' he asked one boy.

The boy pointed and said, 'Over there.'

She was sat on her own around a little campfire.

Cecilio stormed over and said, 'I did not give the order for you and your unit to join the fight.'

He was so mad that his English language subconsciously reverted back to his own language.

'I didn't want you in the fight. We were doing fine. You need to get used to taking orders. Are we clear?' he said.

Annette sat there for a while, then put down what she was eating, pulled back her hood and looked up at the big alien.

'I love you too, Cecilio,' she said.

Cecilio had to hold back a laugh, still trying to look serious. He went to walk off, but quickly turned to Annette's group, as they had all been watching the exchange.

He nodded and said, 'Thank you, men.'

In the light of the fires he noticed the happiness in their faces at this comment, as he had always just called them kids up until now. He turned back again and started walking.

He then stopped abruptly and over his shoulder said, 'Annette. Thank you as well. You fought well today.'

He heard Annette get up and go over to her group. They were all laughing and joking. Cecilio went over to a group of Gogortasana. He had grown to like and respect these beings. He sat down and they all nodded towards him. They respected him as well. Cecilio sat brooding a little knowing that the next day would be another long hard day. Their numbers were down due to injuries. He would have no choice but to use everyone tomorrow, including Annette's kids. He did not like the thought of this. He was brought out of his thoughtful trance, when a Gogortasana handed him some food. For the first time today, he realised how hungry he was and just started to eat.

Cundill was furiously trying to get in touch with Abbott and his group. He wanted to know why they didn't attack and join the fight. He was not even receiving static from their earpieces. Archer suddenly got in touch. He did not like Cundill's report. 'That's very disappointing,' Archer said, 'I wanted to be in that market today. I want all of them. You will have to forget about Abbott and the rest. They must have gone AWOL. We have not got enough men to go find them right now, but find them we will. I will send you Nineham and his men, when their ship is fixed. He has successfully finished his mission.'

This last sentence from Archer was in a sarcastic tone, aimed at Cundill's inability to get anywhere with his mission.

'I want to be in that market soon, Captain,' Archer re-iterated and signed off.

Cundill was left seething in his room on the ship after this conversation. He would probably take it out on one of his men later. He just sat mulling on the idea of having Nineham around, as they really did hate each other.

The following morning, Cecilio was up bright and early. It was so early, he saw the sunrise. He marvelled what a beautiful start to the day this was. He was then brought back to reality, as the lasers the soldiers had stolen from the dead Gogortasana started firing at the shield again. Cecilio went to quickly grab something to eat, as it would not be long before the attack started again.

He had just sat down, when a human boy burst in shouting, 'Cecilio.'

Cecilio stood up immediately.

'What is it, boy?' he said.

The boy came to a halt, panting in front of him.

Still struggling to breathe he said, 'You need to see this, Cecilio.'

Cecilio asked if he had time to eat but the boy said, 'They need you now.'

'They?' Cecilio asked.

The boy grabbed his arm, 'Quick,' he said, as they headed outside.

He noticed as he got outside the lasers were no longer firing at the shield. They were actually firing towards the soldier's camp outside the shield. Cecilio ran down to the shield. He couldn't see much with the laser blasts flying and so much dust. He was sure he could see something flying around the soldiers. Then all of a sudden, a couple of skiffs came into view. Someone must have scattered the soldiers enough that they could get through. The skiffs came directly at the shield. Cecilio was not going to drop the shield. It was too much of a risk, especially if the skiff was full of soldiers and this was a ruse. The skiffs reached the shield, and they were full to capacity with humans and aliens. As soon as Cecilio saw the gaunt and terrified looks of these people, he dropped part of the shield to allow them in. He was willing to take the risk. He could not just leave them out there looking like that. Cecilio did not want the shield down for long though, as the soldiers would become wise to this. The skiffs kept coming. So many of them. He was up to about ten on his count. Then, all at once, lots of Jasny Stern on their bikes started to fly through the shield. There were hundreds of them. They just kept coming. He could see better as the dust subsided, and could see the soldiers had turned and were coming for the shield again. He was going to reform the full shield, when he could see what he thought was one last skiff coming with a few Jasny Stern biking around it. They were nearly at the shield now and it was full of Cecilio's people, the Omorfi Stvar. Huge blaster shots from the skiff were being aimed at the onrushing soldiers. The soldiers were also blasting at the shield now. Cecilio was starting to get

189

anxious. He wanted to save his people and the Jasny Stern, but he also had thousands of lives on his side of the shield to look after. He would hold part of the shield open, as long as he dare. The skiff must have noticed his dilemma, as the skiff seemed to accelerate towards the shield. He was just about to link the spears to reform this part of the shield, when the skiffs and all the bikers shot through. Cecilio linked the spears, but not before some soldiers made it through. Cecilio was quickly joined by some Gogortasana, and they fought them off sending them back over the shield. The skiff was at maximum acceleration and it only just stopped before ploughing into the camp. Cecilio rushed over and was greeted by everyone, both his people, the Jasny Stern and the very thankful humans. They all looked like they had been part of quite an ordeal. One of his own Omorfi Stvar pulled him to one side and took him to his skiff and said, 'Look at who we found over the water on our way here.'

There on his skiff stood a bunch of Tilluke, who were overjoyed to see Cecilio. Cecilio got to work straight away, as it would not take the soldiers long to regroup and they would not be happy. He got everyone ready to fight the soldiers, who were fit enough to fight. Some of the injured also wanted to help, and they would not take no for an answer and would be ready to fight too. The rest he sent back to the market with one of the kids from there, otherwise Cirius would not let all of these new humans and aliens in. Cecilio gathered everyone, now supported by the Jasny Stern and the Omorfi Stvar. For the first time, since this attack started, Cecilio was optimistic about their chances. He could also hold Annette and her group back now. The next two days were a stalemate. The soldiers barely got over the shield, but when they did they were returned to the other side quickly. Innex had also returned. He reported to Annette, who looked a little underwhelmed by what he reported to her.

On the fourth morning, something was different. The battle began as it always did. Then around two hours later a transport ship with Nineham and his men landed next to Cundill's soldier's ship. Thousands of soldiers disembarked to join their colleagues. Near the end of the day they had changed their plan of attack. They had been unable to get enough soldiers over the shield to have any effect, despite the increased numbers of them. Instead of blasting the shield, they started to blast the rock face holding the spears in place. Cundill had them blasting the shield, but it seemed Nineham's influence and intelligence had changed their tactics. The rock face seemed to withstand the barrage. At the end of the evening, as always, the firing stopped and they returned to their camp. Cecilio went up to the shield to inspect the rock face. To his concern, he could see the rock face had begun to crumble in places. He was concerned that a barrage tomorrow could break it further and bring the face down, along with the shield. Cecilio went back to his camp to relay his worse fears. He had expected that the soldiers would destroy the rock face at some time. With the big man in charge, who was Cundill, Cecilio had noticed he was not very tactically aware, so it looked like someone else had come up with this plan of attack. Cecilio planned for the fight to change tomorrow and told them that it would probably be an all-out siege. He gave them all a choice, which was to either stop and fight with him, or go back to the caves. The aliens and humans all together said that they would stay and fight. He gave the order to the Gogortasana and the Tilluke to start blasting the ground around their camp with their powerful weapons, so this would create craters big enough to fit a full-size person in. This was so his men would be able to hide from the soldiers, if they started to fire on them with the stolen Gogortasana weapons again. It would also provide uneven ground, so the soldiers could not run in direct lines at full speed. This should slow them down. To Cecilio's dismay, Annette's unit had also agreed to fight too.

Cecilio took Annette to one side, 'Please go back to the cave and take your unit with you. This is a fight we have to have, but you don't,' he said. He continued, 'These humans we are fighting are your people.'

Annette interrupted and said, 'These things have never been my people. They attacked you all knowing that humans were among you too, but they carried on killing thousands of humans. These people never came to help us, even before you came, when they clearly could have helped. So, no Cecilio. This is our fight too and we will win.'

That night Cecilio sent everyone to bed early, as they would need all their energy and strength for the battle ahead tomorrow. Cecilio could not sleep. He tossed and turned all night long. He got back up for one final look around. He stood at the top of one of the craters, lost in thought. He knew the new day was going to be difficult and he could lose some good people. All these people, both his human friends and alien allies, were under his protection. Cecilio was determined he would not let them down, and he would do all he could to protect them. Cecilio drew himself up to his full height and marched off to get himself ready in his full battle armour. He would wear most of it, apart from that stupid helmet, as he could hardly see out of it! He was ready quickly and outside he went. It was still early, but there were a few of his men up and about. He gave the order for everyone to be up and ready in fifteen minutes, and he meant everyone. Cecilio was not disappointed. Everyone was up and ready for the day ahead. However, the Gogortasana were not too pleased. They were not good in the mornings!

All of his men were now in formation. The time had come. Cecilio was at the head of them all. The Jasny Stern were at the side, ready to swoop in when the shield came down, to hopefully slow the advance of the soldiers. Lutherine was in charge of the Jasny Stern, which delighted Lutherine immensely. He was in awe of Cecilio, which unnerved Cecilio a little. Behind Cecilio were the Omorfi Stvar, along with the Gogortasana. The Mbalame were up in the mountains, ready to fly in and try and protect all the men, when the soldiers got through. The humans were at the back, including Annette's unit. Cecilio still didn't think it was their fight, but the humans were a determined bunch and he had to admit were good fighters too.

At dawn the blasts began as usual. Cecilio and his men were ready. None of the soldiers had tried to start jumping the shield this morning, so the soldiers must have been expecting and hoping the rock face would crumble, allowing them passage to Cecilio and his men. It took about three hours of bombardment, at which time the rock face on both sides gave way and the shield came apart. The soldiers came rushing in within seconds. They were like wild animals, charging forward in no given formation. They were slowed by the craters in the ground that Cecilio's men had created the night before, along with the blasts coming from the swooping Jasny Stern and Mbalame. Cecilio's men had taken a few steps back, watching the onrushing soldiers. So, Cecilio stepped forward and looked at his men, smiled and tipped his head to them. He held in his hand his glowing spears and was spinning them. He turned to face the soldiers and charged towards them screaming. His men must have thought this was madness, but after a few seconds they also started to charge. The Tilluke were in the mountains, and also firing down on the soldiers. From the corner of his eye, Cecilio saw something coming very fast down the mountain face. They seemed to grow in number. Cecilio was hoping this was not more soldiers to attack them, and thankfully this was not the case. As Cecilio reached the charging soldiers, these life forms that had come down the mountain then attacked the charging soldiers from the side. These life forms were dressed in capes and hoods. They charged in and scattered the front rank of soldiers. They seemed to have caught them unaware, and Cecilio was then able to knock some more to the ground. He could see soldiers being knocked all over the place. These caped life forms could fight two soldiers hand to hand with ease, hurt them and knock some out. Cecilio had never been able to do this, without tiring a soldier first. The soldiers quickly split into two groups to help fight the new threat. One group were fighting the new threat, whilst the others continued to fight Cecilio and his men. Many more seemed to be fighting the new threat, so Cecilio's men were managing to push back the remainder of the soldiers. The larger number of soldiers were starting to get the better of these caped life forms, so Cecilio gave an order to the Jasny Stern to provide help. It worked and the soldiers were pushed back a little, but the soldiers were still determined to fight. The caped life forms were starting to tire, but still fighting.

Most of the soldiers that Cecilio and his men had been fighting had retreated back to their camp, so he took some of his men over to help the caped life forms. All the soldiers then quickly retreated to an almighty cheer. Cecilio knew though they would be back tomorrow and angrier. Their retreat was probably just a ploy to regroup and re-evaluate. Cecilio went to find the caped life forms and thank them. There must have been nearly a hundred of them, which amazed Cecilio. So few to cause such carnage. They were all stood there and Annette was there too. Annette noticed him coming and waved him over. She gestured to the caped form stood next to her, 'I take it you know Vaughn?' she said.

The form pulled his hood down and put his hand out to greet Cecilio.

'Long time, no see,' Vaughn said to Cecilio.

Cecilio stood there shocked, not knowing what to say, and then blurted out, 'You're one of them soldiers.'

Cecilio stepped back and grabbed one of his spears, not expecting these forms to be human, as they were clearly stronger than the attacking human soldiers. Vaughn put his hands up quickly.

'Easy friend,' he said, 'We are definitely not one of them.'

Annette moved in between them and said, 'Calm down, Cecilio. It was me who asked for Vaughn's help. I just didn't know if he could come, so I didn't tell you. I knew they had the soldier's strengths and shields, but they have always lived in America, so knew they were not part of these UK soldiers that are attacking us right now.'

'Who are they?' Cecilio asked, still holding his spear ready.

Vaughn stepped in and said, 'We are outcasts. Our group was thrown out of the UK for trying to save lives and do the right thing. This was decades ago. Our ancestors were a group called the SAS. We had to go into hiding here in America.'

A group of humans came up behind Cecilio and Annette, and heard this conversation.

They started shouting, 'Your people caused all this hurt. They dropped the nuclear bombs.'

It was an emotionally charged moment. Vaughn's group stepped back away from them, but Vaughn stayed where he was.

'That was nothing to do with our people,' he said. 'They had already been cast out by Palethorpe. The rumour was that Palethorpe was the one who dropped the bombs.'

The humans were enraged, 'It killed millions,' they shouted. Cecilio stood there listening to all of this. He seemed interested, but did not want to get involved in the conversation for some reason.

Vaughn went on, 'Well the SAS protect the prime minster, and at that time Palethorpe had just become that. He was the scientist, who had designed the formula for the enhanced human programme, and also designed the shield devices inserted in the body. The SAS had volunteered for this programme. He became prime minster not long after his programme had been completed. After a few years in charge, he had become a very powerful and influential person.

However, he had started to not trust the 'enhanced' SAS humans, as they had begun to question and not obey some of his orders. He began to bring in 'mindless brutes,' as the SAS knew them as, who would follow his orders blindly. The SAS were noticing how Palethorpe thrived on power, and was wanting to control many countries using the SAS. The SAS leader at the time challenged Palethorpe about all of this, and was then cast out to live on a remote island. The rest of the SAS team was then disbanded and cast out as well. Many of them just disappeared, and it was unknown where in the world they had gone.

As time went on, without the SAS, Palethorpe started to secretly influence other countries, and was very interested in their nuclear weapons technology. He used his scientific background, as a cover to gain the trust of these countries. Some countries did not like this, and tried to restrict his and the UK's control over them. Palethorpe was furious about this. He wanted to rule the world, and it seemed like he thought he was the most powerful man in the universe.

Not long after this, a country was attacked. That triggered a domino effect of attacks, with countries attacking each other, but not really knowing who the perpetrators were. It was too late and this destroyed the world.

It was found out that Palethorpe had put a shield up around the UK, just before this first attack. Him and a large number of his brutes disappeared. No one knew where they had gone. All that any of the remaining humans knew was that the shield was up, and no one was able to enter or leave the UK.'

Cecilio had remained silent throughout all of this story Vaughn had told them.

He then asked Vaughn, 'Why would they blame your ancestors for the bombings then?'

Vaughn replied, 'Over the centuries, the story has become confused, with different versions of this story being told.'

Cecilio looked at Vaughn sheepishly and just said, 'We have a fight here and now to deal with.'

He looked back towards Annette, and said, 'Please talk to everyone, as we need everyone for the fight tomorrow.'

He then walked away, leaving Annette to calm everyone down, after which they all went their separate ways for the evening.

Cecilio sat on his camp bed thinking that did not go well and he would need to get everyone back on side tomorrow. He needed togetherness. He did not like the thought that he needed Vaughn's group, as he wasn't sure he could trust them. He just hoped Annette knew what she was doing when she asked them to help.

Over the next couple of days, they battled backwards and forwards. Cecilio had some heavy losses. Vaughn and his group did their best to hold the soldiers back, but even they were struggling. Annette and her unit had replaced the injured, and they were becoming invaluable. They were a great fighting unit. Cecilio was proud of them. He had trained them well. The problem was everyone was starting to lose their stamina, after all these days of battle. The attacking soldiers were slowing too he noticed, but they hadn't taken many losses if any, so could rest more. Cecilio was desperately thinking that they needed a way to penetrate the soldier's shields, otherwise they were all doomed. In the evening he walked around the camp. He was slightly injured and very drained. He did not want to show this weakness to his people and tried not to limp.

He stopped and sat with Annette and quietly said, 'Can I tell you something?' and jokingly smiled and said, 'I'm spent.' Annette smiled back and said, 'So am I.'

This was when Cecilio noticed she was covered in cuts and bruises, and his caring nature became evident.

'Are you ok?' I haven't had much time to check on you lately or the kids,' he said.

He moved over to sit beside her and put one of his huge arms around her.

Annette just leaned into him and whispered, 'I take offence at you calling us kids, but yes I'm ok. Just a bit banged up. I'll be ready to go again tomorrow.'

'Sorry,' Cecilio said, 'But with the fight, I forget your unit are just kids. They have fought better than most adults, human or alien. It has been an honour to fight with you. I'm getting a little desperate now. Our losses are great and their losses are small to nil. We can't keep going like this. We might have to retreat to the caves.'

Annette looked at him shocked, but not surprised by what he said. She said nothing, but leaned in even further into his side. Cecilio sighed, 'Tomorrow's another day. Luck might favour us.'

The following morning, Cundill was sat in his room on the ship. He was still sulking about Nineham's idea to start firing at the rock face, instead of directly at the shield, which was Cundill's orders from day one. Of course, he told Archer that it was his idea and this had brought down the shield, and they would be in the market soon. It was starting to upset Archer that they had not made it into the market yet. So, Cundill went outside the ship to see how things were going. He did not like to get too close to the fighting, because he might have to fight and that petrified him. It was chaos out there. The guns fired now and again, but with the men on the battlefield they had to be more selective now and fire at this new threat that had taken their attention. There was fighting going on everywhere. There were flying aliens swooping in, the biker aliens flying around the area slowing Cundill's men's progress, the huge aliens with their glowing spears fighting smartly using their height and speed to their advantage, and humans fighting with them as well which really annoyed Cundill. He thought how dare the humans fight with them. Even Cundill noticed that all their numbers, both alien and human, had now dwindled. So, Cundill made his way back to the ship, so he could speak to Archer in private. It took a while for Archer to get through to Cundill exactly what he wanted him to do. Cundill then went to the bottom of the ramp, and sat watching the fighting with all the toing and froing between the opposing sides.

Men were rushing past him, shouting as they went, 'Are you going to join the fight?'

He replied, 'All in due course.'

He just sat watching the battle, and then a few hours before sunset he got up. He walked over with a purpose. He had been watching for so long, even he could see where the fighting was the weakest. He walked to that position, but did not join the fight. It was still too fierce for him. Cundill crept around the men, and to the side of the aliens and humans. At all costs, he stayed out of the conflict. He was in dark mode, which in this light was worthless. He hoped he could get past the aliens and humans without detection. He thought he had been spotted a few times, but with the fighting they appeared to be too preoccupied to follow him, along with their low numbers so one man was not important. Had he been spotted though? He managed to slip past everyone and headed for the market. Archer knew the market was ray shielded, so he hoped someone would be outside to allow the aliens back in. To Cundill's luck, there was a little man sat outside on a rock. Cundill wore a chest camera, which Archer had made him wear in case he forgot his orders. Archer knew who this man on the rock was. It was Ciruis, the leader of the market. Cundill silently went up to him, catching him by surprise, and grabbed him by the shirt. He was going to throttle him, when Archer said in Cundill's earpiece, 'Let him go, I'll talk to him.'

Cundill let Cirius go, and Cirius stepped back. A little holographic image appeared from Cundill's camera. A small image of Archer stood in mid-air.

'Greetings. It is nice to speak to you. Unfortunately, not in person. My name is General Vinson Archer,' Archer said to Cirius.

Ciruis did not answer and so Archer continued, 'Sorry about my soldier. He is just keen to get into the market, as am I. If you allow us to enter, then I give you my word that no humans will be harmed. We just want that alien scum. I know you have had it hard. I have been watching you for years now, as did the General before me. We have grown to respect your ability to survive against all odds. We would not want to end your existence now, would we?'

To this, Cirius had had enough and said, 'You have been watching us and you have done nothing to help us. We have been dying for years and you have done nothing. Why?'

Archer came back and said, 'I have only been in charge for a short while, so I have not had chance. I agreed with the General before me, when he thought we could not assist you. We have had our own problems.'

Cirius said, 'We have been starving.'

Archer just replied, 'Not my problem, I'm afraid. If you let us in, I will start to help you. I know the aliens attacked you.'

Cirius was angry now. Angrily he said, 'They might have attacked us, but every day since that they have gone out of their way to help us. More than I can say about you. We have been like this for decades and no help from anyone. With the aliens help over the last four years, it's been the best I have ever experienced, and so say all the people. So, no I will not grant you entrance to the market. I don't trust you and your men.'

After listening to this, Archer's patience was reducing. 'You will not speak to me like that,' he said to Cirius, 'I'm a General.'

'Not of me,' Cirius said.

That was enough for Archer, 'I tire of this little man, Captain. Sort this out will you.'

Then Archer's hologram seemed to turn around and he said, 'What's going on back there?' and his hologram disappeared. Cundill carried on regardless and grabbed Cirius by the throat. Annette was sure she had seen a presence go past her, but she was busy fighting. She saw off the soldier again, tiring him until he had to fall back. Annette looked back. She was certain she could see a big presence moving towards the market, so she started to make her way back towards the market. She went past Innex and Nittil, who had their hands full with one of the soldiers. She wanted to help them, but she knew following this person was more important. Innex and Nittil would be able to handle it, so she kept going. At that point, she could see a huge man at the gate and he had Cirius in his hands. Doubling her speed, she was on her way to help. She noticed the man then release Cirius, and some floating thing came out of his chest. She was certain Cirius was talking to this thing, as she got closer. Just before she reached them, the floating thing disappeared, and the big man grabbed Cirius by the throat. As Cundill went to squeeze, Annette smacked him in the back of his knee. His shield was up so it had no effect, but he could not have heard Annette coming, so the shock of the strike on the shield was enough to make him drop Cirius. Cirius ran and now the big man's attention was fully on Annette. He looked her up and down and started to laugh.

'Is this who they sent to stop me?' he said sarcastically. 'Go away and play, little girl,' he continued at Annette.

Annette replied, 'I'm more than enough to take you on, you big dope,' spinning her spear all the time. This infuriated Cundill and he came charging at her. She side stepped him as he rushed towards her, catching him with her spear and tripping him. He hit the ground with a huge thud. Sitting up, he looked at her and she smiled and winked at him.

'Is that all you have got? I thought a man of your size would be more of a fight for little me?' she retaliated back.

He jumped to his feet, and went at her throwing punches. Annette was ducking and weaving, using her spear to deflect his blows. She was spinning and jumping all over, and it wasn't long before he hit the floor again. This was like a training game to Annette, but even Annette was starting to tire now as she had been fighting all day again. Cundill seemed to have lots of energy for a soldier. It was like he hadn't fought at all. He came at her again, after her mocking continued. This time she was a little slow and he caught her a glancing blow. With his strength it was enough to send her flying. Annette was dazed a little, but she got up quickly. She was a determined character.

He was mocking her now and saying, 'Not so clever now, little girl.'

Annette still had her wit and said, 'You must be so proud hitting a girl, mustn't you?'

He replied, 'I'm going to shut that mouth of yours.'

The fight between them carried on for about another ten minutes. Annette was nearly spent, but didn't want to show it. She kept mocking him. He knocked her flying again, but this time he caught her even better. She was sprawled on the floor. She turned onto her back and was going to sit up, when the big man came over.

'I'm going to enjoy crushing you, you insolent girl.'

Annette put her hands over her face and braced. She thought that this was the end and shut her eyes. Then she felt something swooping past her and someone saying, 'Don't kill me.'

She opened her eyes and sat up. Just in front of her, Cundill was being held by the throat by an average sized being. Cundill was pounding the being's arm, but it was having little effect. Cundill was being held up by one arm of this being. The being was wearing a cape with a hood. It looked at Cundill and said, 'If you hit my arm once more, then I will squeeze!'

Cundill stopped immediately and started to cry, pleading with it not to kill him. This caped being stood with its back to Annette, so she had no idea who it was and did not recognise the voice. Annette had not seen anyone as strong as this before. Not even Archer soldiers, or Vaughn and his people, could hold this huge man with one arm. This being was doing it with ease and

201

one arm. It was amazing to her. Knowing that Cundill could have killed her, she took pity on him.

She shouted over to this mysterious being and said, 'Please don't kill him.'

It fell quiet at this comment and then all she heard was the being say, 'Are you sure?'

Annette said, 'If you kill him, then we are no better than they are.'

The being stood there, holding Cundill off the ground.

'As you wish,' it said.

Then suddenly it was off running with Cundill still in his hand, like Cundill was a large sack of feathers. Annette could not believe what she was seeing. She just sat and watched in awe of this spectacle. Cundill was yelling all the way, which Annette smirked at. On the way past Nittil and the stricken Innex, the mysterious being also grabbed the soldier fighting the two of them. Not too soon, as he was getting the better of Nittil. The man carried Cundill and this soldier with ease, and stepped in front of the unit of soldiers. Everyone just stopped fighting, as they witnessed this. They were in complete disbelief. The soldiers had never seen such a feat of strength, and they just stood there not knowing what to do. The aliens and humans had pulled back a little, and were slowly moving back to the market, as Cecilio had given the order for this. Some soldiers became brave and decided that they would try and charge this mysterious being, and get Cundill and this soldier back. They had realised this soldier it was holding was actually Nineham. The mysterious being watched them come towards it, and when they around ten feet away, it literally threw Cundill at the oncoming soldiers taking some of them out. Some other soldiers kept coming, so it threw Nineham at them and took them out too. The mysterious being stood there for a few seconds, looking around at the carnage. Then it turned and was gone. The soldiers just stood there, with shocked looks on their faces. They went over to their fallen friends and picked them up. They were battered and bruised, which was something they had never been before. It was time to fall back to their camp and rest for the remainder of the day. The battered Cundill just hoped that thing was not there at the battle tomorrow. With the soldiers retreating for the night, this gave Cecilio and others time to go out onto the battlefield to retrieve all their injured, and get them back to the market area. Cecilio sat worrying all night about the next day and what it could bring. The shield to the market was old and would not last long.

Chapter Twenty Four

It took a week or so to reach the top of the mountain and Danelaw had lost a few good men. Danelaw would end up being part of history, as they had never lost any men before. It was a little unfair on him, as they had never left the shield until now. Usually they would have reached the top of this mountain in hours, but the huge flying aliens were delaying them. They were knocking them down when they could, and setting booby traps all the way up, but what was causing the loss of his men were the cold temperatures. They were just not used to these weather conditions. The temperature behind the shield was always in the early twenty-degree Celsius range, so anything below zero was new to them and they succumb to hypothermia. Danelaw really struggled too, but tried not to show it as he was in charge and had to stay strong for the men. He was perplexed when they did reach the summit though, as the alien's base must have been about two miles back. He could just see it with his binoculars. He could hear his men complaining behind him.

He turned and said, 'We have got this far, men. We can do this. I know it's heavily fortified, but we are British soldiers and we will finish our mission.'

Danelaw had just finished speaking, when the aliens swooped in out of nowhere firing their impressive weapons. We have to get some of those weapons, he thought to himself. They all managed to reach cover just in time, but the aliens had done what they sought to do. They had slowed the soldiers down yet again. Danelaw was actually starting to respect these things and their intelligent tactics. They were the most cunning warriors he had ever faced. He thought it would be a shame to kill them, but an order is an order, and he had never disobeyed one and especially not one from a General. The men were going to continue their mission knowing there would be more obstacles put in their way. The land was uneven, and the aliens had set bombs and trip wires, and anything they could think of. They would swoop in from time to time as well.

Danelaw's men were becoming more and more exhausted, and starting to struggle. They really could not handle these cold conditions. Danelaw knew they were close now, so told them to set up a camp and they started some fires to try and brighten the men's spirits. They all sat and ate their field rations again, which none of them liked. Danelaw told them that they needed one last push tomorrow and they would reach the base. Then, hopefully not long after that they would be able to go home. He knew that was a bit of a white lie, as these aliens would not surrender without putting up a very good fight. Danelaw slept contently that night knowing that they were nearly there.

Chapter Twenty Five

Evan, Chantelle, Miss Che and her little alien friend left Che's apartment. They had decided that Joan should remain behind, as there was nothing else she could do for them, and what they were about to do could put her in danger. Joan was not happy about this, but understood. She just wanted to do something for the dead General. Chantelle went ahead of them, as she needed to get onto the base first. She would tell security at the base entrance that she was doing overtime, to do an early hour experiment in the laboratory. The security questioned her a little about being so early, but many scientists started experiments early, so they relented and allowed her in. Evan could not be seen on the base, as he would be counted as a deserter and put in the cells, so Evan and Miss Che had to enter the base as cleaners. Evan would hide in the back of their van they had hired, as they had made a little compartment for him. The little alien had also made a device that would scramble the security sensors, and so would not detect Evan. They had also made fake identity documents. The plan was to go in an hour earlier than the usual cleaning crew. This would give them enough time to get in undetected. Getting out of the base again could be an issue, but one problem at a time. Chantelle went to her laboratory and turned on all of her machines. She then waited for the signal from Miss Che, at which point she would make her way to the control room. Miss Che rolled her van up to the security barrier check point. The security man came out looking surprised, as he had not seen her before. He waved to the box and a few more guards stood up ready. The lead security guard tapped on her window and she opened it.

'You're not the usual woman,' he said.

Che said, 'No. She's at another job. The company sent them to a more important job. Their words not mine.'

'You're on your own?' the security guard said suspiciously.

'Yes, a lot off sick at the minute,' she replied to him, 'Meaning the company putting more work on me. I'm not happy about it,' Che said trying to act annoyed.

It seemed to work, as the guard seemed to have empathy with her.

'I know what you mean,' he said. 'We have the same problem.' He seemed to lower his guard a little and soften his stance towards Miss Che.

'Can I have your identification, please? While I check it, my colleagues will do a sensor sweep on your van,' he said.

Che passed across her fake identification and hoped it was ok, as she hadn't had time to do it herself, so she had asked Drake for it. She trusted him, but she didn't know who he would have used to forge one. Che sat there feeling a little nervous, but could not show it. She watched the man checking the identification, and was also watching her mirrors keeping an eye on the sensor team. They kept looking at their equipment and banging it a little. It looked like they were trying to make it work better. To Miss Che, everything seemed to be taking too long. This could all be for nothing if they were stopped at this first hurdle. The security guard in the box suddenly stood up and walked out. The sensor team went over to him. There appeared to be an animated conversation. He left them and rounded the van himself. Che was ready, just in case she had to get out of there in a hurry. She moved her window down and he passed her identification back.

He had a dubious look on his face but said, 'Your ID checks out, Freda. Sensor team had a few problems with their kit though.'

Che was ready to get out the van at this statement, but he went on quickly and said, 'They're happy to let you go, as the eyeball check shows nothing suspicious.'

At that point, the laser barrier lowered and the security guards stepped back and waved her through. She did not wait and went straight through. Che sent Chantelle the signal that they had made it in. Che was trying to remember where the control room was. Then the little alien popped his head out of the bag. He looked annoyed, as he did not like being stuffed into the backpack. He pressed something in the bag, and a small holographic map of the base came up at the side of Che. It showed their position and the control room location. They drove to the hangar where the control room was situated and there were some soldiers walking by, so she waited until they went. There was security on the door, but that would not be a problem for Che. Che pulled up right outside the hangar and got out. One of the security came up to her.

'You can't park here,' he said.

Che acted innocent and said, 'Sorry, it's my first day.'

He nodded and turned. Che quickly knocked him out, without any sound. She quickly ran around the van to subdue the other security guard, before he could alert anyone. She let Evan out of the van and Chantelle met them at the door. They needed both Evan and Chantelle, as there would be soldiers manning the control room. Archer wouldn't have anyone, but soldiers in there. They would have to be quick, otherwise the base would know something wasn't right. The little alien got them into the hangar and shut down the surveillance system. They had to move swiftly now, as it wouldn't take the base long to notice this system had been disabled. Chantelle had her hover skates on and was at the control room door in seconds. She ripped it off its hinges and found three soldiers in there. The soldiers looked extremely surprised, and also shocked at this. Chantelle jumped over the control room desk in the middle, landing into the two soldiers on the other side.

She could hear the other one at the side on his headset say, 'Hurry, we are under attack.'

Evan ran in and ripped his headset off, and they scuffled. The two soldiers, Chantelle had knocked over, were now back on their feet. They were looking directly at her and were livid. Looking at her small stature, they looked at each other and smiled. Exactly what Chantelle had hoped for. The soldiers thought this would be easy for them. Chantelle pulled the hat off her head and her long orange streaked hair fell out. There was no time for hiding now. Chantelle had struggled to believe Evan's story about there being a war on the outside of the shield and that humans were dying. She had always believed no one could go outside of the shield and survive for long, as the ozone layer was no longer there. Evan had told her this was a lie. He had told her the shield was to protect them from nuclear bombs decades before, and was now there to protect them from the remaining radiation. However, in the world some people had survived these bomb attacks and were living in these harsh conditions. Chantelle would now try to help these people from Archer's murderous attempts. The soldiers advanced on Chantelle, but they were too slow. To their amazement they were not strong enough. Their shields were also no help either. She threw a punch at the first soldier, the shield slowed it, but it could not stop it hitting him square on the jaw. He flew across the room unconscious. The other soldier seeing this tried to slow and back off. This was no use, as Chantelle was now spinning through the air and kicked him straight in the side of the head. He just crumpled to the floor. Both Evan and the third soldier had stopped fighting, as they witnessed Chantelle's actions. The soldier looked at Evan, and with Chantelle coming towards them, flung his hands in the air to surrender. They couldn't have a prisoner, so Chantelle knocked him out too. Her and Evan dragged the limp bodies of the soldiers out of the control room to another part of the building. They knew they would wake soon enough, and could have reinforcements with them next time. So, Evan jumped into the command chair in the control room. He had worked there most of his army career, so knew exactly how to use it. He dismantled the jamming on all of the communications, and the communications started flowing in from all over the world, both human and alien communications. The little alien seemed pleased. Evan assumed it could hear its people. Evan saw the smile on its face, but the alien carried on with something he was busy doing in the corner. Evan started to try and contact all of the soldiers fighting out there, that Archer had sent on missions. He managed to reach the soldiers, and gave them the message that the General had been killed and what Archer's involvement had been in it.

Che then brought Dr Simmons into the control room. Drake had delivered Simmons to her that morning and Che had also hidden Simmons in the van. Simmons looked at Chantelle and then down again. He could not look her in the eyes. A call came in and it was Danelaw. He was not too pleased.

'What are you on about, Evan? We are in a war and haven't got time for this.'

Evan came back with, 'What, the truth?'

Danelaw just said, 'The truth is the General died of a heart attack. That's all. That's what the doctors said.'

Evan said, 'They were Archer's doctors, who he brought in from the outside.'

Chantelle noticed soldiers coming towards this hangar, on the surveillance the little alien had turned back on again. She told Evan to carry on talking and she would handle them. On her way out, Miss Che stopped her and told her to remember her training. She was not to give in.

Che hugged her and said, 'You're ready for this.'

Evan carried on his conversation with Danelaw. 'We haven't got long and I can prove what I'm saying is true.'

Chantelle was hiding in a room, on the side of the corridor, that the soldiers would have to walk down. She could hear around four of them coming. She started to panic a bit. She had never taken on so many before, but she knew she was stronger and quicker than them. She put her shield up and waited. The soldiers went past the room she was hiding in. She slipped out and attacked them. She took the first one out by surprise by coming from behind, and left him unconscious. The other three turned around and were now ready for her. She flew at them, getting good momentum with her hover skates, and she bowled them over. Chantelle quickly turned, and as one soldier was trying to get up, she kicked him in the face. The power in her kick was so forceful that it penetrated his shield, which made her laugh. He was now unconscious on the floor. The other two separated, trying to outflank her. She decided to go for the one on the right. She swung punches and kicks at him and he was just able to defend them, but she could see she had hurt him. It gave the other soldier time to grab her from behind though. He was strong, but not strong enough. Chantelle grabbed his arm and swung him over her shoulder, sending him crashing into the wall. The slightly hurt soldier was now trying to kick and punch Chantelle. She was easily deflecting his blows though, and shouting down to Che to hurry up. Chantelle then did a roundhouse kick on him, landing him on the floor with the others. The soldier, that she had thrown against the wall, was now back up and he attempted to catch Chantelle on the way back down from her kick, but she flung a punch and knocked him back to the ground.

Back in the control room Evan had brought in Dr Simmons, and he told Danelaw and the rest of the men who were listening to the conversation about what Archer had done. They were all still struggling to believe this. This was until Simmons sent them all a hologram, which showed Archer telling Simmons what he wanted to do and asking if he could help him. Evan also told everyone that they could not ask anything of Dr Huk, who had got the medbot, as Archer had him killed. Evan sent the autopsy images to the holograms. Danelaw, and all the men in the battles around the world, now stood watching the holograms in front of them in disbelief. These images, that the medbot had taken, clearly showed the General had been killed maliciously. Danelaw was furious.

'We're coming back, Evan,' he said. 'Archer has some questions to be answered.'

Evan got an acknowledgement from all of the men, apart from Archer's soldiers from his Mars days. Evan turned to Miss Che and she said, 'Time to go.'

They got up to go and then heard Chantelle fighting again. As they reached the door, they saw four soldiers on the floor. She was fighting the three they had engaged back in the office the first time. Evan presumed they must have woken up. He was going to help, but Chantelle was more than a match for all three. Her orange hair was spinning everywhere in front of them. She was pushing them back to the entrance.

Evan shouted down the corridor, 'We can head out the back.'

Chantelle had knocked them out again. She turned to look at Miss Che, lowering her shield as she did. She smiled at Che, when all of sudden, Chantelle fell to the floor unconscious. Miss Che screamed and went to go to help her, but Evan grabbed her. Where Chantelle had been stood, Archer was standing over her with a stun stick in his hand.

'I knew you were special,' he said looking down at her.

Then he looked up at Evan and Miss Che, who had the alien hanging out of her bag.

'What shall I do with you three?' he said.

To this, the two of them were off and running. Evan was dragging Che though, as she was crying and distraught. The alien had made a gun again, and was firing it back at Archer and the soldiers Archer had brought with him. They got out of the building and to their van. Soldiers were still in pursuit. They jumped in the van, sped around the buildings, accelerating towards the entrance. At the entrance, there were around five soldiers waiting for them. Evan accelerated the van straight at them. He knew that the soldiers could easily halt the van, but he had to try. The alien was firing the little gun out of the window. The blasts were so huge from the gun that the two soldiers on his side of the van had to get out of the firing line. The other three stayed where they were. That was until they came under fire from outside the base, and they had to disperse quickly. Evan did not know who was firing from outside the base, but he was highly grateful. The little alien destroyed the laser barrier, and Evan took the van straight through, and they escaped to his surprise. When Archer's men got to the barrier, they were not interested in chasing them outside of the base. Evan, Miss Che and the little alien got back to her apartment, checking the apartment for Archer before they went back in. It was empty. Miss Che was still beside herself with grief, at the thought of Archer having captured Chantelle. She wanted to go back immediately, but Evan told her the base would be on the highest alert now and they would need help to do this. Miss Che could not be calmed down and was determined to go back. The little alien was trying to reassure her that they would get Chantelle back, if it was the last thing they did. Miss Che blamed herself for Chantelle's capture and there was no consoling her.

Chapter Twenty Six

Standing on the market walls looking out on the army below, Cecilio was sure this was the end for them. The old shield would soon collapse, and then they would have to try and lose the soldiers in the caves. He did not like that option. It was definitely feeling like this could be the last battle for them. The guns started early morning, as usual. Cecilio came off the wall and joined what men he had left. Annette was slightly injured, but ready as always. Some of her unit were being cared for in the hospital, including Innex who was recovering too. It was a battle weary group of aliens and humans, who would still fight until the end and they stood there waiting. The guns kept wailing on the shield, and they stood there and continued to wait. The anticipation was mounting every second. It must have been around midday, when the force shield finally gave way. The guns now battered the new gate, which for now withheld the onslaught. Then all of a sudden, the guns stopped firing and it went eerily quiet. No-one knew what to do, and strangely there was no firing for nearly half an hour. Cecilio expected they were preparing for an all-out assault. Cecilio would go down fighting. He turned to the group and looked over all of them.

He saluted them and said, 'It's been an honour.'

He fired up both his spears and shouted, 'Open the gate.' With a crunching sound, it started to open. Cecilio was not waiting and he ran. The rest were just behind him. Annette caught up and went past Cecilio. His heart sank, as he thought she would be the first casualty. As they got out of the gate, Cecilio nearly ran into Annette, who had abruptly stopped. Cecilio slid just past her and heard her say, 'They've gone!' Cecilio looked at her dimly and wondered who had gone. She said again, as the others came up behind, 'They've gone. The soldiers have gone,' as she pointed towards the open prairies.

Cecilio turned around and was completely dumbstruck by this observation. He could not believe it. In the distance, their ships were disappearing one by one. Cecilio just dropped to his knees and started to cry. Annette went up and hugged him. 'You old fool,' he thought to himself. He had been overcome by the emotions of the moment.

This left so many unanswered questions though. Why had they left so abruptly? Why had they quit the battle? What had caused them to run away, when they wanted the aliens and humans dead, and would have won the battle?

Earlier that morning, Cundill had been in a great mood. The aliens and the humans had retreated back to the market. Apart from being injured by that being from the night before, he would be finally be getting his hands on the last of them remaining. Not literally of course. He would still be at the back watching, unless there were only a few left and then he might fight. Only then would he get involved. Cundill got the men up earlier than usual to start the barrage, which did not make them happy. They blasted the guns at the shield, and they had more guns at their disposal now. These were the spoils of war. They pounded and pounded the shield, and they finally destroyed it. At that moment, Cundill's earpiece buzzed. It was Archer. 'Get back to the base quick, Captain,' he said.

Cundill was shocked by this and exclaimed, 'We are almost in the market, Sir!'

Archer quickly responded, 'Now Captain, and just our men from Mars. Leave the rest.'

Cundill knew what this meant and which base to go to. He signed off and tapped his earpiece twice. This sent a private signal to all the men, who had originally been based on Mars with Archer and Cundill. These men started to make their way to the back of the group that had been blasting the guns. Cundill and a few hundred of them made it back to the ship, sneakily without being noticed. Then everyone's earpieces buzzed. On them they could hear a message and chat between Evan and Danelaw, and they all heard how the General had been killed by Archer. Archer's men from Mars had now all nearly made it back to the ship, when the message stopped. The guns also stopped being fired then. Cundill could hear everyone getting anxious and saying, 'Get the ship up.

214

The old General's loyal soldiers will be coming back. They'll want to take us into custody.'

The last man boarded this one ship. The ship was up and away, leaving the other ship behind. As it lifted up into the sky, it appeared to veer towards the mountains and was gone. The remaining soldiers on the ground, which were the old General's soldiers, just stood and watched the ship go. Then they quickly boarded the other ship that was left. Luckily Cundill and Archer's soldiers had not had time to sabotage it. The soldiers were aboard this ship in minutes, and they were hoping they could get through the shield to their base and get to Archer. When they arrived at the shield, there was a portal out waiting for them.

Chapter Twenty Seven

Danelaw was incensed. He was running as fast he could back to the ship. He told the men to withdraw and get back to the ship as quick as they physically could. Nothing was going to stop him getting back to the UK and Archer. He could not believe how he had been so stupid and gullible to believe all of Archer's lies. His men were thinking the same too. They felt they had been betrayed. Thankfully, they had no problems running back to the ship. The flying aliens followed them from a distance, but just to make sure they were actually leaving! Danelaw realised that this was another lie from Archer. If these aliens were all so brutal, why were they not still attacking Danelaw and his men as they retreated. Danelaw felt used and angry all at once. He reached the ship first and fired up the engines. He was going nowhere until every last man was on board. It seemed to him to take a long time for this to happen. Eventually, he got the signal that the last man was aboard. He placed the ship into overdrive, and programmed the destination co-ordinates for the UK base. As they got closer to the UK, they could see a ship in the distance ahead of them. The ship appeared to veer off course, away from the open portal. Danelaw did not care about that, as they were nearly back. At the portal, he assumed Evan had left it open for their entry. He shot the ship into it. The portal sent them to a hangar on the base. As soon as they landed, he was out of his pilot seat and off the ship before any other man.

Anyone that came near him he would ask, 'Where's Archer? I want a word with him.'

No-one said they had seen him. Danelaw stormed to Archer's office, with his battle-weary men also in toe. Coming up to the building, he could see a few of Archer's soldiers waiting outside.

On reaching the first one he said, 'Where's Archer? I need to see him.'

He replied, 'The General is not seeing anyone today. You'll have to come back tomorrow.'

The soldiers seemed to form up a little. This did not scare Danelaw in the slightest.

'He will see me now,' Danelaw said, 'And you and your group will not stop me.'

He could see the soldiers shrink a little.

The soldier's earpiece buzzed, and a few seconds after the soldier said, 'Archer will be out to see you in a minute, Commander.'

The soldier visibly sighed, as he did not want to fight Danelaw. Danelaw started to pace from side to side. He was getting more and more frustrated being held here waiting for Archer. He knew it was the last bit of defiance from the man. The soldier noticed Danelaw's frustration too, and in a panicked voice communicated into the earpiece and asked Archer to hurry, as Commander Danelaw would not wait much longer. Archer's reply was blunt, 'I'll be out in a minute, soldier. Stop bothering me.'

The soldier hoped Danelaw did not hear this or it would start something. With the number of soldiers gathering from the ship behind Danelaw now, Archer's guards would not stand a chance. They probably wouldn't stand a chance with Danelaw on his own either! To the soldier's relief, he heard the door behind him click and unlock. Danelaw stopped pacing and all went quiet. The door opened slowly and out walked Archer. He looked directly at Danelaw, as he walked towards him and said, 'What's the meaning of this, Commander? You and your men should be in Beijing sorting out the problem there.'

Danelaw just scoffed, 'You know why I'm here, Archer.'

Before he could say anything else, Archer replied, 'That is General Archer to you, Commander. Show some respect.'

Danelaw ignored this comment and went on, 'I'm here to arrest you for killing the General, and sending our troops to do your bidding.'

Archer said, 'Those allegations are lies, Commander. They are from a man who always hated me. The other accuser we have in our custody. We found Dr Simmons hiding under the desk, when the others escaped, after the attack on the communications control room.'

217

Archer never mentioned that he had Chantelle too.

Archer continued, 'Dr Simmons has already told us what he said was not true.'

Danelaw did not believe any of this from Archer and said, 'Simmons will always be a liar, who looks after number one. So, I don't believe that, and Evan is no liar. Evan has hated you from day one, which he has never hidden. The brain scans he sent to me definitely showed the General did not die of a heart attack. Unlike what you and your Doctor said. The killing of the Doctor by you, who supplied you with your medbot, is clear evidence. Why would you do that, if not to protect yourself? So, I'm still arresting you Archer. Let the courts decide. Take him into custody, men.'

Danelaw was just holding himself back from assaulting Archer. Danelaw's soldiers standing behind him went to grab Archer and Archer said, 'Unhand me, I'm still your General.'

Danelaw turned back to Archer and said, 'Please try to resist arrest, Archer. It will give me the opportunity to forcefully deal with you.'

Archer looked at Danelaw and thought better of it. He tapped his earpiece twice, before sticking his hands out in front of him. Noticing what Archer did Danelaw shouted, 'Shields up men.' Before his words were out, around ten ships flew in blasting at them. It killed a few soldiers, before they had got their shields up. The sheer force of the attack scattered and knocked others off their feet. Dust started to fly up off the ground, as it always did. Danelaw had also been knocked off his feet, but was up quickly.

He shouted, 'Where is Archer and his men?'

Turning to the soldiers remaining he said, 'Come with me, soldiers.'

The ships had turned above them and were coming back again. The fire from the ships was ferocious. Danelaw was ready now though with his shield up, and was knocking the incoming rounds to one side. These things were slowing him down and he needed to get back in that building Archer had come out of. Danelaw was sure he must have gone back in

218

there, but this had all happened so quickly. What had happened to Archer?

When Archer had tapped his earpiece twice, his ships had come in and Archer had been ready. When they blasted the base, Archer had run into the building in the cloud of dust, along with his men.

One of his men was shouting, 'What are we going to do now, Sir?'

'Don't worry, soldier,' he said over his shoulder. 'Go grab Dr Simmons and meet me in the back of the building.'

Archer was running to his office now, whilst in his earpiece thanking the lead pilot of the ships. Archer had ordered all of these ships back from the outer atmosphere, as he had suspected he would need them. He had sent them to the base in Scotland initially, so no one knew they were back in the UK, apart from him.

He asked the lead pilot, 'Is it here yet?' and the pilot replied, 'In a couple of minutes, Sir.'

Archer did not like the sound of that.

He said, 'You need to keep Danelaw occupied then, as he won't be happy.'

Archer got back to his office and there it lay. There was his prize! He was not going to leave her. He grabbed, the still unconscious Chantelle, as he had kept stunning her. With one hand, he picked her up and threw her over his shoulder. He grabbed some other items and then he was off out of his office, running towards the back of the building. He knew there was not a door back there, but that would not be a problem for him.

Archer got to the back of the building and his men were there waiting. Also, there was a whimpering Dr Simmons cowering next to the men, and saying sorry to Archer as he reached him.

Archer looked over to Simmons and said, 'I'll deal with you later, Doctor.'

This made Simmons burst out crying. Archer told one of the soldiers to shut Simmons up, so he knocked Simmons out and threw him over his shoulder.

Archer walked to the lead soldier and said, 'Sergeant, if you will.'

219

The sergeant turned and smashed a hole through the wall. The hole was big enough for them to escape out of. Archer looked out into this open space and there was nothing there. He urgently contacted the lead pilot on his earpiece.

'Where is it, Captain?' he said. 'We are here waiting.'

The pilot replied, 'It's nearly there, Sir.'

Archer and the rest stood there looking out of this hole, and at that moment from behind them they heard the door down the corridor get ripped off its hinges.

Someone shouted down, 'Archer, stop there.'

Archer knew immediately that the voice was Danelaw's. Archer ran out into the open yard, beyond the hole, with his men following. He then heard the drone of an engine he had been waiting for. It swooped into sight. It was one of the troop carriers from Mars. The ramp was down and it had come in low enough for them to start jumping aboard. Archer, still carrying Chantelle, had jumped onto it along with all of his men. The ship started to rise. The ramp was going up. Archer was sure he could hear somebody scream, 'No.' He suspected Danelaw had got to the opening just in time to see Archer's escape. The ship was flying high and its course was set for Scotland. The other ten ships followed the carrier, for any support if required. It took around five minutes to reach Scotland in this outdated ship. They set down at the Scottish base and quickly disembarked. Archer was telling the pilot to fill up with fuel, as they would be setting off again once he had all the men together he wanted. Archer went over to Cundill and all of the others that had returned from battle. Cundill had even found Abbott and the rest of his unit in the mountains, and brought them back from America. Archer thought they had some explaining to do. Cundill told him that Abbott's unit were in a bad way when they had found them.

Cundill said to Archer, 'What now, Sir? What are we going to do?'

Archer said, 'Get all the soldiers on this ship now, Captain. We are leaving.'

Cundill looked at him a little surprised, but as always, he did as he was ordered. Everyone on the base got on the carrier just,

as there was not much room left on it. Nearly all the fighter ships, that Archer had originally sent to attack Blasius, had also been ordered back. They had been loaded with everything they could take, and were now were ready to go. They set off. Archer had left a portal open for them in Scotland, so they could all get out of the shield. Outside the shield, Archer realised he had had enough of the UK. He was upset that he had not had the time or equipment to destroy the UK. The fighter ships went ahead, as the carrier ship was so slow. They waited in the clouds, until it caught up with them. Then they jetted out into the outer atmosphere. Just a few miles from where they were, Archer could see it for the first time. It was the huge alien ship of Blasius's, that Archer's troops had attacked at the start of this battle. Archer was just hoping its sensors and shields were not working, otherwise this would be a short trip. They set the carrier ship to go towards it. Fighter ships engaged in all directions, to keep what ships the aliens had left in space occupied, and away from alerting Blasius's main ship. This hopefully would mean they would not know Archer's carrier ship was coming. Archer slowly advanced the ship, so they did not notice them coming, and they got slowly closer. Archer got the Flight Captain to head towards the cargo compartment of Blasius's ship. To their luck, there was no one in there, so they set down. Archer got the men together.
'We have to be quick and silent, men,' he said. 'We need to take this ship and get out of here.'
They looked at him as if to say, 'Where to?' He gave an order, so they had to obey him. A squad got out of the ship and they headed to the hangar doors. They slightly pulled them apart and looked down the corridor. No one was around, so they opened the doors. They slowly edged down the sides of the corridor, so as not to be detected by anyone. They kept going all the way to the end. It was eerily quiet and they suspected they might have been seen, and the aliens were ready for them. Then they heard something coming their way. They hid where they could, and an alien came around the corner. The alien had three heads, and there was total shock on one of its faces when the soldiers jumped out at it. They subdued it,

before it could sound the alarm. They took it back to the hangar and onto their ship. Archer went in to see the creature, who was also joined by Nineham and Cundill. It did not take long before it talked. It was difficult to understand it, but it spoke a little English. It told them that there was only a skeleton crew on board now, as most had gone down to Earth to help their people. Archer hated this fact. He knew they could take the ship without much of a struggle. They brazenly went down the corridors, knowing the aliens could not really stop them, and reached the command centre of the ship. The aliens knew they were coming and put up a fight. It took Nineham and some of his best men to take down the alien, who seemed to be in charge. It was a big alien too. Probably about ten and a half foot tall, but looked older than any of their race they had seen before. There were hundreds of aliens on their knees in front of Archer now. They had captured all of them or so they thought. Archer started, 'I should really kill all of you, but I need something to fly this ship.'

All of the aliens stirred and the big one spoke English, to Archer's surprise.

'Where do you want to go?' it said.

Archer walked over to it, with Nineham and Cundill just behind, in case it tried to attack him.

'Out of this god forsaken galaxy. That's for sure. Hopefully to find some more of my own people,' Archer said.

The creature stirred and said, 'We will not help you.'

'Well, aliens will die at your hands,' threatened Archer.

Archer looked at Cundill, and Cundill went over to the smallest alien he could find and ripped it's arm off, smiling as he did it. The huge alien tried to get to its feet, but Nineham and some others held it down.

'Believe me. You really do not want to find your people,' the alien said. After a pause, the alien continued, 'Our ship is still severely damaged from your attack on us. It really is not safe to fly.'

Archer just asked if the engines were in operation. The big alien went quiet, when asked this.

222

Archer repeated the question and said, 'You better answer me this time or your friend will have no arms.'

The alien looked over to Cundill, who was still smiling at his exploits.

The alien said 'Okay,' in his broken English.

Archer could feel the hatred coming out of all of the words the alien said.

'The engines were fixed two days ago. The ship is still unflyable though, as we are struggling to fix the shield, sensors and communications,' replied the alien.

Archer seemed to ponder this news.

Then Archer said, 'The engines are fixed, so I want to be gone from this sector. It won't take Danelaw long to find out where we have gone and come after us. I want to get out of here long before that.'

The alien went to argue, but Archer held his hand up signalling to him to be quiet, whilst Nineham and the others held him down further.

Archer continued, 'I need some of your people to pilot this ship, and the rest of you I don't need will be locked in the hangar. If any of the pilots among you try anything, then I will open the airlock.'

Archer looked at the big alien again and said, 'Would you like to relay that message to your friends?'

The alien looked scornfully at him with his big silver and gold eyes.

'They all understand you.'

'Good,' Archer said.

They separated out all of the pilots and escorted the remainder down to the hangar, which would be the new cell. The pilots got themselves situated, ready to fly the ship.

Archer shouted, 'Get us out of here!'

One of the aliens responded and said, 'Get ready for hyperlight speed then,' and pushed a lever.

They accelerated off, which caused Archer and his men to be violently sick with the sensation.

As they got used to the hyperlight motion, Archer stood there thinking that all of these weird colours must be the moons they were going past. He had to have the bridge cleaned, as it smelled so badly from the vomit! Cundill came over and said, 'What about Dr Simmons and the girl?'

Archer laughed and said, 'Oh I forgot about those two. Bring the Doctor to me, Captain. Just throw the girl with the aliens for the time being. I haven't decided what to do with her yet.'

Cundill headed back to Archer's office on their ship. As soon as he entered, Simmons was crying and saying, 'Don't kill me. It was her.'

He pointed over to the still unconscious Chantelle.

Cundill just said, 'That's not up to me, Doctor,' and grabbed him.

Simmons was now uncontrollable, kicking and screaming. Cundill said, 'You best calm down Doctor, because if you don't and you wake that girl, then I will kill you.'

Cundill did not want to have to fight Chantelle, as from what he had heard he would not stand a chance. Simmons calmed a little, although he was still crying. Cundill did not want to take a chance with Chantelle, so he stunned her again. Then he picked her up and threw her over his shoulder. He dragged Simmons with his other hand. They got to the hangar, where all of the aliens were. Cundill slid the door open, threw Chantelle inside and closed it quickly. He did not fancy going in.

Simmons exclaimed, 'Are you not going to put me in there with her?'

Cundill said, 'No, Doctor. Archer wants you on the bridge with him.'

To this comment, Simmons went pale and fainted, so Cundill dragged him off.

After a few hours Chantelle finally awoke. She was very groggy and felt nauseous. She was sure she was moving, but could not be certain. She felt weak, and for the first time she could remember in her life she also felt sore. She thought she was bruised too, but it was so dark she could not see a thing in here. However, where was 'here'? This did not feel like anywhere she knew. When she moved, it echoed in this area. She suspected this was a large area. She tried to sit up, but collapsed back down. She tried again and this time she stayed upright, but it wasn't easy. Then to her surprise, she heard something move behind her. She heard whispers in languages she had not heard before. Then it started to get louder and louder, and it felt like a lot of things moving towards her. Chantelle turned slowly, aching all over as she did. She was met by thousands of bright eyes staring directly at her. She said, 'Oh sh….!'

Printed in Dunstable, United Kingdom